About the A

Paul Devine was vocalist and frontman with Sheffield Post-Punk band Siiiii between 1983 and 1986, and again from 2005 to 2014. He has published two previous books, the autobiography *The Devine Comedy* and the semi-fictitious *Here Be Hermits: The Year of Covid*. He lives in Somerset with his wife, two fully grown men with beards and a Siberian Husky called Jack.

The Hallow Man is his first novel.

By the Same Author

The Hallow Man

By

Paul Devine

Sheffield General Cemetery, circa 1840

This book is for the people at the Soup
Showground and the Secret Red Car Sliding Door
Gallery, who made me remember that good folk
still do good things. And for making me welcome.

A Table of the Contents Contained Within

2015

PROLOGUE

THE INCOMERS came in boats. They brought with them vessels hewn from mud. Their clothes were filigreed and ornate, and their long dark hair was hung all about with red beads. They were tall, men and women both. And they were devoid of pity.

They had come from windward, the bloodied runner of the woman's people told them. She had fallen, a flap of peeled scalp blubbering into her eyes, at the edge of the village. She gasped through her newly-broken teeth that they must all hide within the forest or among the stones. The woman had given the poor runner water and comfort. She held the runner close as she was dying. The woman looked around at her people as they stood, silent, with their children. And then her lap suddenly filled with the runner's blood.

Later. The woman fled along the edge of the forest, following the contours of the brook. Her grey hair had come loose from its hide binding and hung in damp fronds against her wet face and back. Summer birdsong and the cries of animals echoed through the closely growing trees. A long gash on her forehead drooled thick blood into her eyes. From time to time she wiped it away, sticky, with her sore and dirty palm. She could smell her own sweat, winey and acrid. Her breath came in hot, rapid bursts.

She stopped to listen, her chest heaving, behind a broad horse-chestnut tree. The leaves whispered above her. Were they still coming? A dog barked somewhere. The breeze gently hushed as it teased the branches. She turned towards it and let it momentarily cool her face. Then the shouting and clatter of the men again. The woman gathered herself and ran on. Now she veered away from the brook and began to scale the hill. Here the forest thickened, the invaders having only taken their wood from the lower reaches so far.

She could still smell the smoke and broiling flesh from her decimated people. The men of her village were beheaded and emasculated, their parts rammed into their mouths and added to the great fire the invaders had set in the village. The children were all beaten senseless and burned alive on this fire, while she and the other women were forced to watch. The grease and fluid from the men's heads fuelled the blaze, making the flames blue and green and fatty. The silence of the children, their blood sizzling as they cooked and hunched, was monstrous. There was as much steam as smoke coming from the poor, small, shriveling bodies. The women were either summarily executed and thrown into the brook along with what was left of the menfolk's bodies to poison the water downstream, or taken as trophies. Or perhaps as breeding stock.

Bent double, the woman grabbed handholds of ferns and tussocks of grass as she climbed. Not daring to look back for fear of losing her footing, she scrambled, panting, upwards. Had they let her run so they could have their sport? Or had her sudden escape in the face of this horror been a surprise for them? Just inside the darks of the forest were blocky stone outcrops. The roots of great trees had grabbed this bedrock and crafted grottoes and caves from it. The woman backed into one of these sanctuaries, keeping low and breathing as quietly as she could.

She squatted. Drew herself into herself. She could smell her womanhood, ripe and earthy, like the moss she shivered upon. Animals had been here. A hint of piss. Maybe a whiff of dung. She breathed long and deep. Her eyes closed, she pictured herself elsewhere.

Stealthy footsteps, where she had just been. Men whispered in a language that sounded like their mouths were filled with mud. From where she sat, low, she saw a thick limb. The shaft of a spear. It moved leaves and soil around. Then another spear. More men. She thought they were listening. She made a hole of her mouth to breathe as quietly as she was able. Could they smell her?

A strange droning horn blew in her valley. The gathered men talked loudly for a moment then they began to descend. She sat, hugging herself. Her whole world in ruin. Her children. Her man. Her people. All gone. All ash or poison. She began to weep. The woman wept tears of sorrow and loss and incandescent, impotent fury. She wept in utter silence until the forest became dark and the night creatures began to venture quietly abroad.

Time passed. And passed again. And the woman realised that she was not alone after all. Had one of the incomers remained behind or returned? No. She could hear them laughing in the slaughtered ruins of her village. She could hear the pop of the fire. A cheer as a woman was raped or killed. The blowing of the horn. A long arm reached into her refuge. There was a vague scent of rot. A huge hand covered her mouth and nose, blanketing her whole face. She could not breathe. The hand pressed and pressed. In her utmost extremity she realised just how much she wanted to live. Struggling noiselessly, her feet jerked on the mossy floor of her den. She tried to see her new assailant. To see who was killing her. Her eyes became huge, as blood struggled to work its way around her body. Her lungs burned. Her mouth was a useless dead-end. She felt her heart begin to fail. And fail. Then nothing.

Later. The woman awoke. She was alive but she was changed. The forest lifted its mighty brow in the wind. The night was strewn with stars. Her killer and saviour laying alongside her on the leaved-and-needled floor of the forest, spoke for the first and last time. His voice was all holes. All hollows. Like a well.

'It is done,' he said.

·1954·

THE DOORS OF PERCEPTION

HERE ARE TWO young men.

Bunny Reeder and his housemate Simon Glass, both students at Sheffield University. They look at each other across the old Willow Pattern teapot as it sits on a matching metal tea-tray. It is almost a dare, what they about to do. It is also a quest. They grin. And Simon stirs the oily contents of the pot with a tablespoon.

They have been in the front bar of The Barfield pub on Abbeydale Road since six o'clock that evening. They have played darts and talked about Aldous Huxley and their plans for the night. It is past eight o'clock now. A warm July night. And sunny.

The Barfield serves good ale. It is Simon and
Bunny's local pub. It was less than crowded
tonight because their usual student drinking
companions have gone home for the summer
holidays. These two, though, decided back in the
Spring that they would stay on for the Summer.
A taste of freedom. After their fourth pint of
beer, they had walked back to their house on
Vanguard Road in the Sharrow area of the city.
A tram had ambled past them, trailing a scent of
tobacco smoke and valves.

Bunny and Simon share an interest in beer
and books. And the burgeoning folk and rock
and roll music coming over from America. And
Blossom Dearie, Hieronymus Bosch and
Salvador Dali. They met on their first day at the
University Halls of Residence, and within a
week had decided to rent a house together
elsewhere. It would be more fun, they agreed,
and either louder or quieter. And at least the
choice between noise or silence would be their
choice, rather than that of the trad-jazz mad
residents of the Halls.

They had found the details of this house
pinned to a corkboard in a tiny and grimy open-

door cubicle near the town centre called The Sheffield Student Accommodation Office. The details, written in pencil on a torn beer-mat, and drawing-pinned up, announced: **"ROOMS FOR TWO STUDENTS IN SHARED HOUSE IN QUIET AREA. FULLY FURNISHED. GAS AND ELECTRICITY METERS. MALES ONLY. RATES INCLUDED. 10 2/- P/W. MONTH DEPOSIT PLUS BOND. CONTACT MR J TORODE. TEL SHEFFIELD 340."**

Bunny and Simon met the landlord, an asymmetric man who was almost as wide as he was tall, on an October Saturday the year before. He had presented the house to them by walking through the rooms and pointing at beds, the cooker and various wardrobes.

The two boys said that they were happy with the house. Mr J Torode produced a grubby-looking contract from his pocket, and they signed it. They handed over their deposit and their bond.

Apart from that first, wordless meeting, they have not seen their landlord. Mr J Torode insists on the weekly rent being left on the kitchen worktop on Fridays, and he comes in and collects it at the most peculiar hours. The house suits them. The front door has been locked for years. With a heavy red velvet curtain drawn across it on the inside, it is simply part of Simon's bedroom wall.

We access the back door by walking through the narrow alleyway formed by their next-door neighbour's wooden fence and the adjacent house wall. The fence ends a few feet from their living room window, giving them their own small, tarmacked yard with a few gravelly loose stones dotted around. The back door opens onto a galley kitchen containing a gas cooker, shelves that are currently filled with tinned food, and a small pantry.

If we turn right, we are in their living room. With its geometrically patterned carpet and bright yellow curtains, this is the main room in the house. There is a swirly-beige tiled mantelpiece along the living room wall that adjoins their neighbour Mrs Bron's kitchen. A brass-and-wood lozenge-shaped clock stands upon it, and a Constable print, *The Lock*, hangs above it.

On an alcove shelf to our left sits a large wireless radio and a gramophone player. Long-player records are stacked alongside them. Next to the alcove is the small, latched door to the cellar, where the shilling-operated gas and electricity meters hang amongst the cobwebs.

The door from the living room takes us to Simon's room, dead ahead. And the narrow, white-painted stairs to the right. Up the stairs we go. To the left and we are at Bunny's bedroom door. The bathroom is on the right. A small boxroom, full of suitcases and shoes, and an ancient canvas tent that already was here when they moved in, lies straight ahead.

Huxley's new book has awakened a yearning in them both. *The Doors of Perception*. Its title taken from William Blake's *The Marriage of Heaven & Hell*. Simon and Bunny also like Blake. His line, *If the doors of perception were cleansed, everything would appear to man as it is, Infinite. For man has closed himself up, till he sees all things thro' narrow chinks of his cavern*, is, to them, the Huxley book in microcosm.

The age in which they find themselves is filled with the most wondrous events and the most marvellous changes. Watson and Crick described the DNA Double Helix last year. Heezen and Ewing discovered that the abyssal canyon in the Mid-Atlantic Ridge proved the theory of Plate Tectonics. And in 1952, Salk had produced a vaccine for Polio. But, they feel, the dour society they inhabit is, as Blake and Huxley suggested, blind to these wonders.

They have acquired the nearest hallucinogen to mescalin available in Yorkshire, the liberty cap mushroom *Psilocybe semilanceata*. And they are putting into practice another gem from Blake's book. *The road of excess leads to the palace of wisdom.*

They plan to take these fruits, harvested by an older student friend last October in the Peak District and then dried in an airing cupboard, and attempt at least a partial replication of Huxley's adventure. Neither of them has tried to alter their minds before. But that only makes this experiment more succulent.

Bunny Reeder bears a striking resemblance to the actor Farley Granger. He favours pegged jeans, a leather jacket and heavy boots, and his hair is carefree. As is the way with handsome boys, Bunny has quite a fan club at the University. Unlike many handsome boys with fan clubs however, he prefers to treat his devotees with an unusual respect. This only serves to stoke their ardour.

Simon doesn't think Bunny is even aware that he has admirers. But girls, and boys, sometimes appear at Bunny and Simon's door at unearthly

hours. These waifs, often in tears and sometimes
the worse for drink and in need of nothing more
than a cup of tea and an island of solace, often
stay the night. And they invariably, if not always
willingly, spend the night on the living-room
sofa.

Bunny's given name is Richard, but he has
been known as Bunny since he was evacuated
from Bristol during the war at the age of ten. He
found himself living on a farm in South Wales.
Soon after he arrived, the farmer, Mr Gerries,
took Richard, a dog and a shotgun out one dawn
morning to shoot rabbits. The taking of this
edible wildlife was an important part of the War
Effort. Food was in very short supply and
rabbits were not. Once he realised what was
happening though, Richard ran, clapping and
hollering in the dewy silence, in front of Mr
Gerries and his gun. The rabbits all startled and
disappeared into their various burrow entrances.
Richard was determined to protect these little
creatures with his ten-year-old life. And Mr
Gerries, a kindly, humorous and now astounded
man, christened him Bunny. And he told
Richard that he would shoot just one rabbit a
week if Richard helped around the farm every
day except Sunday.

From there on, as well as attending the local school and Sunday School, Richard mucked out the cattle and tended the smallholding in which grew potatoes, runner and broad beans, peas and tomatoes. He fed and cared for the farm dogs. And he learned to drive a tractor. Mr Gerries, having lost his own son in Burma, came to depend on Richard.

And when the boy returned to Bristol after the war, Mr Gerries cried real tears as he embraced him at the railway station. Mr Gerries said that he would remember him as Bunny Reeder. And Richard Reeder decided that it was a good enough name for him to keep hold of.

Simon picks up the teapot. The mushrooms have brewed long enough for a first cup. He can feel the heat from the contents on his knuckles, and he can smell sour earthiness. He pours.

Simon is thoughtful. On his nose rest thick NHS glasses that he says make him look like Arthur Miller. He has a stillness about him. Away from his studies, Simon writes poetry and plays his guitar, making up chords and words as he goes.

He likes the Beat Poets. They both do. Diane Di Prima. Kerouac. Ginsberg. Michael McClure. These writers have Simon and Bunny in an almost visceral grasp, with their authentic and spontaneous way of spinning their ideas onto the page. Simon says the Beats are like potters. Throwing down lumpen words and moulding them to their will with the physical spinning of the wheel. Their writing and their disdain for materialism and conformity, their use of hallucinogenic drugs, and their love of visionaries like William Blake mean that their plan for the night has a circular reality. Like snakes eating their own tails.

A few months ago, Simon attempted one of the new Rock and Roll slicked-back DA hairstyles. But he didn't like it. Now his black hair falls over his face, and sometimes it prods at his eyes behind his lenses. He dresses flamboyantly though, for all his introspection. He wears pencil-thin trousers and a short light-blue drape-jacket like the new Teddy Boys. He has decorated the back of his Edwardian coat with an embroidered Pax Cultura, the three red dots in a red circle that is Nicholas Roerich's Arts and Science symbol. Some of his friends think this a pretention. But Simon believes in the veracity of the symbol's message of peace through culture.

He is a Northerner to Bunny's South-Westerner, being from Bramley near Rotherham.

He could visit home in an hour if he wanted. But he doesn't want to. Not until he has something his parents can understand and be proud of. Simon excelled at Grammar School, as did Bunny. They both see a bright and meaningful future before them. Simon thinks that his path lays in the arts or music. His parents are not wealthy people. His father is a miner, though now engaged in what are laughably called "light-duties", owing to a fall in the pit and suspected emphysema. More than anything, Simon wants his parents to be able to speak to their neighbours about him with pride. He believes that tonight's experiment will hasten this. Right now, they both think he is wasting his life and getting ideas above his station. He is, after all, the first in his family to receive any education beyond his teens.

They raise their Willow Pattern cups, housed on their Willow Pattern saucers, in a salute, still grinning. This is a new experience for them both, and it will be delicious. The Huxley novel is at the forefront of their minds. And they are keen to be, as Huxley says, men who come back through the Door in the Wall totally changed. Simon has made a rough map of their in-journey destination and has put it somewhere safe.

'Ready?' asks Simon
'Come on then!' says Bunny

They drink the first cup in one hit. It tastes like dirt. They gag a little. Simon goes to the kitchen for some sugar lumps. He plops them into the teapot and swirls it. Sinewy things bob around in the brown water. Bunny pours this time. The second cup, sugared, tastes like sweetened dirt. No less repulsive.

Time to rest awhile. How long does it take? It doesn't matter. They regard each other, and then Simon shuffles across the room and turns Test Match Special on the wireless. England are playing Pakistan at The Oval. They can hear the crowd. But the commentary becomes muffled and inconsequential after who-knows-how-long? Who is bowling? Who is out? Nobody cares in this house. Not now.

Later. They sit on the floor. Their tray of mushroom tea sits between them. Simon pours again and, upending the pot, realises there is only a tiny dribble of weak liquid left in the Willow Pattern pot.

'I can refill?' he says.

Bunny looks at him and blinks. 'Let's see what's in there.'

Simon lifts off the lid and, hidden within, are what look like hundreds of tepid and canoodling slugs. 'I'll get a fork!' Bunny exclaims. And, getting up with an effort, he manages to get to the kitchen and the cutlery drawer.

Years pass. Bunny reappears in the doorway with two forks. On the radio, Fred Trueman is speaking in tongues. The familiar living room is plunged into nothing as Bunny turns off the light. A sudden vacuum.

Simon cries, in near terror, 'Bun for Christ's sakes! Turn the bloody light back on!'

Bunny flicks the switch. The room comes into being but is now plump with unfamiliar shapes and colours. Sitting across from each other again, in the light, they both calm a little. Momentarily. Or longer.

The tray is aslop with dark liquid, syrupy with sugar. Bunny upends the teapot onto the tray. The grey and penile slug-larvae slither across its surface. They are cold and repulsive, but Bunny and Simon devour them with the forks, chewing them into a paste to wring out every last atom of unreality. Bunny picks up the tray and licks it.

There is a roar from the Test Match spectators. Simon opens the curtains. He is astonished. It is still light, even if that light is starting to fade. For an instant he thinks he has emerged from a cinema matinee. That strange unreality of going from a synthetic dark into sudden, natural brightness. The coming night outside is almost tropical.

He sits once more. The furniture feels reptilian. The carpet sucks at his feet. The light in the room undulates as if someone is swinging the shade. Bunny's face is leering and ugly and making its way across the room toward him on its own. To distract himself, Simon studies the magnolia wall. It keeps not being magnolia and then being magnolia again. Bunny looks at his hands. They are writhing like spiders, but he isn't moving them.

Later still. Bunny leaps to his feet. He parts the curtains and cries, 'Let's do it then!'
It is full dark. Bunny wonders when that happened. He can't make any sense of the lozenge-shaped mantelpiece clock. It tick-tocks,

but it seems to be fighting against the actual passing of time. For Bunny, the lozenge clock is telling the time in repetitive cycles, instead of something linear and constantly evolving. And the streetlamp on the road beyond their yard is dripping amber.

Simon, full of fungal poison, gets to his feet. He is pale. He can still smell the loamy tea and feel it mossy on his tongue. He makes the kitchen, just, before he reels through the door and vomits in the yard.

'Jesus!' says Bunny, somehow suddenly next to him. He holds him up and avoids the next torrent. 'You okay?'

Simon, after a few moments, coughing and spitting: 'Ah fuck. Yes. Oh God, that's better. I can see again. It's clearer. Sorry I was sick. Bun. Have you got the map?'

Bunny: 'We don't need the map. We have eyes. The sea flows in our veins. And the stars are our jewels! And don't be soft. It's a whole new world. Let's go and look at things. Now.'

Simon: 'Yes!'

Bunny manages to lock the door, but he forgets to take the key. Such matters mean nothing. The key hangs, slotted within its keyhole. The wood around it, routed out by someone's hand in the 1870's, holds the heavy pin within itself. As Simon and Bunny's footsteps recede, and their voices become faint, a nearby door opens. A shuffling and the fall of a shadow. A sigh. The key is removed and pocketed. A gate clicks. Then a door. Then the turning of a different cam. The click of another tongue.

Bunny and Simon make their way from their house and along Vanguard Road, walking as if suspended from rails of light. The few people they pass all bare their teeth or seem to rear up as if to attack. Their horror at this is real, but the faces that sneer and wink at them as they walk by are not. A man in a baker's outfit performs a ballet for Simon, while Bunny sees him, with horror, as a white-cloaked and damp cadaver, dripping with rot. A tram driver, walking home from a late shift, bristles his moustache at them both and pokes out his huge, flaccid tongue. They can smell mud and plaque. A constable, on his beat, looks at them with both suspicion and fury. They make sure to behave like young men on a late-night stroll until he has passed. And then they collapse into silent hilarity until they are nearly sick. This is the drug.

A solitary car whispers past leaving trails of white light in its wake. More rails for Bunny and Simon. Bunny stops near a hedge and looks at a line of poplar trees. They are stark and black against the lights of the city and the pale summer gloss of the stars. The trees nod their great heads in the soft, hot breeze.

From Vanguard Road, they turn left. Sharrow Lane. The streetlights along this road are white rather than orange. Simon is astounded by the sudden colours.

"Look Bun!" he cries. "Look. Green. Red." A tortoiseshell cat creeps from under a parked blue Vauxhall Cresta. Its eyes are sparks of yellow.

Right onto Washington Road. A wider road, this. Bunny cannot remember how they know the way. Then he realises that he is following Simon. Simon, after all, made the map. The map they left at home. Bunny needs to look at it when they get back. He knows where they are going but he is forgetting why they are going there. Huxley? Blake? The Beats? He thinks his ears are

thrumming in time with his pulse. But if it is his
pulse, it's too rapid. He looks at Simon.

'Is it bang bang bang?' Bunny asks.
'It is. It's bang bang Bun bang Bun bang!'
Simon falls onto the warm pavement. He begins
to shriek in his hilarity. Bunny panics.
'Shut up Simon! You'll have that bloody
copper back here!'
Simon freezes. He looks Bunny hard in the
face. His focus is perfect. Bunny and Simon
regard each other, eye to eye.
'Bunny. Something about this whole evening.
This night. It is the closest people can be to each
other. We are sharing so much right now. I
mean, really.'
'Okay.' Bunny feels stranger than ever,
confronted by this outpouring. Is this still the
drug?

At the top of Washington Road is Cemetery·
Road. Nearly there. They head left. The
streetlights are orange. All of the colours are like
earth again.
'At night all cats are grey.' Bunny says.
'Benjamin Franklin.'

Not far now.

Here are two young men. They have drunk of the soil from Willow Pattern teacups. Their eyes are opened. They are wrapped within their youth and their friendship and their hopes. They feel invincible and they are journeying. But for their tapping footsteps, the street is silent as they approach the huge concrete cemetery gate. The ten-minute walk has taken twenty because they kept stopping to look at wonders they had never imagined. And now they stand. Gazing at the cemetery entrance.

'What the hell are those things?' asks Bunny, unsteady on his feet himself now. This is his first and only visit. Simon came last week and drew the map. He remembers this again. 'On the gate?'

'They're snakes eating their own tails.' says Simon. 'They represent infinity. Or the opposite. And that there in the middle, at the top… whoah! Steady on Bun! That world with wings… I think that's Masonic. I'm not sure though.'

The snakes suck themselves into themselves as they watch. Eaten and not-eaten. Not-eaten and eaten. On and on. Forever.

The carved stone globe rustles its wings and its feathers shiver against each other. Barbs and quills and vanes.

'Is this place still used? For burying people?' asks Bunny.

'It is.' says Simon.

They look at each other for the last time.

And they pass through the great gate.

.1984.

THE CLUB

SHEFFIELD IS RAINING. It is warm and slight. Late June rain. Damp coats smell old like house-clearance clothing. Like a charity shop. This elderly, grandparenty perfume is almost sexual if you live in this town. When he smells it, he knows. The queue for the club is only twenty-people-long. But it moves slowly in the failing daylight because of the hanging-up of damp coats in the hole-in-the-wall cloakroom.

It is Wednesday. Student Night. Doley Night. There is music. Equally musty. Equally squalid. Bauhaus? Difficult to tell from up here away from the speakers above ground. Killing Joke? The Virgin Prunes? Ah yes. *Baby Turns Blue*. Pounding through the pavement up here. The girls with dreadlocks will have commandeered the stage, marching about. The shrivelling queue absorbs rain. Waiting to descend.

The club is subterranean. There are, count them, thirteen descending stone steps to reach the cloakroom below. And then another five to

enter the club itself. Once inside, there is the
smell of ancient sex and new sweat. And fresh
snakebite breath and old darkness. The people in
here are silhouettes, until they are close.

Sex Gang Children's *Sebastiane* now. And he
can guarantee that the dreadlock girls are
stomping around down there on the raised
stage. They all scream *Jezebel!* to each other at the
appropriate moment in the song. Is one of them
called Jezebel? Some people say that the
dreadlock girls travel to London on National
Express every other month to have their hair
done. Nobody has ever spoken to them though,
so no one knows. It's just a rumour. While he
shuffles along the shiny pavement, his hair
dampening, he wonders. What did this place
used to be? Was it a cellar? A Georgian storage
space? A crypt?

Now, at last, he is inside the club, and his
damp suit jacket is being hung up by the
distracted student behind the counter. The
student is distracted by an all-in-black girl who
had handed over her leather coat. The distracted
student palms him his cloakroom ticket. He
tucks it into his black jeans pocket. Better not
lose it or he'll go home on the bus without a
jacket and have to come back for it tomorrow. If

nobody else has claimed it for themselves. These are catch-as-catch-can times.

He calls himself Ptarmigan. His friends call him Ptarmigan. Or Tarm. It is neither an affectation nor his given name. He chose it on a holiday to Canada with his Mum and Dad when he was seven and stroked a wild ptarmigan. The bird sat, perfectly still, plump and white, while he smoothed its soft feathers. He loved its barnyardy scent. He was entranced by its snowy down, and the way it closed its eyes upside-down in pleasure. His Mum and Dad had to bribe him with the promise of poutine to pry him away from it. When he got back to school, he told everyone to call him Ptarmigan. And they did. His bedroom wall was soon filled with posters and cut-outs of ptarmigan. And, although the obsession was short-lived, the name stuck. His family had been on an earlier holiday to the Isle of Wight, and he stroked a marmot that had escaped from Robin Hill Zoo. But, he thinks, who wants to be called Marmot?

He has been in Sheffield for a year, give or take. He lives with two friends in an area called Sharrow. Sharrow is nice enough. There is an Asian Sweet Centre over the road from his

house. They make proper Pakistani food as well
as the sweets, and serve it up in a little cafe.
Tarm likes to sit at a Formica table on Saturday
lunchtimes with Mohammed, the owner's
twelve-year-old, football-mad son. He enjoys
chewing goat curry on-the-bone and basmati rice
with elderly Pakistani fellows who sport great
orange beards, while watching half an hour of
Grandstand on the little black and white TV on
the wall. Neither the proprietors nor customers
appear to care about his black spiky hair, his
make-up, or his occasional wearing of a black
leather kilt. Mo and Ptarmigan sometimes go
onto the field at the back of the house and kick a
football about.

He moved to this city on a whim. Living in
rural Lincolnshire, with its stinks of cut sprout-
stems and its dull and insular attitude, had
become unbearable by the time he reached
eighteen. Sheffield, a Cultural Mecca according
to John Peel, was close. A few miles away. So, in
1983, he upped sticks and left. His parents said
he was making a terrible mistake, and what the
hell did he think he was doing? Ptarmigan said
that he was young and that he wanted to live
some of his life before he was too old to enjoy it.
He hasn't got a job, but this city is so inexpensive

that he feels he can bide his time. The council pay his rent too. He sometimes thinks about joining a band. Everyone seems to be in a band in Sheffield. But it's summer. And he's still in his teens. And he's having a ball. So all of that can wait as well.

Sheffield is a different world. From the curious freshwater fish in the Hole in the Road tank, to the mindbogglingly cheap bus fares. From the gigs and late-night discos at The Hallamshire and The Leadmill, to the friendliness of the local people. Sheffield isn't a city, Ptarmigan thinks. It's more a collection of villages and communities, each with its own specific charm and character. And he is charmed. Not least by the strange destinations displayed on the fronts of the omnipresent buses. Intake. Beauchief. Herdings. Blubberhouses. He thinks he will hop aboard a few buses one day and investigate some of these exotic places.

Ptarmigan leans on the bar, waiting to order a snakebite. His hair is its natural brown, but has so much dried hairspray and gel (and now rain) in it that it looks black and moist. His fringe covers part of his face, which his friends describe as "pretty, rather than handsome". The cider and beer in here are rough. But mixing the two turns them from something foul into an almost passable, and somehow more incendiary drink. Some element of the ultraviolet light in the club reacts with something in the plastic snakebite glass, making it look a solid and glowing blue, like haunted milk.

There are five thick equidistant Doric-style pillars marching along the middle of the club, giving it an almost Classical feel. Although these columns are here to prevent the three huge floors above from crashing into this place, generations of merrymakers have carved their names, and more mysterious sigils, into their soft plaster surfaces. See "Darren Fly". "Kingor The Culprit". And "Zoon". These stanchions parade from the back of the club, past the bar, and come to a halt ten feet from the raised stage. Dancers are fond of using them as handy props as they cavort around to The Cult or Echo and The Bunnymen. Spontaneous and drunken games of hide-and-seek are sometimes played after midnight, using the pillars as comedic sanctuaries.

The quietest and most comfortable part of the club, tucked away from the pounding speakers, has mirror tiles along its perimeter.

These give the club an aura of having more space. It also offers an opportunity for the clientele to tweak their hair without having to brave the toilets. The squalor of the club's toilets is legendary. Especially late of an evening. The men's toilets are always full of women after eleven o'clock. And nothing in the cubicles actually flushes away. Sex in here is apparently regular, although Ptarmigan can't see the attraction. It's another rumour.

At the far end of the club, just beyond the final pillar, is the stage. It isn't a high area, but those on it can be seen from everywhere else in the club, unless a column obstructs their view. Tarm suspects this is why the girls with dreadlocks frequent it so often. Although he has never been able to figure out why, because they only ever talk to each other.

'Tarm!'

He turns around to see the currently matching and back-combed aubergine hair of Seb and Rita from his house.

'Alright!' he grins, 'Pint?'

'Twist that arm!' smiles Rita. 'We'll grab a table.'

Seb has wiped the slopping tabletop with a bar towel by the time Tarm gets to them and puts down the full plastic beakers. The music is loud and pulsing. *The Wheel.* Spear of Destiny. Around this corner you can talk without needing to bellow. They watch the dancers for a while, Tarm paying particular attention to a small white-haired girl in a paisley dress and suede waistcoat. He sometimes gets lucky. It isn't hard in here. This is the eighties. And the eighties are like the sixties as far as casual sex goes. But it's still early. The club doesn't close until 2am. If something happens, it happens. If not, he thinks, there'll be a takeaway from the Gandhi.

Rita lights a Benson with a match, flicking the blackened stump into an ashtray. Seb describes Rita as "sturdily built". She and Seb are both from South Wales and were a serious item long before they came to Sheffield to study at the Polytechnic. Their villages were only a mile apart, a short drive from the port city of Newport. The name of his village, according to Seb, has so few vowels that you pronounce it by clearing your throat. They are both nineteen like Ptarmigan, and their relationship has been in full spate for more than five years. It was a difficult romance to begin with, with them both having embraced Punk Rock and its attendant raucous clothing at fourteen. Neither set of parents wanted their offspring "seeing someone who looks like that!" But the young couple persevered, striding down the respective sides of the valley separating their villages. To catch a bus into Newport to see a band. Or walk to a local pub. Or lay in the gorse and bracken, talking and smoking. In part due to Seb's charm, their parents eventually saw past the spiked-and-dyed hair and aggressive music. They came to realise that they were both gentle, intelligent young people who loved each other and had ambitious plans for their futures.

They arrived back at Vanguard Road as second years last September, in a vortex of laughter, patchouli, crimpers and a huge collection of vinyl records. Ptarmigan had been ricocheting around the house on his own for weeks. So he was delighted to have some company. And the three of them get on better than they had any right to expect. Maybe it's their shared interests. Maybe it's their mutual upbringings in rural locations. For whatever

reason, Ptarmigan, Seb and Rita have become
the closest of friends.

'Now then,' says Ptarmigan, putting a Camel
between his lips. 'You two have been a bit thin
on the ground.'

Seb pinches a cigarette out of Rita's pack. He
lights his and Tarm's. He is taller than
Ptarmigan. His purple hair is crimped and
spiked, but lazily. Giving him an unkempt,
swashbuckling appearance.

'Well I'm up to my arse in Beowulf right
now. I kept having rows with Geoff last term
about it, but I'm with Grendel and his Mum. All
they wanted was a proper bit of peace and quiet.
And these hooligans are kicking up a racket day
and night in their stupid banqueting hall.
Imagine if Mrs B kept having Heavy Metal
bands playing at three-in-the-morning. I'd
complain. Rita'd go fucking mental! And, by the
way, she's Grendel's Mum in this scenario.
Anyway, the thing is a brilliant nightmare to
study. Bloody Vikings.'

Ptarmigan isn't familiar with the saga, but he
is used to Seb's unusual take on his course
topics. When he was studying Lord of The Flies,
he thought the little boys with sticks at the end

should have taken one look at the Naval officers who were there to rescue them, and then beaten them to death. He looks for the little white-haired girl, but she has either left or is at a dark table.

There is some movement near the entrance.

'Oh for fucks sakes!' Rita blows a dragons-worth of smoke. 'Emma bloody Smith and her coven.'

A woman with black Siouxsie-style hair and a leather mini-skirt has come in, followed by four similar-looking people.

'There goes the neighbourhood,' Ptarmigan smiles.

Seb looks round and waves.

'Jesus Seb! Don't get them over here!' Rita gives his ear a pull.

The newcomers either haven't seen Seb's gesturing or they're ignoring him. The three women and one of the men sit at a table. The other man walks to the bar.

Rita takes a deep breath, crushes out her cigarette, and finishes her drink. 'I've got months of the Rebecca Riots to look forward to.'

She sighs and fishes in her bag for her purse. 'Rebecca bloody Riots. I bet it was fascinating while it was going on. So was the snooker final. But I don't want to write a dissertation on it. And I'll tell you something Tarm. It's a good job the desks in our room face in opposite directions. All the bloody grunting he does. I'd kill him if I could see him.' She pecks Seb, who is looking outraged, on the cheek. Then she gets up and stomps to the bar in her Doc Martens, red and black dress swishing around her fishnet legs.

Seb watches her go. 'I love that woman mate. I'm going to make her my wife once all this education stuff is over. I'm going to give her children. I'm going to honour her. And she, Tarm… she is going to obey me.'

Ptarmigan chokes on his cigarette. 'Course she is! You can see obedience all over her face. You watch when she comes back. She'll be dripping with submission.'

They sit, tapping their feet to The The's Uncertain Smile, looking at Rita at the bar. When she returns and sits back down, they regard her with blank faces.

'What?' she says. They remain silent. 'What? Oy Seb, you knob. What?' Rita puts her fingers into her pint and flicks it at Seb.

'Fucking hell woman. That's my eyes!'

'And?' says Rita. She swigs at her pint and then she gets up to dance. The Clash have come on. Should I Stay or Should I Go.

Ptarmigan is almost helpless. Seb shakes his head. 'What's happened to us Tarm?'

'I don't know,' Ptarmigan replies. 'But it's funnier this way. Oh bloody hell. Hang about.'

One of Emma Smith's friends has come over to the table adjacent to theirs and is leaning on it, snakebite in hand. It is George Cave. He is staring at Tarm.

'They keep doing this,' Ptarmigan says, avoiding George's glare. 'I have no idea why. The thing with her lasted a month, if that. When I first got here. Then she realised I wasn't the cool and fashionable character she thought I was and that was that. As far as I was concerned anyway. And her. I assumed.'

'They'll have been in the Tea Clipper,' says Seb, louder than necessary. 'He'll be half-cut. He's a wanker. The only reason that lot have anything to do with him is because he reckons he's related to Nick.'

They both peer at George Cave's curly ginger hair and wispy red beard. Seb crosses his eyes at him. George's colour increases, even under the lights of the club. He wanders off and sits back down with Emma Smith and the others. They all put their heads together and look over at Ptarmigan's table, whispering.

Seb looks back at them. 'Left to Right!' He says, pointing and counting them off on his fingers, 'George Cave. Dick! Simon McBride. Dick! Caroline Swift. Dick! Fiona Handy. Dick! Emma Smith. Megadick! All moved here in a big stupid clod from the leafy Home Counties! All fucking entitled. All social climbing in the heady world of Sheffield studentdom. Not an original idea between them.'

Emma Smith's table have not noticed Seb's appraisal.

'What the hell happened to moving on?' Tarm says to Seb. Emma Smith's strange behaviour only bothers him in here. Not being a student, he rarely sees her anywhere else now.

'Ah that's the thing. She don't want it. She don't want nobody else to have it. Even though nobody else do have it. She don't want it. And yet! She still want it. She wants you and she don't want you Tarm. Simultaneously!'

'Also, did you gnash and grind your teeth when she dumped you?' Rita asks, sitting down, having caught the gist.

'Not a bit. Her choice. It was pointless anyway. Plus, they're all vile.'

Seb grins and swigs his pint. 'There we are then. Textbook spoiled, pretentious arsehole. Lucky escape there, Sunshine!'

Ptarmigan rubs his eyes and smiles. 'Great!' he says.

THE GANDHI

THE ASIAN SWEET CENTRE keeps normal shop hours. But the Gandhi Indian Restaurant, across the road from their nearest bus stop, stays open until 3am. Ptarmigan always finds this reality both amazing and a comfort. On the long nights before Rita and Seb came, when he was broke or wanted to sleep, it somehow reassured him to know that men in bow-ties were serving hot food to the tipsy in the long reaches of the night. Sometimes, if the wind was in the right direction, he could detect the Gandhi aroma as he lay in bed. Back in Lincolnshire, he says, you get arrested for being at large after nightfall.

They had left the club early, at eleven, and caught a bus back to Sharrow. It was a quiet night. Most of their fellow students have gone home for the summer. Rita and Seb have decided to stay on in Sheffield rather than returning to Wales. Partly due to their summer workload. And partly to have fun. Ptarmigan's white-haired girl never reappeared tonight. So, at the appropriate stop, they hopped off the bus, walked over the road, and grabbed a takeaway.

To save on washing-up issues they always sit with the full aluminium trays on dinner plates on their laps rather than dishing out. The lads at the Gandhi are very generous with the turmeric, and it's the devil to get off ceramic. Ptarmigan has his usual lamb masala and chips. Rita and Seb are eating king prawn biryanis and onion bhajis with mint yoghurt sauce. Tarm likes Sheffield masalas because they always have sliced boiled eggs on the top. He also likes chips with a curry, salt-and-vinegared, which the others think is plain weird.

Seb is fiddling with the big wood-effect colour TV, while trying not to let his plate of food slide off his lap. The television has a great picture, but it is hard to tune in.

'Bloody hell,' he says. '*The Thing* is on in a bit. The only horror film in history that starts with a Husky galloping about in the snow. John Carpenter.'

'Can't you put the plate on the floor while you're doing that?' Rita forks a king prawn between her lips.

'Not with you in here.' says Seb.

Ptarmigan wipes his mouth with a tissue. He always has tissues in his pockets. 'Did you know that in the original movie the monster looked like a giant carrot?'

Then the lights go out and the TV goes dark, leaving a strange grey oblong of luminescence where the screen was.

'Oh shit.' Rita says from somewhere. 'Anyone got any fifty-pees?'

'I have. I think. In my room. Hang about.' Ptarmigan carefully places his tray-on-a-plate onto the invisible carpet, trying to remember exactly where it is, and gets up. He feels his way across the room.

Rita and Seb hear the bottom of the living room door rub against the carpet as it opens. Tarm's door opens with a squeal. Then a yelp as he stubs something. A clink of coins. Then his dark form appears back in the room as their eyes become more accustomed to the gloom.

'I've got three here,' he says. 'Want me to do the honours?'

'I'll do it.' Seb's voice is surprisingly close. Tarm feels Seb's fingers trying to locate his own.

'Wrong hand! And mind where you're putting yours!' Seb snorts and Ptarmigan grabs his wrist and turns it. He makes sure that Seb's palm is facing upwards and feeds the fifty-pence-pieces into it. There a torch hanging on the back of the cellar door, which is in the corner of the living room. Seb makes his way in its general direction.

'Oh bugger!'

'What?' Rita hasn't moved but is still eating. She crunches a bhaji.

'I'm standing in someone's tray,' Seb says.

'Oh for fucks sakes!' Rita's cutlery rattles irritably on her plate.

Ptarmigan stays where he is. He thinks it's the safest thing to do.

The old latch on the cellar door clicks open and they can hear Seb's hand hunting for the hook with the torch hanging on it.

'Got it!' he announces. Rita tuts.

He turns it on. 'That torch is crap,' Rita has said this before. They have changed the batteries but it still has an anaemic beam.

Seb plays the meagre light across the living room floor. Everything looks monotone but there are obvious signs of curry among the geometric shapes on the carpet.

'Fucks sakes!' Rita says again.

Seb goes through the door and creeps down the stone steps into the cellar, where the gas and electricity meters hang among the blackened cobwebs. There is some muttered swearing, the sound of wood shifting, then a distant clicking sound. The light comes back on, followed by the television. Ptarmigan and Rita examine the ruins of the carpet. Egg, chips, rice, lamb and prawns are trodden across the room in two directions.

'He didn't only stand in his tray. He got mine too.' Ptarmigan was enjoying that. He has a feeling of genuine loss.

Seb comes back upstairs looking triumphant. Tarm and Rita look at him sternly.

'What?' he says.

GERDA

THE NEXT WEEK and Rita and Seb sit at their
usual table in the club. There are even fewer
people here than last time and Rita likes it like
this. Fewer bodies mean that the club is cooler.
And, should they want to dance, there is far
more room. The bar is less crowded too. 'Bloody
students!' she says under her breath and smiles
to herself. She is happy with her life right now
and can't imagine things changing. . She's doing
well on her course and, like Seb, is putting in
more hours than most. Although the bloody
Rebeccas are intensely dull. Road tolls? Wow! As
ever, Seb seems to be sailing through everything
without having to make much of an effort. Rita
looks across at him as he taps his fingers to the
music. He is wearing a floral shirt tonight, with
some sort of grey chiffon scarf around his neck.
His hair is all primped up on one side. She
pointed this out when they left the house and he
had laughed. She loves him more than she
would have thought possible. He is like a book.

The cover stays the same, but the story inside changes every day. And she knows he's comfortable too. They've been talking about their plans after qualifying, and they are both adamant that they're staying together. Seb has actually mentioned marriage. Rita had expected this, but it was also a wonderful surprise. She smiles a small and secret smile to herself.

It has been raining again today. Showers. A few meagre puddles. She had popped into town after the library to buy the *Dead Can Dance* album from Virgin Records. Walking through the Hole in the Road, she had felt as disoriented as ever. The angles in that place always seem wrong to her. And she had stopped to look at all the weird fish swimming trance-like in their thick glassed tank.

They haven't seen Tarm for a few days, Rita thinks. He hasn't missed a Doley & Student Night here since they've known him. He likes the cheap snakebite, and he thinks the music is great. He says it's like being able to play your own records at an ear-splitting volume. Seb gets up to dance to The Sisters of Mercy's *Floorshow*.

Emma Smith and her friends have taken up residence at a table near the stage. Emma Smith is standing and talking to a local Chicago House

Music DJ called Marriott. She appears to be enamoured with him, fiddling with her hair and touching his arm. Her hair is now short and blonde, and she is wearing a shiny black bomber jacket and ripped jeans. Her friends all appear to be in varying stages of morphing into a similar style.

A girl from Rita's course, Cat, is on the next table. Rita beckons to her and asks her to mind the table while she goes back to the bar. It is now 9.30, so she orders three pints. If Ptarmigan doesn't turn up she'll share his with Seb. Rita sits back down. Seb, sweaty, has returned to the table. He looks at the extra snakebite. Ptarmigan is usually here by now. He glances towards the entrance and, yes, here he is, blinking in the bright flashing lights, looking around for them. He is wearing a Butthole Surfers tee shirt and black jeans. His hair is a riot. Rita waves. He wanders over and sits down looking mysterious.

'What?' she says
'What what?' says Tarm.
'What are you looking so smug about?' she looks from Ptarmigan to Seb and back again. Seb looks vacant.

Tarm, watching the entrance, waves at someone. A small girl with vertical white hair has come through the door. She waves back and makes her way over.

'Hiya!' she says.

Ptarmigan pats the empty space next to him and she sits down. Tarm leaps up and goes to the almost empty bar.

Emma Smith sees him as he stands ordering a drink. She looks him up and down. 'My God Ptarmigan! You look so old-fashioned!' She dismisses him with a look of disdain and continues her conversation with the DJ. The DJ is wearing a green fedora, red braces and brown loafers.

Ptarmigan sits back down with Gerda's drink, makes an "introducing my beautiful assistant" gesture and says, 'This is Gerda.'

'Girder?' Rita raises her eyebrows, gesturing a vague lintel shape.

Gerda smiles broadly. 'It's Gerda. My Mum's German. Tarm's been at mine all weekend. I only live down the road from you.'

'Ah. Right. Hiya!' says Rita

'Hi!' Seb shakes her hand. Gerda bats her eyes a little.

Ptarmigan points at her snakebite. 'That's okay isn't it?'

Rita appraises her. Her hair is white and vertical. She is very pretty and is wearing a knee-length dress patterned with large red and purple roses and a suede waistcoat with badges on it. It's too dark to make them all out but she can see the black and white Birthday Party one clearly.

Gerda picks up her drink, downs half of it, looks at the few dancers on the stage, and then belches so loudly that Cat on the next table turns around to look and her friends laugh and applaud.

'Yep. Lovely old job!' she says.

The other three look surprised for a split second, then they start laughing too. Gerda joins in.

Emma Smith obviously heard as well. She sends a disgusted look towards their table. The DJ has gone elsewhere.

'Brilliant!' Seb takes a swig and starts laughing again, snorting a mouthful of snakebite out of his nose onto the table.

'You filthy bastard!' cries Rita.

Tarm looks round the table, puts an arm around Gerda, and is as happy as he has ever been.

'Emma Smith just told me I look old-fashioned,' he rolls his eyes. 'I am bereft!'

Gerda peers over at Emma Smith's table. She bats her eyes again. 'Anyone who's anyone thinks you're old-fashioned, dah-ling!'

Ptarmigan throws his head into his arms.

'Where did you meet him then?' Rita gestures at Ptarmigan with her thumb. Tarm lifts his head up and flashes his teeth at her.

'It turns out this one has been holding a torch for a while,' Gerda says, making a give me a fag gesture at Tarm, who hands her a Marlboro, takes one himself, and lights them both.

'He didn't know it was reciprocated though. Neither did I. So… Anyway. We actually met on the 17 bus.'

Seb begins to sing *Some Enchanted Evening*. Rita gives him a kick.

'Shut up. Are you at the Poly then?'

'Uni.' Gerda says. 'Physics. Batchelors. I'm wanting to stay on for a Masters. Maybe a doctorate.' Ptarmigan offers Rita and Seb an even bigger grin. They look impressed.

Gerda's accent is soft and curved. West Country, Rita thinks. She asks her.

'Somerset,' she says. 'Near Frome. Except it's spelled F-R-O-M-E.'

'That's near Glastonbury isn't it?' Seb asks her.

'Not far. We don't get too snarled up with Festival traffic though.'

'You can see Somerset from Newport in Wales.' Seb pulls at his lopsided hair. 'Weston-Super-Mare. Across the Bristol Channel. The Bristol Channel used to be called The Severn Sea you know.'

Rita raises her eyebrows. 'I'm going to the loo,' she says to Gerda. 'You coming?'

'Yeah.' They get up and make their way to the ladies.

Seizing her opportunity, Fiona Handy sways over to their table in her tie-dye tee shirt and baggy jeans. She sits heavily next to Ptarmigan, nearly tipping him off his seat. 'You've got a proper fucking nerve coming in here,' she says to him. She isn't quite focussing, and Tarm doesn't really know her. Seb sits opposite them with a huge grin on his face.

'Fiona?'

'Yeah.'

'Right. Fiona. I have no idea what you're on about. And you're in my girlfriend's place.'

'Girlfriend?' Fiona turns to Emma Smith's table and back again. 'Girlfriend?' Fiona laughs a little too loudly to sound natural. She looks back at Emma Smith. 'More fucking pity her, you bastard!' Fiona heaves herself up and weaves back towards Emma Smith's table. Emma Smith glares at Ptarmigan with a perplexing combination of smugness and fury.

Ptarmigan looks at Seb, who shrugs. 'La belle dame sans merci.'

'Less of the "belle", Seb. Why do women do that?' Ptarmigan asks, taking a mouthful of snakebite. 'Not that!' he gestures at Emma Smith's table. 'You know. Go to the toilet in gangs?'

'No idea. And I've never asked. Some things... y'know. Just bloody leave it man!'

Tarm laughs and, when the girls get back, they've been to the bar.

Later on, Rita says, 'Me and Seb were in the cellar earlier. We thought we'd make the path to and from the meters a bit less lethal after the curry fiasco the other night. Seb found an old suitcase full of records down there.'

Ptarmigan explains the electricity meter running out and ensuing Ghandi-marinaded carpet to Gerda.

'Yeah It was under that bloody pallet near the wall. Dusty old thing. Splintery. There's Bill Haley. Some old blues. Somebody called Odetta.

God knows. We can stick some on after. The
vinyl was wrapped in some old newspapers.
Three or four editions of the Star I reckon. Not
the national one. The Sheffield one. It smelled a
bit chapelly. You know, frowsty. So we left the
pages on the settee to air off before we came out.
I love that shit. Old minutiae. Dead people's
lives. Local intrigue. Terrible clothes. Brilliant
hair. Cheers you twats!' Seb takes a swig and
grins. 'Give us a fag Reet!'

Rita hands her pack of Benson & Hedges to
Seb, who takes one and offers them to Gerda and
Ptarmigan. 'Nah. You know I can't stand those
things.' Tarm pulls out his soft package of
Marlboro from a seersucker shirt-pocket and
lights one with a match. He only smokes Camels
or Marlboro and thinks English tobacco tastes
like soap. Usually. Gerda takes a Benson.
Seb and Rita get up to dance before they go
back to the bar.

NEWSPAPERS

THEY GET OFF THE BUS bus together and lean against a shopfront laughing about the Stonehenge scene in Spinal Tap. Seb sits on the window ledge and passes out cigarettes. He is a little pensive.

'We're all a long time dead you know,' he says after a while, almost to himself. 'We owe it to ourselves. To have fun. You know? To explore. Gather knowledge. Or at least not to end up sad fucking sacks like Emma Smith and George bloody Cave! There's all this… stuff. All around us. All these possibilities.' He moves his foot around on the pavement. 'And most people don't even know what's there if you scratch the surface of the world. You know? Underneath here,' he gestures downwards. 'There's sewers and electricity and gas. There's tunnels carrying water from the Sheaf and the Porter Brook. I heard last term that there's a cathedral underneath the train station. Not a Christian one. It's a huge cave made by the Victorians to stop the place flooding. The size of a cathedral. I want to know about this stuff. I think people are duty bound to go and discover what's out there. And under here'

Rita clutches the arm of his jacket. 'You're going nowhere, fuckface!'

'We're all going somewhere.' Seb hugs Rita. Lifts her off her feet.

'Put me down you bloody oik!' she cries, laughing.

Seb sets her down, grins, and says, 'And right now we're going to the Gandhi.'

Gerda has never had a meal from the Gandhi. Ptarmigan, Seb and Rita order their usual (Rita telling Seb to keep his fat feet out of hers). Gerda decides on a fish madras. With chips, Tarm is delighted to note. They sit on the plush red chairs in the takeaway waiting area. Seb and Rita are reading today's *Daily Express*.

Ptarmigan eyes them, pulls Gerda towards him, and whispers. 'Those two think I'm weird for having chips with curry.'

'You are weird.' Gerda whispers back, giving him a kiss on his ear.

Their meal collected, they walk back to Vanguard Road, passing through the narrow

alley created by their neighbour's wooden fence.
They go through the back door. The house
immediately smells mouth-watering. All spiced
and warm and opulent. Before they retrieve their
food from the grease-patterned brown paper
bags, Rita stacks the old newspapers near the
settee so Tarm and Gerda can look at them while
they eat. Sitting on the floor, with his curry to his
right and Gerda to his left, Tarm is turning the
manila-coloured pages. This was a broadsheet
paper, like The Star during the week. Not a
tabloid like the Saturday Star. The pages are
crisp, and they still smell old. Chapelly. But
they're not fragile. Old faces peer out of the
paper, smiling about long-forgotten events. Old
typefaces, set by real printers, and printed on
real printing presses. Ptarmigan wonders if any
of the men who produced these elderly, yellow
pages are still alive.

'This curry is great!' Gerda says, swallowing a
mouthful and taking a swig of cold Becks. She
glances at the newspapers now and then, but she
is hungrier than she thought.
'Firth Park was flooded like hell in the fifties!'
Ptarmigan says, a little shocked at the grainy
pictures of his half-submerged adopted city.

'So when are they from?' asks Rita, dissecting a bhaji with her fingers. 'We just unwrapped the records and set the papers to air a bit earlier.'

'1954,' says Tarm. 'From, hang about… July, July, August, more August, September… another September… and… this one's October. So there are seven editions. Or bits of seven. The Queen was coming here in November. Loads of kids were going to pile into the Sheffield Wednesday ground to see her. Funny to think she was knocking about that long ago isn't it? Oh. And there's one from 1961. That's a bit odd.'

Seb spills a forkful of oily yellow rice onto the carpet. Rita rolls her eyes. 'For fucks sake Seb. Not again!'

He looks abashed but opens his mouth, which is full of curry, and displays it to Rita.

'You disgust me.' she says.

'The ads are amazing! There's one for some sort of Viking outfit.' Tarm laughs

'Let's have a look.' says Seb, wobbling a little as he leans across to grab a paper. Rita keeps her eye on his plate.

'*Let Brylcreem Give You Clean Grooming! The Hillman Minx, Leadership Won By Craftsmanship. The Dance as you Farm Camp!* What the hell's that?' Seb grins and swigs Becks.

Ptarmigan turns to the front page of the later August edition and reads for a few moments. 'Bloody hell! Listen to this!'

The Sheffield Star. Wednesday July 28th 1954

'UNIVERSITY STUDENTS MISSING'

'The whereabouts of two student housemates studying Politics and Fine Art at Sheffield University has been unknown since last Saturday, July 24th. Richard Reeder, 21 and Simon Glass, 20, are reported to have been drinking in The Barfield public house on Abbeydale Road until around 7pm that night and have not been seen since.

Richard Reeder, known as 'Bunny', is 6ft tall with light brown hair. On Saturday last he was wearing blue jeans and a short, black leather jacket. Simon Glass, also 6ft tall and with dark hair, was wearing black-framed spectacles, a 'drape' jacket with a circular red design on the back, and blue jeans.

Their neighbour, a Mrs Bron, said today that she may have heard the students leaving their house on Vanguard Road in Sharrow late on the night of the 24th, but could not be certain.

Anyone with information is requested to call Sheffield & Rotherham police on Sheffield 165.'

'Bron?' exclaims Rita. 'That's next door isn't it?'

'Well. She's a Bron. Not necessarily the Bron.'
Tarm looks at the magnolia-painted wallpaper
on the dividing wall between the houses.

Seb and Ptarmigan carefully lay the
newspapers down on the floor in date order.
Rita fetches a pair of scissors from the kitchen.
Curries forgotten for the moment, they sit
together on the carpet, turning the rigid pages.
After half an hour they have created a makeshift
incident room like they have seen on The
Professionals. The clippings are placed in date
order on the sofa.

Gerda reads the next article aloud.

The Sheffield Star. Friday July 30th 1954

'MISSING STUDENTS TRIGGER MANHUNT'

**The Sheffield & Rotherham Constabulary have
launched a major investigation following the
disappearance of two popular Sheffield University
undergraduates. Simon Glass, 20, and Richard
Reeder, 21, were last seen in The Barfield public
house on Abbeydale Road at around 7pm on
Saturday July 24th and left the premises together.
Reeder and Glass are known to live at the same
rented house on Vanguard Road in the Sharrow
area of the city and have not been seen since they
left the public house.**

As stated in our previous report, Richard Reeder, known as 'Bunny', is 6ft tall with light brown hair. On Saturday last he was wearing blue jeans and a black leather jacket. Simon Glass, also 6ft tall with dark hair, was wearing black-framed spectacles, a blue 'drape' jacket with a circular red design on the back, and blue jeans. Both students are keen fans of both Rock and Roll and Folk music. However there have been no related events occurring locally or nationally.

Their neighbour, a Mrs Bron, said that she may have heard the students leaving the house late on that Saturday night but could not be certain.

Following house-to-house enquiries, officers are now expanding their search to include Porter Brook and the nearby Mill Pond.

Anyone with information is requested to call Sheffield & Rotherham police on Sheffield 165.

Rita grabs Ptarmigan's sleeve. Then she nudges Seb, who is next to her on his knees. She is looking at the record on the top of the pile in the old suitcase. The others look too. Bill Haley & the Comets.

'Rock and Roll.' she whispers.

And they read the press clippings again.

MRS B

THURSDAY. A BRIGHT morning on Vanguard
Road. The road shines. A shower before dawn
has made everything sparkle. Dewy birds sing,
and Ptarmigan wakes to them. He lays warm in
his ground floor double bed and watches the sun
peep over the top of the maroon bay-window
curtain. Gerda's white hair pokes out of the
duvet next to him. The rest of her is nestled,
purring, in the folds of the bed. Now day is here,
last night's strange investigations feel vaguely
ridiculous. They had talked into the small hours
about the disappearance of Simon Glass and
Bunny Reeder. Eventually, Rita said she needed
to sleep because she had to go to the library this
morning, and she and Seb had turned in. Gerda
and Ptarmigan sat on the settee drinking Irish
Whiskey for a while, talking. Did these two
young men live in their house? It seems likely.
They had looked at the collection of 1950's music
but had not played any for fear of disturbing

Mrs Bron or the never-seen neighbours on the other side of the house.

The record covers are all beiged with the years. The corners all dog-eared and frayed. None have the inner lyric or picture inner sleeves they are used to. But the vinyl itself, the couple they had examined at any rate, is almost pristine, at least to their eyes. Later, he thinks, they should listen to some of this unexpected bounty.

He slides out of bed and covers Gerda back up with the duvet. She gives a little snore. He looks at her sleeping face. He thinks they might make each other very happy. But it's early days. He touches her hand. Her skin is warm and silky. Then he shuffs on his slippers and grabs his purple towelling dressing gown from its hook on the door. Wandering through the living room he glances at last night's debris-field. Part-eaten curries on the floor. Fifties records popped back into the ancient suitcase. Two overflowing ashtrays. Old newspaper cuttings still laid out in date order along the settee. Jesus! It's all a bit strange. Like Scooby Doo. Only real. Possibly. He thinks he might warm some of the curry up for his breakfast later if the flies haven't been at it.

Kettle on, he glances at the old lozenge-shaped mantelpiece clock. Has this thing been here since the fifties? It looks old enough. He picks it up and sniffs. It smells oily and metallic. God knows. He doesn't know who used the kettle before. Or this Willow Pattern mug. He doesn't even know how many people have slept on his mattress. He doesn't know who they were or how much sex they had on it. Plenty, he thinks. The kettle howls. Into the mug goes the teabag. Tea is the only way to start the day.

Sitting in the armchair opposite the huge colour TV, he places his scalding mug onto the beige tiled fire-surround, hops up, and turns it on. The TV warms up. Tick. Tick. He twiddles the station button around. Morning television. Frank Bough in a mustard jumper. God it's early! Seb probably won't be up for hours, and Rita must have left already. Her mug is in the sink, and she's had toast. Her crumby plate sits on the kitchen worktop. Tarm lights a Camel, realises he needs to buy some more, and slurps his tea. He thinks about the girl sleeping soundly in his bed and grins at Frank Bough. The sound of a gate latch outside. Ptarmigan leans back a little and moves the yellow curtains aside. Mrs Bron is sweeping her patio.

'Hello Tarm!' she smiles over her fence at him as he emerges into the full of the sun, carrying his mug of tea.
'Morning Mrs Bron.' he says, blinking.

Mrs Bron is, as far as the housemates can figure, somewhere between forty and sixty years of age. Although, with the additional information gleaned from the old Star issues, Tarm now thinks that she could be a little older. If so, she wears it very well. Her round face is almost unlined atop her slight, slim body. She wears a flowery apron over her skirt and a usually pastel-coloured blouse. Her hair is blonde-going-on-grey, and she wears it in a long, plaited ponytail. Seb says she looks like the woman on the Aunt Bessie's Yorkshire Pudding boxes apart from the hair. If Aunt Bessie was a bit hotter. There was a Mr Bron at some point. Nobody next door has felt comfortable asking about him though. So his whereabouts is a mystery. Mrs Bron has a large and primitive stone angel-like figure in her garden that she keeps polished. Seb thinks it's an old piece. He says that this is proven by the way it survives the frosts.

'It was so hot in my bedroom last night that I
could smell your curry through the window.'
she smiles, leaning on her broom. 'Nice?'
'The Gandhi's always great Mrs Bron,' says
Tarm, shielding his eyes from the glary sun. 'The
others think I'm a lunatic for having chips with
it.'
Mrs Bron smiles again. 'What do they know?
Chips are manna!'

She is full of these little phrases, which is one of
the reasons everyone in the house likes her.

'Mrs Bron,' says Ptarmigan. He takes a swig of
his tea. 'We found some records in a suitcase
yesterday. Vinyl. Albums. LP's. You know?'
She nods and puts her head to one side.
'There were some old newspapers with them.
Well, the records were wrapped up in them. In
the old papers. Sheffield Stars. From 1954. And
one from '61. They all had reports about a couple
of students who went missing thirty years ago.
A bloke called Glass and another one called
Reeder? Was it you who talked to the papers
about it? We wondered if they lived in our
house. They mentioned your name. Well, they
mentioned a Mrs Bron.'

'Simon and Bunny. Oh god yes.' Mrs Bron looks into the blue sky. Swifts are screaming up there. 'They were great lads. They were the first students here after Joe Torode started renting. Joe was Julian's dad. Julian's your landlord? Aye! Nice work if you can get it. But yes. Lovely young men. Very quiet. Up and left one day. Or one night. Nobody knows.' She looks at him then sweeps at a fallen leaf.

'I'd love to know what happened. We're all fascinated!' Tarm says. And he means it. He finishes the last of his tea, dangles the mug by its handle.

Mrs Bron flicks her duster at a fly. 'Well I don't know. Those lads going off like that. Maybe they are dead like the papers said. Maybe they went journeying. Like I told the police back then, I thought I heard them go out. I heard something anyway.'

'Was Mr Bron here back then?' asks Tarm, pulling his cigarettes out of a top shirt pocket.

'No. He wasn't.' says Mrs Bron. She looks up to the sky again, and then back at Ptarmigan. 'He was long gone by then. Right. Must crack on. See you later Tarm.'

And with that she shuts the yard gate and goes back into her house, glancing at her primitive stone angel figure.

Tarm lights his Camel. He looks around the yard and up at the terraced house roofs. There are three magpies there, on Mrs Bron's side. They hop along the roof ridge yelling their cracked music. Then they fly away.

THE SECRET OF BLOSSOM DEARIE

RITA'S DOC MARTENS crunching the loose stones in the yard announce her approach. She comes in, damp and puffing. After dropping her scuffed leather schoolgirl satchel onto the sofa, undoing her DM laces and kicking them off, she walks into the kitchen. The gas burner tick-tick-ticks and puffs on. The Willow Pattern kettle is filled and scraped onto the hob.

'Jesus!' she says, 'Bloody library. Bloody Rebecca Riots. I know I'm Welsh. But the ins and bloody outs. Jesus! My fingers are killing me!' There is silence from Ptarmigan and Seb. A crowd whoops on the TV.

She stands in the living room doorway. Seb and Ptarmigan are watching Blockbusters. 'Hiya! I'm here you know!'

'Ah, sorry love.' Seb smooths the settee next to him and pats it, 'It's a Gold Run in a minute.

We're rooting for the Northern girls with the make-up. The bloke's a right tit.'

'He is!' Ptarmigan laughs.

Gerda emerges from Tarm's room. Her white hair is feathery and falling around her face. She has been in the bath. She sits by Ptarmigan in the middle of the sofa, Seb on her other side. She lights a Marlboro.

'Hallo Rita!' she says. 'Good day at the library?'

'Don't ask.' Rita throws herself onto the chair in front of the slightly open window. She lights a cigarette. 'But that was twice as much study as I needed to do. Again. So I'm off it for a few days. Thank fucking God.'

Gerda chuckles and sits, fluffing her hair. Then she stops dead, staring past Rita.

'What? Is it a wasp?' Rita looks behind her, following Gerda's gaze.

Ptarmigan looks at Gerda, then at the window. 'What?' he asks.

'I thought I saw someone out there. Looking in. Can't have been. They'd still be there. Ignore me.'

Seb, also looking at the window, appears to wilt. He looks as if he is about to say something. His mouth moves.

Then Rita throws her box of matches at him. The spell is broken.

'I was going to make a cup of tea,' Rita says, 'Fancy getting off your fat arse and doing it for me? I've been up to my eyes in cross-dressing farmers all day.'

'Me! Me! Pick me!' cries Seb as he leaps up, throwing the matches back at Rita. He dances towards the kitchen like John Cleese.

'Twit.' says Rita, slapping his bottom hard.

Ptarmigan is always charmed by the comfortable depth of his friends' relationship. He knows they come from adjacent villages in the South Wales Valleys, now decimated by Thatcher's policies, and so they are likely to have many points of reference. But still, the ease they have with each other means that it looks to him like they will be together for a lifetime. He hopes so.

The yellow curtains puff. Rita pulls another Benson out of her pack and lights it, flicking the match into the odd twirly ashtray-on-a-stand near the coffee table. She inhales, then breathes out fragrant blueish smoke, tucking her feet under herself.

'Alright?' she asks Tarm.

'Yeah. Weird.. I spoke to Mrs B earlier, after you'd left. Seb was snoring his head off upstairs.' ('Fuck off!' shouts Seb from the kitchen)

'And?'

'And. Well, she did know those two students. They did live here.'

'Christ!' Rita rolls her cigarette about in the ashtray. 'So, what did she say?'

Seb comes in and hands Gerda and Ptarmigan a mug of tea. He sits down and puts his and Rita's on the coffee table.

'Not much. She says she thought she heard them go out late. She says they might have gone abroad. Well, she said journeying.'

'Well that doesn't wash,' Rita says. 'Passports. Tickets. Sounds like they were easy to spot as well, with that red thing on the Teddy Boy jacket. And who goes journeying for thirty years without telling anyone?'

'That's what I thought.' says Tarm.

Seb has swigged some of his tea and is rifling through the suitcase of albums again. He pulls a few out. The worn covers make a soft slooshing sound as they rub together. Here is an exotic lady surrounded by moustachioed, baggy-sleeved men holding ukuleles. Here a black and white saxophone breathing crotchets and quavers. Here is Bill Haley, grinning next to his Comets. Here a sad-looking couple hugging acoustic guitars.

'God Alive! Who the hell are these people? Joe Hill? Charlie Gore? Look at this thing. 'The Lure of The Tropics'! Let's put that on. Oh no. Hang about.' He slides another threadbare record out. *Blossom Dearie and King Pleasure*? Fuck off! That's not real is it?'

Ptarmigan grabs the album. Judging by the blurry sleeve-notes it is a French release, and it looks like a bootleg. Were there bootlegs back then? A vague picture of a woman wearing glasses is on the front, along with what look like instruments and maybe other women. The image is so primitive and faded that it is hard to make much out.

'Here, pop this on.' Ptarmigan says, sliding the record from its cover. It is in mint condition.

Seb takes the album out and places it onto the turntable. When the needle reaches sound, a smoky female voice and ornate jazz guitar tumble into the room. The three friends look at each other. The music is delicious.

'Wow!' Rita says, 'This is lovely! Like Julie London or something! Let's have a look at the cover.'

Tarm passes the album sleeve to Rita. And as he does so, something falls out of it. They all hear and see something hit the geometrically patterned carpet. There it lays. It is creamy and shiny. Seb reaches across and picks it up.

Thick paper. Or is it vellum? It is heavily foxed with rusty-looking pockmarks. There is further discolouration sown along the four creases where it has been folded for three decades. At the top of the map runs a bluish line with PORTER BROOK written along it. There are other words here, but they have faded. Below this is a vague oblong marked SHEFFIELD GENERAL CEMETERY. Whoever made the map has reinforced this fact by drawing little skeletons all over the area. The cemetery is dissected by several intermittent lines, noted as TERRACE. And there are drawings of a church, a building that resembles The Pantheon, and a large, chunky Arc de Triomph shape. These three sketches are numbered. 1 – THE ANGLICAN CHAPEL. 2 – SAMUEL WORTH'S CHAPEL. 3 – THE GREAT GATE. The mapmaker has drawn two snakes near this one, along with a circle with feathers coming out of its sides. Two lines of XXXX's run through the cemetary site, marked STEEP PATHS! BE CAREFUL!. To the left of the cemetery is a plankton-like blob with what look like cilia poking out of it. It looks like an afterthought. This nebulous shape is filled with tiny writing. And there is a primitive heart-shape in the centre. At the bottom right of the map is a childlike drawing of a house, with smoke puffing from the chimney. Arrows lead from the house to THE GREAT GATE. More writing. Illegible. And written boldly down the right hand side, the words WE WILL EXPLORE!

Seb studies it. 'Well, it's a map!' He passes it to Tarm and Gerda, who move their fingers along the arrowed lines. 'Wow! Do you think those boys made it?' Gerda is reading the words on the sepia-coloured paper.

'Pass that here!' demands Rita. Ptarmigan, having looked, passes it to her. She studies it for a while. 'It's the cemetery up the road. The massive one. It goes from this house as well. This house! Look. Down here at the bottom. It says *Our House On Vanguard Road*.'

They crowd around Rita.

Gerda looks closely. Some of the writing is badly faded. 'Bloody hell, it does as well! It must have been made by those students who went missing. Surely? What's that stuff in that amoeba thing on the left?'

Seb, who has been studying his mug of tea, leans across Rita and pushes his face so close to the paper that his nose almost touches it.

'That's Huxley!' he says, 'Definitely Huxley. Look. In that blob thing on the left? *To become enlightened is to become aware.* That's from *The Doors of Perception.* You know. Riders on the Storm. There's even an 'AH'. Aldous Huxley. And it says '1954'. And "Bunny & Simon". With a heart. Is it a heart?'

'That heart looks like a willy.' says Tarm, pointing.

'Looks like yours.' cackles Seb.

Ptarmigan sticks the v's up at Seb, and reaches for the final Star cutting. He reads aloud:

The Sheffield Star. Wednesday August 30th 1961

'STUDENTS GLASS & REEDER PRONOUNCED DEAD'

Despite the weeks of effort conducted by The Sheffield & Rotherham Constabulary and other agencies in 1954 and subsequently, and with the

agreement of their families, the Sheffield High
Court has announced that missing Sheffield
University students Richard Reeder and Simon
Glass are Missing, Presumed Dead. The students,
aged 20 and 21, vanished after being seen drinking
in The Barfield public house in the early evening of
Saturday 24th July 1954. The landlord of The
Barfield, Mr Bryn Marr, was the last person to
report seeing the young men. Following extensive
house-to-house enquiries and several searches of
both the Mill Pond and Porter Brook at Frog Walk,
the authorities widened their enquiries. Lecturers
and the student body were interviewed extensively,
and every hospital and Constabulary in the country
were contacted. Officers travelled to Glass and
Reeder's family homes in Rotherham and Bristol to
gather information but, having had no contact
from either young man for more than a month, and
with no financial transactions or sightings since
that period, court official Mr Charles Sixsmith, has
pronounced their tragic deaths.

The students' neighbour, one Mrs Bron, said
shortly after their disappearance that she may have
heard the pair leave their house very late on the
night of the 24th July, but that she was in bed at
the time and could not be certain.

Richard 'Bunny' Reeder, originally from Bristol,
was studying Politics. He was a popular student
with a love of Folk and Rock and Roll Music. He
leaves behind his parents.

Simon Glass was a Fine Art student from
Bramley near Rotherham. An accomplished
guitarist and also a Rock and Roll and Folk-music
afficionado, he had expressed an interest in a

career in music. He leaves behind his widowed mother.

Dr Stephen Clare, dean of Sheffield University, has sent the faculty's belated condolences to their families.

THE BARFIELD

IT IS NINE O'CLOCK on Friday night, and Gerda, Ptarmigan, Seb and Rita are in the front bar of The Barfield pub. Rita and Seb are playing pool. Seb is being defeated. The bar is only a quarter full. Like the club, this place depends in good part on the students who live nearby.

'Oy! Tarm! You putting your money down?' yells Rita across the room. 'This bloke's bloody hopeless!' Seb flicks her on the arse with his cue, leaving a blue dash.

'I need a couple more pints before I'll be any good,' says Ptarmigan. 'Then I'll whup you.'

Gerda asks him, 'Are you any good at pool?'

'Not as good as her. You?'

'Wait and see.'

Rita gives a snort. Her hair is now blue-black, and she has had it shaved into a thick mohawk. She is wearing a light, floral cotton dress, thick black tights and her DM's. Gerda, her white hair defying gravity again, is in knee-length black shorts, baseball boots and an old Virgin Prunes tee shirt. Seb is wearing a too-long black t-shirt with the Sex Gang Children logo on it. His purple hair is growing out to his natural light brown. Tarm has a black polo neck and black jeans on. He's had a bath and ruffled his hair up with a towel so it's fallen flat. Seb says he looks like a lounge-lizard or an assassin. Gerda likes it.

'Bastard!' says Seb as Rita pots the black. 'Pub sticks!' He peers down the length of his cue. 'This thing's like a bloody oxbow lake!'

'It's the same as mine.' Rita grins. 'You're just crap. Come on. Tarm? Gerd?'

'In a bit. Nobody else looks interested. I'll get a round in.' Ptarmigan reaches for their glasses.

'I'm in!' Gerd bounces out of her chair and over to the pool table. They rack up, giggling about something.

Tarm is back within two minutes with four pints and a bag of tomato flavour Wheat Crunchies on a Greenall Whitley tray. The tray features a colour photograph of a 1970's man with a perm. He is holding a pint mug full of richly coloured ale in one hand and is doing a thumbs up with the other. He wears a chunky knitted gold jumper and is grinning at the long-ago brewery photographer.

'Flash the ash Tarm!' Seb gestures, waggling his fingers.

Tarm throws his Marlboro onto the table. Seb helps himself. Ptarmigan takes one. He opens the crispy snacks and offers them round. Rita comes over from the pool table and takes a huge handful for herself and Gerda. Seb shakes his head.

'Simon and Bunny.' Ptarmigan says quietly. 'I wonder whose rooms they had.'

The door slams open. Emma Smith, George Cave and Fiona Handy. Emma Smith scans the room. She is wearing heavy gold earrings. Her hair is still blonde. It is now shaved around her ears. Her shiny black bomber jacket is worn over a pink tee shirt that announces *POLO*. She spies Tarm, Rita and Seb, turns, and walks back out. George Cave and Fiona Handy gaze blank-eyed at them for a few seconds. Then they turn and follow her. Fiona Handy throws Rita a look of disdain.

'Shame.' says Seb, sipping his pint. 'I was just wondering what was *en vogue* right this moment. I thought they could help.'

Rita, standing next to Tarm and crunching her snacks, glances at Gerda, who is clearing the table.

'She's a bit good!'

'What?' Ptarmigan is still thinking about Emma Smith.

'Gerda. Pool. Back in the real world. Where we live. Where Emma Smith doesn't live. She's better than me.'

'She's a physicist,' Ptarmigan says, 'She understand stuff.'

The black goes down. Rita sits down on her chair and sighs. 'Bloody hell. Three shots I got in that game!'

Gerda disappears to the toilets.

Seb has been thinking about Simon and Bunny, and which rooms they lived in at Vanguard Road. He says, 'I don't know. It makes me a bit goosey actually. I mean, there were two of them. Could be either way. Our rooms are a bit of a squeeze, but they both take a double bed. I don't suppose double beds were encouraged back then though? Not in the fifties. Hays Office and all that.'

Two hippies have suddenly appeared from the back bar and are putting money into the pool table slot. The balls rumble out.

Gerda comes back into the bar looking troubled. She sits down.

Rita says, 'Our double bed fits in our room a bit better than yours does, Tarm.'

Seb leers and rolls his tongue about in his mouth making a squelching noise.

'You filthy sod!' Rita clouts him on the arm. Seb mock-falls off his chair.

Ptarmigan looks at Gerda over the rim of his glass and rolls his eyes. She looks back at him blankly.

'Gerd? You okay?' Ptarmigan gets up and sits next to her. He takes her hand. 'Have I done something?'

Gerda studies him for a few moments. She considers, weighing things up. Then she smiles so widely that he can see bits of Wheat Crunchy in her molars.

'No Tarm. You haven't. You've done nothing but what you should have done. Give me a kiss, Mister Lincolnshire!' They wrap themselves in each other.

Seb climbs back onto his chair and says, 'Put him down for Christ's sake!'

Later. 'You've not read any Huxley have you?' Seb asks them, shifting in his seat.

'I have,' Gerda says, 'But it was ages ago.'

Seb nods. 'He wrote loads, but it's *Brave New World* and *The Doors of Perception* he's known for. I studied *Brave New World* at school. By mistake.'

'How the hell do you study a book by mistake?' ask Tarm. He looks at the bar, his pint is nearly gone. It's getting dark outside now. He can see sodium light through the curtains. A taxi grumbles at a red traffic light.

'Summer holiday project. Just before O-Levels. Mr Gripper wanted us to do *The Go Between*. You know? Hartley?' Ptarmigan nods. Nobody else says anything.

'Anyway, I'd read that one and it was okay, but I wanted to push things a bit. I asked him if I could write about the Huxley book instead. Mr Gripper looked at the itinerary or whatever it was and said it didn't matter what book it was. So I did *Brave New World*.'

'I've seen the movie of that.' says Tarm. Seb always amazes him, the way he can flip from being a clown to a deadly serious intellectual in a heartbeat.

'I haven't. I didn't know there was one. Anyway, it's an amazing book. Set in the future.

Humankind grown in tanks. Hideous demarcation of classes. Eugenics. Pretty grim old stuff. Epsilons. Gammas. Alphas. The Alphas were in charge, and they were all off their tits on this drug called Soma all the time. If an Alpha was good in the sack, they got a reputation as pneumatic. It's a hell of a book. I got a great mark from Mr Gripper as well. Anyway, those two students put a quote from him on that map. In the amoeba thing. From The Doors of Perception. *To become enlightened is to become aware*. Aldous wrote the book in 1954. So those blokes were on the ball. Or one of them was at any rate. It's about when Huxley took Mescalin in 1953. Mescalin's a Mexican cactus derivative. Like natural acid or magic mushrooms or something. He was with his wife and a psychiatrist while he was tripping. Once the stuff kicked, in vases of flowers became like pure light. Time lost its meaning. He existed for the moment, every moment. The there and the then. And he began to understand ancient philosophies and ideas. That was the opening of the doors. Although at one point they put some Mozart on the gramophone, and Huxley became terrified by some lawn furniture.'

'No thanks!' says Rita.

'Don't knock it til you've tried it!' Seb finishes his beer. 'I'll get them in.'

'You haven't tried it!' Rita laughs.

'A man's history is full of dark secrets.' says Seb, getting up.

'Your history's full of beer.'

Seb gives them all a smile, sticks out his tongue, and heads to the bar with the Greenall Whitely tray.

Ptarmigan shrugs. 'I have no idea where this is going Reet.' he says. 'Bloody hell. Gerda, I'd like to introduce you to Seb. The fucking maniac.'

Rita looks at Seb's back while he leans on the bar.

Gerda finishes her pint.

'Lovely old job!' she says.

The hippies have given up on their game of pool. Rita gets up and pots the balls, one by one, with ease.

Seb sits back down with the beers. 'I hope they'd finished playing.' he says.

'Look what I've done with your bent cue.' Rita says.

'That's your cue. Anyway. I think that Bunny and Simon had both read the Huxley book. And I reckon they got hold of some sort of trippy shit and planned to go and explore that big old cemetery after dark to get the bona-fide Huxley experience. Although Aldous went to a big chemists shop in West Hollywood rather than a cemetery. Anyway, I can't think why else they'd make a map.'

Tarm thinks. 'Yeah, but if they took the map to the cemetery then disappeared for ever, how did it get back into the house?' He hands out some Marlboro.

Seb downs half his pint. 'I don't think they took it with them in the end.'

'Why the hell not?' asks Gerda, lighting their cigarettes.

'Because they were off their fucking heads.' says Seb.

THE DEAL

JACK MARX IS LEGENDARY among the students of Sharrow and their friends. He is the go-to dealer for those wishing to expand their psyches beyond academia. A local ex-student himself, Jack realised during his first year in 1978 that there were easier ways to make a living in this town than three years of Technology and Design lectures, followed by working until he keeled over and died. Jack doesn't supply drugs that can kill people, his ethos being 'why kill your customers?'. Added to which he dislikes "hard" drugs because of the familial and societal damage they can wreak in the wrong hands. But his business has been healthy enough to enable him to buy a large house with a large garden in pleasant Nether Edge at the age of 26. And he buys a new car every other year, even if they're always sensible ex-demo second-hand models. The police have thus far turned a blind eye to Jack's activities, because his wares, in effect, keep the youth of the area a lot calmer than the local off-licenses and pubs.

As well as his soft but illegal trade in mind-altering items, Jack is also a talented recording engineer. He is in some demand from Sheffield's thriving music scene. He has a small studio, off the city centre, which is rarely idle. Jack has worked with acts who have become, if not household names, then at least renowned in alternative and Post-Punk circles. His records are regularly played on Radio One by John Peel and Annie Nightingale. Jack Marx is grounded enough to have never let his success go to his head, unlike many with his enhanced reputation.

Although Seb is a keen beer drinker, he also buys an occasional wrap of speed or block of Red Leb. So he and Jack are acquainted. And they get on well. In a long leather coat and a trilby today because it has been raining on and off, Seb opens the squealing gate and walks up the path to Jack's front door. He brushes past a small azalea. Thin rivulets of water from its flowers and leaves run down his coat. Seb pulls the old-fashioned bell-ring. It dings twice somewhere in the house. He hears soft footsteps on a tile hallway floor.

The big black front door opens. 'Hi Seb!' says Jack. He glances up and down the road. 'Come in then.'

Jack Marx is a slim man with a day's blueish stubble on his cheeks and chin. His black hair is curly and combed back with some sort of preparation. Brylcreem, Seb thinks. That's traditional! He is wearing a Damned tee shirt and what look like cycling shorts. He always looks like he wears eyeliner, but this is the result of his jet-black lashes.

Seb follows Jack down the hallway and into a high-ceilinged lounge with highly polished floorboards. They sit. Seb looks around the room and rests his hat on his knee. Here is a bookshelf heavy with paperbacks, there a vinyl collection that stretches along two walls, over there a huge, framed poster of the Cabaret Voltaire album Jack worked on. And a new Gibson bass is hanging on the wall.

Seb looks around the room and rests his hat on his knee. Here is a bookshelf heavy with paperbacks, there a vinyl collection that stretches along two walls, over there a huge, framed poster of the Cabaret Voltaire album Jack worked on. And a shiny Gibson bass is hanging on the wall.

'That's a pretty thing!' says Seb, admiring the guitar.

'Yeah. Second-hand mind! It's in great nick. Just have to learn how to play it now.' Jack pours a glass of a reddish liquid from an ice-cubed jug that sits on an occasional-table next to his armchair. 'Pimm's. Simone's at her folks. So I can day-booze.' He glances at his watch. 'Well, teatime booze anyway. No studio work tonight either. Fancy one?'

'No ta.' says Seb. 'It always tastes weird. Bit alkaline. What have you been up to?'

Jack lights a large spliff, takes a draw and offers it to Seb, who shakes his head again.

'Quite busy. Been in with Repulsive Alien. The Box. Some lot called Siiiii. There's some cracking stuff around here right now. How's Rita?'

'Oh she's fine. She's doing the Rebecca Riots right now. Tenant farmer protests. 1840's. It's driving her scatty. She says it's the most boring period of Welsh History. And that's saying something. Anyway. I'd like some mushrooms mate. If you've got any.'

Jack clears his throat and sips his cold Pimm's. 'How much?'

Seb hasn't even considered this. He thinks.

'Enough to give three people a proper experience? We're doing a Huxley. I might write a book!'

'Okay Timothy Leary. Well, it's by weight. There's about four hundred in my bags. I got them last Autumn up at Foxhouse. They dried lovely. That'll do you easy. It'd do a football team.'

'Sold!' says Seb, smiling.

Jack bends down and lifts a foot-long section of floorboard to his right. He puts the board on his knees and pulls out a black plastic container about the size of a shoebox. He lifts the lid, rummages around, and produces a crisp-packet sized plastic Ziploc bag full of little twiggy stems wearing helmets. The Ziploc bag is tossed to Seb, and the floorboard goes back down with a gentle thunk.

He sees Seb looking at the secret hidey-hole and smiles. 'Hey! I love Simone and everything, but I don't know all of her secrets. And she doesn't know all of mine. Well, I don't think she does!'

'Fair do's' Seb agrees.

Cash changes hands. The hands are shaken. The bag goes in a leather coat pocket. Seb puts his hat back on. They go to into the hallway.

'Have a good evening with your No.1 Cup Jack!'

'I will Seb. I'm getting that bass of the wall in a minute. Got to start somewhere. See you soon buddy!' says Jack, closing his front door.

ANGER

IT IS SEVEN in the evening on Tuesday July 23rd, the following day. They are in the front bar of The Barfield again. Once more they have the place almost to themselves. It's nice, thinks Gerda. This airy place with the evening sun's rays hitting the carpet. It is quiet too, unless they decide to pop a song or two on the jukebox. No hassle. Good friends. Things are fine.

They are sitting around a different table tonight, near the bright window. Rita prods Seb in the ribs. She has told him that she doesn't feel like drinking tonight and is still only a quarter of the way down her first pint of Castle Eden. A bus growls past on the road outside. It blocks out the sunshine and darkens their faces. Somebody rings the service bell in the back bar.

'What were you being so shifty about earlier then?'

'Ah,' he says. 'I'm glad you've asked me that. There's something odd in your knicker drawer.'

Ptarmigan and Gerda's eyes go wide and they laugh.

'What?' Rita prods him again, harder.

'Something unexpected Reet.'

'Jesus Seb. Talk bloody sense will you?' Rita is looking at the pool table.

'I went to see Jack Marx.' says Seb.

There is a definite pause.

'Oh Jesus!' Rita eyes him. 'Why?'

'Well. It's Wednesday July the 24th tomorrow.'

'And?'

'And what?' Seb is half-drunk and feeling playful.

'And? And what the hell has Wednesday July the 24th got to do with Jack bloody Marx?'

'Bunny and Simon. Aldous Huxley. The map. The disappearance. The cemetery. Rita, I have a plan.'

Gerda looks bewildered. 'What?'

'You've got to be joking!' Rita is beginning to look concerned. 'What have you done?'

Seb offers her a smile that usually pours oil onto troubled waters. 'I've got us some magic mushrooms. You know. *Psilocybe semilanceata*. Dried. Enough to fell a pony, according to Jack.'

'Again. Why?' Rita has crossed her arms. Her eyebrows are clumped together.

'What are you lot on about?' asks Gerda again. Then she gets it. 'Ah god! Those boys. They went missing didn't they. What…' she calculates and looks at Seb with something approaching awe. 'Thirty years ago. Tomorrow.'

Seb grins at her, 'Well, tomorrow night.'

Rita sits playing with her hair for a moment. Then she says, 'I hope you're not thinking about doing what I think you're thinking about doing.'

Seb makes the mistake of finding this repetition hilarious, and Rita immediately gets up and walks out of the pub. They see her furious head make its way past their window and then she is gone. Tarm and Gerda study their drinks. Seb cranes his neck up to the window to see if she is coming back. He looks a little lost and very young.

Thirty seconds later the doors open and Emma Smith, Simon McBride, Caroline Swift, Fiona Handy and George Cave come through it.

'I just saw Rita storming away!' Emma says with an innocent smile as she stands against the bar.

Seb gets to his feet. 'Yeah, well when my life is any of your fucking business I'll drop you a line.' He is livid. The blood has emigrated from his face to his limbs, giving it an almost blue colour. 'So why don't you take your poisonous clique of airhead fuckwits somewhere else before I fucking do it for you?'

Simon McBride looks like he might take Seb up on the challenge. Then he takes a proper glance at his face and decides against it. Emma Smith appraises Seb as he stands breathing hard. She smiles again and then, once again, they all retreat into the back bar. A few moments later, Emma Smith's shrieking laughter can be heard.

Gerda puts her head on Ptarmigan's shoulder. Ptarmigan takes a drink and glances up. Seb is furious. He sits down and takes a deep breath. 'I'll go after her. Rita. I'll see you later. No worries. It'll be okay.' He puts on his hat and leaves, slamming the door behind him as he goes.

'Bloody hell!' says Ptarmigan. 'I've never seen them argue before. Not in over a year. And that's the first time I have seen Seb actually angry. Ever.'

'Let's go back to mine tonight.' Gerda takes his hand. 'Give them some time?'

'I'll need to grab some bits from my room,' says Ptarmigan. 'Let's go now before it kicks off. If it's going to kick off. And before that bloody woman in the back bar decides that the front bar is on trend at the moment'

Gerda prods him and gives a little snort.

They walk to Vanguard Road hand-in-hand. The night is light and warm. Two warbling blackbirds vie for attention in adjacent trees. They walk through the miniature alley formed by Mrs Bron's fence, enter the house, and find Seb sitting alone on the living room sofa. There will be no takeaway curry tonight. Rita went straight to bed after her lonely and furious walk home. She has left Seb, and now Gerda and Tarm, downstairs to drink the chilled white wine she had left in the fridge to go with the Gandhi meal.

'She'll be right.' Seb says, trying to get a decent picture on the TV again. 'Just. New ideas. She worries. A bit.' Seb sounds like he is trying to convince himself. 'That's all. Are you two up for it though?'

Gerda has been looking through the clippings again, and at the map. She turns to Ptarmigan, who has sprawled on the floor with his back against the settee. 'What do you think? I haven't taken any mushrooms for ages, but it might be an education. Or a laugh. Or I'll just chuck up everywhere like I did last time.'

'I thought you were going to chuck up after you belted that first snakebite down in the club the other week!' Seb says, finally getting *Alien* on the television. He is trying to make things normal. *Whistling past the graveyard*, thinks Tarm.

'I'm up for it,' he says. 'As long as it won't make Rita think badly of us all? No? Okay then. Nothing I like more than tripping my tits off in a disused cemetery late at night in the pitch dark!' He pauses. 'Seb. She'll be okay? Really? Rita?'

The Nostromo is in trouble, and Bishop is dribbling white gunk.

'Ah yeah. You know. She's probably a bit drunk. She'll come round.' He's still whistling, thinks Ptarmigan. She only drank half a pint. If that.

Gerda swigs the last of her wine and stands up. 'Right. You coming with me, Mister Chumley?'

'Yeah!' says Tarm, grinning wider, getting out of his chair and mouthing 'Jamesons and Weed' to Seb.

FURY

I AM NOT HAVING this!' Rita is up in Seb's face. He is pinned against the kitchen sink. It is eight o'clock on the evening of the following day. Seb's bag of mushrooms sits on the coffee table. Rita had pulled them out of her knicker drawer and shoved them into Seb's sock drawer when she stormed upstairs last night. She has been out of the house all day. She returned home a while ago, expecting Seb to comfort her that, yes, she's right. And yes, it's a stupid idea. And yes of course it's ridiculous Rita. Because it's potentially lethal.

'I don't see the point. Bunny and fucking Simon? I've told you this. It's bloody stupid. That place has massive drops in it, and that torch is fucking rubbish!' Rita gestures towards the cellar door. 'It'd be bad enough in the dark anyway. But after that amount of mushrooms?' she looks at the huge, plump bag on the table. 'You're out of your fucking mind!'

'Look, love,' Seb holds his palms up, surrendering, 'No problem. You can stay here.

Great idea actually! You can stay here and record everything we tell you when we get back. We won't be long anyway.'

Gerda and Ptarmigan, sitting on the settee with a can of beer each, out of Seb and Rita's lines of sight, are feeling uncomfortable. Tarm has never seen Rita this angry. And Seb last night as well. Two in a week! Rita and Seb don't even have minor spats. They just rib each other and seem to know where the boundaries are set instinctively. They are as comfortable as a well-loved book in its well-loved dustsheet.

'Look. Okay Reet. You know. We'll be really careful. You don't have to come like I said. But I just want to recreate things. And it's thirty years to the night. And it's Huxley!'

'And? Fucking *and*, Seb? You're a fucking idiot and you need to fucking grow up. Grow the fuck up Seb!'

'Reet. Sorry lovely. This is important. We'll be fine. I'll be fine! It could tell us something. I'm more than curious. And you don't know Aldous. Aldous Huxley. I mean, look Reet. Who knows?'

'Who knows what? That you'll fall down something and break your stupid fucking neck?' Rita has reached the zenith of her fury. 'Right.

Fuck this, Fuck Aldous Huxley and fuck you!
You do what you want. I'm going to Cat's.'
   She grabs her astrakhan jacket. She pokes her
head round the door into the living room.
'Sorry,' she says. 'I'll see you tomorrow.' She
glares at Seb, who is still up against the sink.
'Probably.' Her coat knocks Seb's cigarettes and
a plate from the work surface as she leaves. The
plate shatters. The cigarette packet bounces into
the shards.

   Seb sits down on the settee, smiling
uncomfortably. He has swept up the plate with a
dustpan and brush, grabbed a cold beer from the
fridge and popped it, sucking the foam from the
top.
   'Listen mate,' Ptarmigan looks worried. 'She's
really bloody upset. I've never seen her like this.
Maybe you should go and get her back. We can
do the mushrooms and sit about in here, or go
for a walk in the park or something.'
   'There's no problem Tarm. Honestly. I've
known her long enough to read these moods.
It'll be okay tomorrow. She's probably hormonal
or something.'
   Gerda flashes him a glower.
   'Ah hell. Sorry Gerda. Look. I know. It's not
like her. She's acting weird. But I think this is

important. This Bunny thing has got under my skin. It's got under Rita's as well, I know. And yours. She'll be gagging to know what's happened tomorrow. We'll go to The Bradfield and have a drink, and she'll wish she'd come with us. You know. Alright? Good. I'll get the kettle on.'

Seb dances into the kitchen singing *Light My Fire*. Tarm turns to Gerda. 'You okay?'

'Yeah. I just don't like conflict.'

'Me neither. But they've been together forever. If Seb thinks it's okay it should be okay. I hope. You looking forward to this?'

'I don't know. I told you. I was as sick as a dog up last time I took these things. You'll be straight enough to look after me won't you? If it goes badly?'

Ptarmigan kisses her mouth. 'Of course!'

THE TRIP

SEB HAS DRAWN the yellow curtains and Blossom Dearie is breathing smokily through the stereo speakers. Her voice wraps around them like satin. Evening daylight, pale lemon, diffuses into the room through the yellow curtains. They sit on the carpet and look at each other across the old and crackled Willow Pattern teapot where Jack Marx's mushrooms have been mashing for ten minutes. The teapot sits on a metal Willow Pattern tray with matching cups and saucers. Gerda picks it up.

'I'll be mother,' she says, and pours.
They lift their cups in a salute and sip.
The warm liquid tastes like dirt. 'This stuff is still vile!' says Tarm, grimacing.

'Don't bother trying to sweeten it,' Gerda says, poking her tongue out in disgust. 'After the first cup you can't taste it. I put some honey in it last time I had it. It made it too heady or something. That's why I was sick all over the place.'

Seb sits cross-legged on the floor sipping the foul-tasting brew. 'Tastes like shit!' he announces with a friendly, manic grin. 'Let's have some more!'

A further kettle is boiled on the gas hob. The room begins to change, subtly at first. They sip the tea once it is tepid. Then they gulp it when it is cold. It is like drinking liquid compost.

'I think I have greenfly!' Gerda cries, and they all laugh until they can hardly breathe.

Ptarmigan turns the record over. They may have already listened to both sides, but it doesn't matter. Not now. Not in this house. Blossom Dearie's languid voice is beginning to sound threatening to Gerda. She asks if they can turn it off. Ptarmigan takes the needle off with a loud swipe. The sound of amplified scratching vinyl startles them all. 'You've damaged that,' Gerda mumbles. 'And it's lovely too. As a rule. She sounds like she's having a go at me tonight.'

Later. Seb sits in front of Ptarmigan and Gerda.

'How long have we known each other?' he asks them

'About a year? Year and a half?' Tarm says and looks at Gerda.

'A month. Two months? Three?' she says. 'I'm not sure. Why?'

'Because tonight will bind us together. And Rita. When she comes around. Something about this whole evening. This night. It is the closest people can be to each other. We are sharing so much right now. Tarm, Gerda... Rita. I love you all.'

They stare at each other for a while and then Seb embraces Gerda and Tarm. They all sit, huddled and warm. And then they come apart.

Silence inside the house on Vanguard Road now. Outside, the sound of magpies chattering and clattering in the still-sunny evening. A blackbird sings his sweeping tune. Seb takes the teapot back into the bright kitchen. Gerda and Ptarmigan gaze at each other, watching their faces change and disintegrate and change back again. There is the sound of sploshing and swearing from the next room. And then Seb walks back in carrying a dripping aluminium sieve full of rehydrated wormlike fungus. Drops of murky water fall onto the carpet.

'*Psilocybe semilanceata.*' he cries. He pours them out all over the Willow Pattern tray. The tiny mushrooms look repulsive, like something from an anatomist's specimen jar. But Gerda divides them into three equal portions with her fingers and they eat them like baby birds. Heads up, mouths open.

Later. Seb puts the television on, but he can't get a picture. He leaves the hissing white noise and snowy non-channel playing. The TV ticks as it warms up. The sound and strobing light is somehow a comfort.

'What's the time?' asks Ptarmigan. His head is on Gerda's lap.

The mantelpiece lozenge clock must have stopped because it tells one-in-the-morning or one-in-the-afternoon. And it was nine-in-the-evening half an hour ago. The mantelpiece tiles, a pale beige swirl, are swaying like kelp in a gentle current.

'I wish I had Jack's watch!' Seb says. Tarm and Gerda have no idea what he means. 'It tells the time! And he keeps his secrets under the floorboards. Under the fucking floorboards! He's like Agatha Christie or something!' He laughs.

Later. They sit, still but fidgety, as the drug continues to grab at their minds.

The room is too small and too hot. Ptarmigan leaps up, walks into the kitchen, and opens the back door. Cool air streams into the house like a blessing. 'It's dark!' Tarm is astonished. 'It's like when my Dad took me to the pictures in Lincoln to see *The Vikings* one afternoon when I was a kid. Kirk Douglas. Tony Curtis. Only the other way round. It was light out after the pictures.' Ptarmigan finds this concept hysterical and has to steady himself against the door.

'Well, we should go then. I've got the map. Up we get! Let's go!' says Seb, elbowing himself up from the carpet. He sees that he has cigarette ash down one trouser leg and rubs it in, leaving a grey smear. 'It's like Aldous Huxley,' he says. Gerda and Ptarmigan know what he means this timeseb marches. They both nod and smile. 'Let's go and see what Simon and Bunny saw. Thirty years? Thirty years is but a drip. A drop! A bop!'

Gerda is full of life now the door is open and the heat is radiating away from the house. She had started to fade. Now she grabs Seb and kisses him on both sides of his face. Then, turning her face up, she pulls Ptarmigan down to her and kisses him full on the mouth. 'I love you two!' she says, swaying a little and smiling. Her breath smells like fresh coriander and mint.

'Let's go!' Seb says again. He clips the cellar torch to the belt-loop of his jeans, slips on his long leather coat and strides away out of the yard. He looks like an outlaw or a spy.

In the yard: Gerda says, 'Do I need a coat?' Tarm says, 'I don't know. I want the coat I had when I was a kid. It was sort of tartan with a massive furry collar. I used to go fishing in it.' Gerda says, 'Where is it?' Tarm says, 'I was fourteen! It's gone.' Gerda says, 'Well, have you got another coat?'. Tarm says, 'Yeah. Do you want it?' Gerda says, 'I'd like a coat. But it's nice and cool.' Tarm says, 'I'll get you a coat.' Gerda says, 'I've got a coat.' Tarm says, 'Do you want it?' Gerda says, 'Yeah. Please. If you can find it.' Tarm says, 'Hang about.'

Ptarmigan goes back into the house, which is so, so bright and unfamiliar, all filled with curves and angles and strange buttresses. He emerges with both his and Gerda's leather jackets. They set off out of the yard. Seb is hanging about near the phonebox across the road smoking a cigarette. 'Come on!' he whispers. 'Let's fuck off!'

The street is dry and dusty. It has been very warm today. The sodium streetlights appear more yellow than orange, like venomous insects. They shed their toxic light onto the road. Ptarmigan, Seb and Gerda have no idea what time it is now, but there is hardly any traffic. Only three cars pass them as they walk the ten minutes to their destination. Seb marches ahead with the buzzingmap in his hands like an old-time preacher with a bible. The cars' head-and-tail lights stretch out behind them like a timelapse photograph. Gerda shuts her eyes, but the traces of white and red light are still there. At least she hasn't been sick, she thinks. Not yet, anyway.

Nobody is around. Ptarmigan can hear the tick-tocking of bedside clocks and the odd snore coming from windows opened against the night's warmth. Profoundly late then? He wonders. Must be. There is a dull and hazy half-moon. But there are no stars. Apart from the poisonous streetlighting, the night is dark. Ptarmigan is beginning to think that Rita made a good call by not coming, and in wanting them to cancel this expedition. What the hell are they doing? He feels the first webs of trepidation creeping into his unravelling mind. He draws Gerda tighter to him. She feels small and vulnerable and somehow alone.

They see the Great Gate looming and growing as they approach it. It has red wrought-iron double gates. The edifice itself stands belligerent, legs apart. Like a challenge. On the two red wrought-iron gates are two large, brassy snakes. They have their tails in their mouths. And atop the massive stone gate itself, perfectly centred, is a large globe sprouting feathered wings.

'Ouroboros!' says Gerda, looking at the gate snakes. 'Wow!'

'Those snakes? Meaning what?' asks Tarm, still hugging her close. She hugs him back.

'Cyclic renewal? Rebirth? The interruption of eternity? You name it,' says Gerda, still gazing at the gates. 'And that world? Globes with wings? That's bloody Egyptian I think. God this is so weird! I'm not sure about this now Ptarmigan. It feels as wrong as hell and we're not even peaking. Going in here won't bring those young boys back from 1954. I can't see how this is a good idea. Not now I'm here. Let's go home?

Have a smoke. Seb'll come with us. I've got some weed! We can go and grab Rita?'

'Suits me if I'm honest,' Ptarmigan whispers to her. 'I'm fucked. And I've forgotten why we're doing this.'

The snakes slither around on their gate-prison. They devour themselves. They consume and they are whole again. And once they are eaten, they are lost. Then they are not lost, and they suck themselves up once more. They turn their faces, full of tails, to Gerda, Seb and Ptarmigan. The snakes bite into themselves and their thick blood spatters onto the pavement, black in the toxic sodium light. The globe above grows dark, glistening eyes and observes them. Its feathered wings whisper and tick as it watches. Tarm and Gerda are horrified. The snakes grab their unruly tails once more.

'Fuck that!' Seb marches through the cemetery gate. 'Come on in. What's the worst that can happen? The water's lovely! And Jack Marx didn't secrete this shit under his floorboards for nothing!' He laughs again. Ptarmigan and Gerda glance at each other. And then, hand in hand they too walk through the great gate.

As soon as the three of them are in the cemetery, the air itself changes. There is stillness, baited with the heavy scents of damp undergrowth. Stone and lichen. This place is filthy and abandoned and forgotten. So many old memories have escaped from so many old, dead minds in this soil that they can almost smell them. The path underfoot feels soft and yielding, almost liquid. Gerda and Tarm try to see where they are walking but it's impossible. This is a darkness of time and loss. Those long-ago faces in the Star clippings? They could be right under their feet. Although their faces would be long gone now. Their families would have wept here, right here. For fathers and mothers and children. And those mourners, in turn. They sleep here. All forgotten. Almost as if they were never alive at all.

Ahead, Seb's jerking torch sheds feeble light on an earth-wall to his right and a dangerous precipice to his left. Ivies and roots have infested and investigated the eyes, bibles and wings of the angels and urns here. This fecund life looks grey in the wan torchlight. Seb, definitely peaking now, whispers to Gerda and Ptarmigan in the darkness.

'Come on you lot! Onwards. We need something good to tell Rita tomorrow! There'll be some fine things tomorrow. Rita. Yeah! She's in a mood with me. I've never known her like this. Come on you two. We're doing this for Simon and Bunny. We're here to discover. Remember Aldous fucking Huxley!'

He turns to the others and gives them his big, stupid, carefree grin. He nearly falls over. He rights himself. He grins at Gerda and Ptarmigan. Gerda and Ptarmigan grin back. The deeper into the cemetery they have come, the more static the air has grown. He turns around and carries on.

Two terraces down, Seb turns his torch beam onto a gravestone. 'Look at these!' he whispers, beckoning. The epitaphs, on two adjacent headstones, read:

Clive Ather
1827 - 1864
Husband, Father, Grandfather
Sorely Taken From Us
'I am unsafe here
Deliver me from this'

John Aaron Dixon
1840 – 1841

A Child Is Taken
'Coil about me
I am hardly born
Yet I am rended'

'What the hell does that mean?' asks Seb, rubbing a piece of moss from the inscription.

Ptarmigan is frightened. He looks at Gerda. In the dark, her eyes are huge and terrified. Things aren't right here.

'And this,' says Seb. 'And here!'

A slight creaking noise from ahead. They all look into the darkness. And they all assume it is tree branches. Rubbing. In the dead, still air.

Seb shines his torch.

Henry Collins
1871 – 1894
Beloved
'I am but death-soap
But I was once as you
And you shall be as I
And all I shall suffer'

Victoria Louise Cullum
1839 – 1924
Our Grandmother

'I have seen much
But my dead eyes
Shall see more'

Seb says, 'Death Soap?'

He shines the cellar torch around. 'Death soap? Fuck alone knows. I'll come back and take a rubbing or some photos tomorrow. Maybe this was normal. The Victorians were fucking grim at the best of times.'

He stands back up. He giggles. The drug again. Then a further low creaking from the darkness. Like someone heavy standing on old floorboards. They all stand still, terrified, attuned to every sound. It doesn't come again.

They walk for a further twenty minutes in the almost pitch dark. Seb turns off the torch for a while. Their eyes become used to the buzzing darkness. The slim moon offers them a more spectral view of their surroundings. The effigies and weeping angels glister and glitter in its muted light. In their confused state, they whisper together that they might be going round in circles. The same narrow lanes, hazardous drops and huge edifices march towards them over and over again. Or did early Victorians pick monuments from a catalogue? Like Kays or something?

Ptarmigan wonders if they are learning anything. About Huxley? Or the missing long-ago students? Or about themselves? Surely that was the point? He reaches for Gerda's hand. It feels chilly, even though the night is warm and still. Their fingers cling to each other. Seb is ahead of them, blundering. Why are they here in this sad place, unable to trust their senses? More than anything, Tarm wants to go home and watch the television A movie or even some late-night sports. Fight Night would be good. Until the hallucinogens are out of their systems. He knows from experience that coming down from a trip can be a lulling, peaceful time. He hasn't read the Huxley, so he's ignorant about Aldous's comedown story. But, peaking now, he wants this to be over. In the dreariness that is passing for light here, he sees that Gerda is frightened and upset. They have to leave this place. He is about to tell Seb that, if they can find a way out, they're going. He is about to try and convince Seb to come with them.

And then. 'Hold up,' whispers Seb, coming to a halt. 'There's something moving about to our right.' Gerda and Ptarmigan freeze. Something is there. They can hear the sound of a huge man, or a large living object, creeping through the undergrowth. Soil flattening. Plants shifting. Being brushed against. Making its way toward them. Seb turns on his flashlight and points it into a tangle of ivies and bramble. Nothing. Other than the weak torch beam with its sallow yellow middle and its pointless darker rings playing on the complex plant-patterns.

Seb shushes them again. There is a further suggestion of movement somewhere in the darkness. Something big. It stops. A vague low and furtive sound. A creaking. Then stillness once more. They stand together and listen.

Ptarmigan takes a breath to say his piece. Seb hisses at him. There is a further suggestion of stealthy movement somewhere in the darkness. It's big. It stops. A vague low and furtive sound. Then silence. They stand together and listen.

'Stick this in your pocket will you Tarm?' Seb says, handing the old map to him. 'I can't hold the torch and this.' He is whispering. His breathing is rapid. 'And I can't see anything anyway.'

A towering plinthed angel rises in front of them as they edge down one of the steep paths Seb thinks was marked on the map. His torch is now so feeble that he cannot see where they are going. Cannot tell solid ground from void. Still, that subtle creeping of something huge. Keeping up with them. A terrace away. The continuous, inexplicable, ancient groaning.

'This is wrong,' Seb says. 'There's something fucking wrong.' He sounds scared.

Gerda agrees. The fact of Seb's fear has now galvanised her. She is sweating and can feel that Tarm is as well. She clutches Ptarmigan's jacket sleeve, hissing loudly, spitting through her teeth, 'Let's go. Come on Seb. Those guys died. We're okay. Let's go back. I'll pop to Cat's house and get Rita back. There's beer. And Jamesons! We can have a smoke? Watch whatever's on the TV? Let's get out of here!' Ptarmigan is once more about to tell Seb that they've had enough.

From their right, on an avenue running along the side of a steep drop in the terrace, they hear a noise like the groaning of a ship's mast. Seb shines his useless torch in the direction of the sudden sound then, seeing nothing, into his own face. His eyes are wide. He illuminates Gerda and Tarm, who have also pulled up short, swaying, their mouths open. Then the smell. Unpleasant yet remote. Like fish rotting on a distant wharf.

Seb turns. He takes one step further. And one more. And then he slips and falls onto his face over the crumbling edge on which he had stood.

His torch tumbles twice and shines its weak light back at where he lays. It exposes six large holes dug into one of the terraces. These are remnants of the few cemetery catacombs. Seb has trodden onto one of these hollows and it has given way. He begins to push himself up. A squat, square Classical tombstone stands in front of this unexpected honeycomb of collapsing dirt. Ptarmigan and Gerda begin to scramble down the incline to help him back up. Seb begins to kick and try to back away from something they cannot see. The creaking starts again. Much closer now. Much louder. Gerda and Ptarmigan back away. In the glow of the dropped torch, a huge, grey, impossibly lined face rises from behind the squat tombstone. It turns its head about slowly as if trying to figure out where it is. Its skin moves as if it is slowly falling. Like cold lava. Its tendons, or whatever they are, sound like old fibres tightening as the great head rises further to reveal a black elongated void where its mouth should be. It turns, mostly in shadow, and coolly regards Gerda and Ptarmigan with its dirt-filled, egg-white eyes. Then it stands with a sound like shrieking dead sinew. A towering eight-foot tall, almost transparent horror, with limbs like long, lined insectile mandibles and a pregnant belly. It tenderly picks up the now paralysed Seb as if he were a baby. It holds him close to itself, takes a last look at Gerda and Ptarmigan, and slides, with a sound like rotten hinges, backwards into the dark. From their left, very close, comes a soft, despairing sigh. Less than a second later, as if struck by a cudgel, both Ptarmigan and Gerda fall unconscious onto the soil on which they stand.

WITNESSES

SOUTH YORKSHIRE POLICE

WITNESS STATEMENT

DATE: 5th August 1984

NAME: Shaun Houghton

It was probably the most stupid thing I have ever done in my life. But even so I can't remember the most important parts of it. Sebastian Corkerry, Gerda Willis and I drank a lot of magic mushroom tea on the night of the 24th July, and afterwards we all walked to the Sheffield General Cemetery. We had arranged to do this because of the disappearance of two students from our house in the nineteen-fifties. And for a laugh, I think. Sebastian Corkerry was laughing about watches and floorboards, I remember that. I know we went into the cemetery. I know we wandered about in there like idiots for ages getting lost. Please remember that I was under the influence of a huge amount of psilocybin. We found some weird headstones. Weird inscriptions. Then there was something. Something happened. But I don't know what. I'm really sorry but I don't know. There's nothing. Not really. The drug made Gerda Willis and I pass out.

We came round on a terrace in the Sheffield General Cemetery while it was still dark. It had obviously rained because we were wet. I think the rain might have woken us up. We made our way back to Gerda Willis's house at 17 Empire Road where we fell asleep until about 7pm on the 25th July.

When we woke up we went to my house on Vanguard Road. We thought we'd find Sebastian Corkerry and Rita Bevan there. We thought that we were going for a drink to talk about everything. Sebastian Corkerry was not in the house. Rita Bevan was in the house and she was really upset because she and Sebastian Corkerry had had a row on the evening of Wednesday 24th July, and he had not returned home.

I have no knowledge as to the whereabouts of Sebastian Corkerry. I wish I did.

Signed: SHAUN HOUGHTON

SOUTH YORKSHIRE POLICE

WITNESS STATEMENT

DATE: 5th August 1984

NAME: Gerda Willis

My new boyfriend, Shaun Houghton (he is known as Ptarmigan), and I drank a lot of tea made with psilocybin mushrooms at his house on Vanguard Road in Sheffield on the evening of 24th July 1984 with Sebastian Corkerry. We did this so that we would be in a similar mindset to two students who vanished from Shaun Houghton, Rita Bevan and Sebastian Corkerry's house on the same night in 1954. After we had drunk the tea with the drug in it, after a while, we walked to the Sheffield General Cemetery. Sebastian Corkerry had a torch, and also a map that the two boys who disappeared had made. Sebastian Corkerry fell over and dropped the torch at one point. And there was a really terrible smell. Then Shaun Houghton and I woke up in the cemetery. It was still dark and we were still under the influence of the magic mushrooms. We walked to my house at 17 Empire Road and slept in my bed until about half past seven that night, 25th July 1984. I assume we had blacked out. Like when you've drunk too much. All I remember is Sebastian Corkerry falling over and the horrible smell and then I woke up. We were both soaked so it had been raining.

We walked to Shaun Houghton's house that evening and found Rita Bevan in a very distressed state, in which she remains as far as I know.

Signed: GERDA WILLIS

SOUTH YORKSHIRE POLICE

WITNESS STATEMENT

DATE: 5th August 1984

NAME: Rita Bevan

My boyfriend Sebastian Corkerry was at our house on Vanguard Road on the 24th July 1984. He took some dried mushrooms in some tea with our friends Shaun Houghton and Gerda Willis. I did not accompany Sebastian Corkerry , Shaun Houghton and Gerda Willis into the Sheffield General Cemetery on the night of 24th July 1984. That night I stayed at my friend Catherine Eddow's house because I had had an argument with Sebastien Corkerry. I did not want him to take the drugs and walk around that cemetery in the dark because I knew it to be a dangerous place. It was our first real argument in years And our last. And it was my fault. I wish I had gone with them. Or stopped them. I have not seen Sebastian Corkerry since the night of the 24th July 1984.

I know this is supposed to be an official witness statement and report, but it might help your investigations to know that my heart is in a billion pieces. I want to scream. I am empty, Please find him. I am alone and scared and I want him back. I want Seb. I want Seb back. If

I don't I will die. Please. Please. Please. I am broken.

Signed: RITA BEVAN

The Sheffield Star. Wednesday August 8th 1984

'UNIVERSITY ENGLISH STUDENT MISSING'

South Yorkshire Police are appealing for information on the whereabouts of Sebastian Corkerry, a popular student of English at Sheffield University. Sebastian is known to have been in the old Sheffield General Cemetery in the early hours of July 25th with two friends. However, he appears to have left the group at some point and has subsequently disappeared.

Sebastian was last seen wearing an ankle-length black leather coat. He has long purple hair and is 6ft in height.

Anyone with information on his whereabouts is requested to contact South Yorkshire Police on (0742) 411411

The Sheffield Star. Monday August 13th 1984

'POLICE APPEAL FOR MISSING STUDENT WITNESSES'

Sebastian Corkerry, the Sheffield University undergraduate who disappeared on July 25th has still not been found. Sebastian is described as slim, 6ft tall with long purple hair that he sometimes spikes up in a 'punk' style. He was last seen in the Sheffield General Cemetery by his housemate and another friend. South Yorkshire Police have confirmed that Sebastian has not returned to his family home in South Wales and are appealing for anyone with information on his whereabouts to call their incident room on (0742) 411411.

The Sheffield Star. Wednesday August 22nd 1984

'LOCAL MUSIC PRODUCER LAST TO SEE CORKERRY'

Sheffield music producer Jack Marx was the last to see missing student Sebastian Corkerry apart from the two friends who were with him when he disappeared. Marx, who has produced songs for Cabaret Voltaire, Abby and Niceville among others, has told The Star that Sebastian visited him at his Nether Edge home early on the evening of the 24th July to see his new bass guitar.

South Yorkshire Police have now reported that, during their initial search of Sheffield General Cemetery, where Sebatian was last seen, a large amount of a waxy substance was found. Following forensic examination, this has proved to be animal in origin. Sebastian Corkerry is described as slim, 6ft tall with long purple hair that he sometimes spikes up in a 'punk rock' style. He was last seen in the Sheffield General Cemetery by his housemate and another friend. Police are appealing for anyone with information on his whereabouts to call their incident room on (0742) 411411.

The Sheffield Star. Friday 16th November 1984

'CASE CLOSED ON MISSING STUDENT SEBASTIAN CORKERRY'

South Yorkshire Police said today they have closed the case on missing student Sebastian Corkerry, having received no information on his whereabouts since August. Assistant Chief Constable Kevin Hartley said, 'We regret that we have no leads at this time as to the young man's movements after the early morning of July 25th, and we therefore have no option but to suspend our investigations. Obviously, should further information become available in the future, we will resume our inquiries.'

The Sheffield Star. Thursday 29th August 1991

'SEBASTIAN CORKERRY PRONOUNCED DEAD'

Former Sheffield University English student Sebastian Corkerry, who went missing in July 1984, triggering a large police investigation, has been pronounced 'missing presumed dead' by the Sheffield High Court following an application by his parents.

.2014.

EMAILS (1)

Email
From: tarm@ptarmigan.com.uk
To: bevanreet@goto.com.uk
Saturday June 14th 2014

Hi Rita

Thanks for accepting me on Facebook. Your profile doesn't have much info on it. Not even a picture! Then again, my photo is from back in the day so I haven't got much to shout about. And thanks for sending me your email address. It's a bit weird this isn't it? After thirty years?

So. How are you doing? Ack! Such a stupidly crass way to start a conversation. But what else is there? People all over the world are probably doing this right now.

Seriously. I'm interested to find out how you're doing Rita. I've thought about you almost every day since then.

What are you up to? You married? Kids?

I'll let you know my news as and when you respond Rita.

You take care.

Love

Tarm. x

Email
From: bevanreet@goto.com.uk
To: tarm@ptarmigan.com.uk
Tuesday June 17th 2014

Dear Tarm. It is great to hear from you. It's taken me a few days to reply because there's just so much weight to this and I needed to get my head straight about talking with you.
But, keeping things light... no I'm not married. I'm working for a charity. I know! It's not exactly what I

had planned, but as you might know I moved back to Wales and that was the end of my Polytechnic life. I just couldn't bear staying in Sheffield, let alone in that bloody house. But it's good work. There's no dress code (ha ha) and at least I'm doing something positive with myself. What about you? What are you up to now? Kids? Do you ever see Gerda? I seriously have no idea.

Rita

Email
From: tarm@ptarmigan.com.uk
To: bevanreet@goto.com.uk
Tuesday June 17th 2014

Hi Rita

So brilliant to hear from you.

Charity work is Good Work. Please don't downplay yourself because of circumstances. You were always a lovely person and your career choice only proves that.

Well, I hope you're sitting down. Because Gerda is making a cup of tea in the next room as I write this! I moved into her place on Empire Road afterwards. Couldn't bear to stay where we were either, and we haven't been back since I shifted my gear out. We've been together ever since. She got her degree (she took some time out but she caught up) and now she works at the Uni doing research. It's Physics, as you know. But don't ask me ANYTHING about it because it's like trying to read Cyrillic for me. We're not married and haven't got kids, but we keep talking about it. (Marriage. Not kids. We have a ginger cat).

After you left I decided that yes, I'd join a band. It was tough going in Sheffield. A few venues wouldn't put us on. But we got a fair following and we got an album out and it was great. Peel played us! It became clear that I wasn't much cop at playing bass for an hour-and-a-half at a time, but I discovered (by mistake… and aren't a lot of good things discovered by accident?) that I was a natural in the recording studio. Good ears Gerda reckons. When my Dad died in 2005 he left me a bit of cash, so I set up a studio here at the top of Abbeydale Road. We're nearly in Dore! Posh eh? That was a struggle to begin with as well, but I do okay now. Me and Gerd live upstairs in a nice flat. My Facebook page is the studio one. Which is why there's not much info on my personal one. It's also how I have my 'name' on my email! It's called Ptarmigan Sounds. The studio I mean. Yeah I know. What a twat!

Anyway. I have a band coming in now so I'll say cheerio Rita. Please let me know more. I'm so happy to be in touch. You take care.

Love

Tarm x

Email
From: bevanreet@goto.com.uk
To: tarm@ptarmigan.com.uk
Wednesday June 18th 2014

Hi Tarm. Jesus you've done well. And say hi to Gerda. Good Grief! I didn't see that coming!! I'm really happy for you both and very proud of you. You always seemed a little lost back then, in a very sweet way. Or maybe not lost. Maybe journeying. Strange isn't it. This sudden way of talking? My mind still lives in the era of mixtapes and phones with curly leads! So much has changed. So. What do we talk about now?

Love Rita

Email
From: tarm@ptarmigan.com.uk
To: bevanreet@goto.com.uk
Thursday June 19th 2014

Hi Rita

I think we're all journeying in one way or another. Don't you? And yes. It's a Brave New World! Ha!

Well. There actually is something specific I wanted to talk to you about. I'm going to be honest and say that, apart from the fact that you're brilliant and I think about you all the time, you're the only person I have to talk to about it apart from Gerda. I'll understand if you want to end both this conversation and our email communication right now as a result. If you do, that's fine. I haven't even spoken to Gerda at any length about much of this either.

So. Okay. (deep breath) I'm guessing that you haven't done any digging into what the hell happened to Seb?

(further deep breath) I have.

It's easy to find information now, with everyone throwing information about absolutely everything online for everyone else to read, if you know where to look. Which I do.

I have discovered stuff that I don't want to go into in depth by email. It's not that I think people are reading it, or that The Illuminati will find out or any of that foil-hat crap. It's just so bloody weird and horrible that you'll think I'm a maniac and never speak to me again. I'm being deadly serious Rita. Really.

I'll just share one thing with you. One bit of information. I have other records that go much further back. Whatever happened to Seb, and to Simon Glass and Bunny Reeder, and, I believe, hundreds of others, has been going on for centuries at least. Really, Rita. And it happens, for some reason, in July. Every thirty years. I have no idea why. And if I'm honest I don't care why. But I loved Seb too. He's one of the best people I have ever met. And, if I can, I want to find out the truth and if I can. I want to stop it happening again. And next month is thirty years since July 1984.

(breathes out deep breaths)

The information is attached.

Rita. I hope to hear from you soon.

If I don't, I wish you happiness, love and luck in everything you do.

All My Love

Tarm x

Email
From: bevanreet@goto.com.uk
To: tarm@ptarmigan.com.uk
Friday June 20th 2014

Jesus! Tarm I haven't stopped crying on-and-off since I received your email. For all the right reasons. I think. I wanted to fire one back at you straight away. But I needed to think. So I have thought. I know you loved Seb. A lot of people did. He was that sort of bloke. But I loved him the best of all. And if I can help, I want to. He was the love of my life. I have never met anyone who holds a candle to him, the big daft berk. And I have felt ragged with guilt ever since that night. I have never been able to decide if I should have kicked him in the bollocks to stop him going or come with you. It has haunted my life. Sorry Tarm. Sorry. I'm gushing. I needed a few down me to deal with this (not snakebites!). That article is. Well. It's amazing. And it reminds me of you and Gerda's statements. So. My darling Ptarmigan. What do you want to do?

Email
From: tarm@ptarmigan.com.uk
To: bevanreet@goto.com.uk
Friday June 20th 2014

Dear Rita

You have no idea how relieved I am. Thank you so, so much.

Okay. Let's synchronise watches! We are now only ten days away from July. July is, for some reason, THE month. Our place over the studio is huge. Do you want to come and stay at ours for a few days while we look at this thing? The spare room is well-appointed, and our wine cellar is bursting. As is the fridge. And (drumroll) the Gandhi is still going up the way!

Have you got a car? I can help with fuel costs. If not I can also help with a train fare.

Let me know.

Lots of Love

Tarm x

Email
From: bevanreet@goto.com.uk
To: tarm@ptarmigan.com.uk
Saturday June 21st 2014

Dear Tarm. It's holiday season. I have about a month owing. I have a car. You don't need to help with petrol. I can arrive on Saturday next, which is the 28th. What do you reckon? I need your address and parking info obviously.

Love and Excitement!

Rita x

Email
From: tarm@ptarmigan.com.uk
To: bevanreet@goto.com.uk
Saturday June 21st 2014

Hi Rita

That's just brilliant. Gerd's taken some time off from Uni too. And I can do what the hell I want! I'll pop everything you need over on a separate email so it doesn't get lost. There's private parking. I'll air the bed out! The cat's been on it, the little swine!

See you on Saturday!!

Love and Anticipation

Tarm xxx

RITA AND KATE

PTARMIGAN HAS BEEN wandering around
in front of the two big windows that look onto
the flat's car park for an hour. Rita had some
things to get done back in Wales, she said. So she
had set off towards Sheffield at five o'clock that
afternoon. The AA website put her journey time
at three hours. It is now half past eight and Tarm
is fretting with a bottle of Proper Job Ale in his
hand. Gerda has prepared a selection of olives,
cold meats, salads and tofu that she calls Nibbly
Bits. There is a marguerita pizza keeping warm
in the oven.

'Have you set the table Tarm?' she calls from
the kitchen.

Ptarmigan checks to make certain he hasn't
missed anything. 'Yep!' Three plates sit ready for
to be filled. Cutlery. Glasses. Ketchup. Brown
sauce for Gerda. There are three open bottles of
red wine too, and two bottles of white chilled in
the fridge. There is beer and cider too, if anyone

feels like taking a walk down memory lane and having a snakebite.

Gerda and Ptarmigan don't usually bother sitting at the dining table, preferring to eat on trays in front of the TV. But this is a special day. Gerda has even put their tartan tablecloth out. She thinks their little meal looks welcoming.

A neat little red Corsa pulls into the car park.

'She's here!' he calls through.

Gerda trots into the living room and watches the car pull into an empty space. The driver's door opens, and Rita gets out, puffing. And, by the look of it, swearing under her breath about something. She peers up at the window they are standing at with her hand shielding her eyes. She squints a little, sees them both, smiles, waves and yells, 'Hiya!'

Rita pulls a small white suitcase out of the boot, shuts it, presses her key fob. And the car beeps locked.

'She doesn't look any different!' Gerda says in amazement. 'Apart from the hair. I wonder if she still smokes?'

'God knows. I'll go down and get her,' says Tarm, 'I'd get that wine out of the fridge if I were you. She looks like she needs it!'

Gerda is placing the fourth wine bottle onto the table. A chilly white. She hears voices and laughter on the stairs. The door opens and Rita comes in, followed by a sheepish-looking Ptarmigan carrying her suitcase.

'Gerda!' cries Rita. 'Jesus! You look fantastic!' Her Welsh accent has become stronger over the last three decades. She pulls Gerda into a close and effusive hug. Gerda's head comes up to the top of her nose. Rita pushes her away then embraces her again. Tarm stands a few feet away.

'I got that treatment in the car park,' he says, 'Then she said I'd got fat!'

' I said plump. Not fat. And you were always too thin anyway. Like a bloody coathanger.'

Ptarmigan is a little heavier now. His midriff pushes the band tee shirts he still wears away from him slightly. He has a short beard now too, greying a little at the sides. He says it's there to stop him looking so youthful until Gerda tells him to shut up. His hair is still there, cut into a scruffed, easy-to-wash style. It, too, has the odd hint of grey. Ptarmigan abandoned tight black jeans and leather kilts long ago, in favour of loose-fitting joggers and cargo-shorts.

Gerda has thickened a little. Her hair is her natural light brown right now. No greys yet. She wears it short at the back and long at the front and she sometimes colours it with the new and now easily available reds, blues and mauves. She still wears DM's, charity shop dresses and her old leather jacket. Neither Ptarmigan or Gerda have aged badly.

Rita, as far as they can tell, has hardly changed. Apart, as Gerda said, from her hair. Rita's long hair is silver-grey, and she has it in a long plait that reminds Tarm of Mrs Bron, their old neighbour. Up close, she has the obvious evidence of three passed decades. She looks great

Like Gerda and Tarm, Rita has that *older-yet-still-alternative* way of dressing. She is wearing a Butthole Surfers tee shirt and a checked cotton skirt. She has a chunky silver vape battery around her neck on a leather lanyard. Her make-up is still perfect.

They stand in a triangle for a moment, looking at each other and remembering.

Then Ptarmigan says, 'Right. I'll show you your room.' He leads Rita into the hallway, asking about the traffic. Gerda shouts, 'What are you drinking Reet?'

'Snakebite!' Rita yells back, and they laugh.

Rita wants to see Ptarmigan's recording studio. Once she has deposited her suitcase in her room, Tarm takes her downstairs. Gerda waits. And here we go. The faint sound of a drum kit being assaulted comes through the floor of the flat. When they come back up, Rita is breathing hard and grinning. And her face is red. Ptarmigan is grinning and delighted to have shown off his workplace to her.

Rita takes a seat at the table and gulps at her cloudy snakebite. 'Whooo!' she says. 'That brings me home! Your studio's great Tarm! And this place looks like a normal house from the street. I wasn't sure if I was at the right place.'

'I don't like to advertise,' Tarm says. 'All that gear down there cost a fortune. That's why I invested in the best soundproofing I could afford. I'm not sure if the neighbours even know what I do. And that's great. The number of bands who get their equipment nicked from their vans outside venues is like a pandemic nowadays. Besides,' he looks at Gerda, 'This flat has precious cargo.'

'You silly soft sod.' Gerda pinches his bum and Ptarmigan yelps.

'And there's that little bit of exclusivity too. Bands arrive at the back. Nobody notices. In they come. The people I work with all like the fact that I'm off the beaten track. The only way they can find out the location of Ptarmigan Sounds is by having a chinwag on the phone with me.'

'Nice!' Rita says.

Later. They sit around the kitchen table helping themselves to wine and Gerda's *Nibbly Bits*. They talk. Ptarmigan watches his two friends. One so familiar that he would know her in the pitch dark. The other resurrecting both fond and awful memories. Rita's voice and presence is bringing back visions of spilt curries and dancing to The Clash. And Seb's goofy laughter. And them all laughing And utter, utter loss and horror.

He watches this wonderful woman as she refills Rita's glass and wipes her eyes from laughing. He remembers the times they spent together. He wonders whether he will feel the same about this experiment, this investigation, as he did when he, Gerda and Seb were in the cemetery in the dead of night. He wonders if he will, eventually, want to end it all and run from the darkness.

But, for now, around the easy table, Ptarmigan has stories about appalling gigs in London and Glasgow with his band. And about almost-famous musicians who he has worked with in his studio and had chronic, perpetual flatulence. And terrible band vans with dead pigeons under one of the seats. And about the issues he had securing gigs for his band and making Ptarmigan Sounds a going concern.

Rita tells them about some of the disgusting things people donate to the shops her charity runs. She tells them about her little house in South Wales. And about her Mam and Dad's passing. And, now she has pummelled Tarm's studio kit for a while, she is adamant that she wants to learn to play the drums.

Gerda talks about her life with Ptarmigan and all its ups-and-downs. Mostly ups, she says. She explains Fusion Energy, her specific field of study at the University. And she attempts to explain what she does. The other two nod along sagely along for a few minutes.

'Tarm, why are you bothering to pretend you understand any of this you idiot?' Gerda says after a while.

'Because it makes you think I'm sexy.' says Ptarmigan with a poker face.

Rita laughs explosively.

Later in the evening, when the traffic outside has slowed and the meal is just debris, they sit around in the comfortable living room. Rita has Cadellin the ginger cat purring across her legs. She has curled her feet underneath herself. Like she used to. She does it a little more carefully these days. She had one snakebite, for old times' sake. Now she tips her glass of red wine back until it's empty. Her lipstick leaves a smile on the rim.

Ptarmigan gets up from his seat next to Gerda and refills her glass. Rita pulls on her vape. She blows out a fragrant billow of caramel. Then he sits back down and tops up his and Gerda's drinks.

'When did you give up the fags Rita?'

Gerda watches the musky blue-grey water vapour crowd about on the ceiling and then disappear into itself.

'1984 actually,' Rita says. After. I never picked up a cigarette again. And then we had a works do about three years back. And someone had a primitive version of this thing,' she waggles her big vape battery. 'And that was it. I can get all the pleasure of smoking my head off without killing myself or anyone else.'

The bottles that were on the table are empty. Two more have been opened. But none of them feel as drunk as they should. This is such a charged event, their meeting again, that they're running as much on adrenaline as anything else. Gerda has a Spotify playlist playing on the flat's stereo. Rita's ears pricked up when Blossom Dearie singing Manhattan came on. She has remembered.

This day is full of memories. The living room is cool, with the windows open enough to allow a comfortable breeze to play around them. Gerda and Ptarmigan's ornaments and pictures are everywhere. More memories. An original print of a Wayne Coyne *Yoshimi* from The Flaming Lips album. Several ginger porcelain cats. A framed poster commemorating Tarm's band when they supported *Getting The Fear* in London in the late eighties. A willow pattern teapot perched on a bookshelf amidst hardback books about films and music. A Jim Morrison cushion with the picture from *An American Prayer* on it. A stuffed ptarmigan with googly eyes. A strange series of balsa-wood boxes featuring dead wasps hanging from fine wires. A green man's ceramic face. A Waterhouse wall-hanging, *Circe Offering the Cup to Ulysses*. A huge, dead cuckoo clock.

'So, what made you delay coming up earlier today? Apart from the traffic?' Ptarmigan asks Rita.

Rita swirls the wine in her glass and sips at it. 'It's one of the things that made me want to come. Jesus. The main thing actually. I went to see my little girl.'

'Oh! I didn't know you had children!' Gerda says with a smile. 'Did you leave her at your folks?'

Tarm feels that something is not right. He rubs his hair with his hand and takes a large swig of Cabernet.

'My folks are dead. So is my baby. She's in a Garden of Remembrance in Caldicot. She was mine. And Seb's.'

Gerda puts her glass down. She goes to sit at Rita's side, on the floor, her back against the settee.

'Oh no, look. Gerda. Jesus it's fine,' Rita says ruffling Gerda's hair. 'It was a bloody long time ago. I cried for Seb, and I cried for Kate and I cried for me. And now it's. Well, it's what it is. I went to see her today though. I don't go often. She's not there. Not really. But there's nowhere else. So I took her some flowers. A nice bunch from Tesco actually.' Rita smiles. 'And I talked to her about her Dad. And I told her I was coming to see you to find out what happened to him. If we can find out. At least I know what happened to Kate.'

Gerda rubs Rita's leg. And she goes back to sit next to Ptarmigan.

'So. What did happen to her? In the end? To your daughter?' Ptarmigan asks. 'If it's okay to ask.'

'Oh sure, yeah. Well. I got back to my Mam and Dad's after everything had happened here. I already knew I was pregnant. I knew before. I knew at The Barfield that night. It's why I was so angry about that psychedelic fucking Monster Mash down at the cemetery.'

'Fuck!' says Tarm. He glances at Gerda.

'Yeah. Fuck. I'd done a test. Big blue plus sign. You weren't to know. But... So anyway. I got back home. And they were all fussing about and all *Here's your old room* and *You don't need boys* and *We're sure they'll find him* and I was all *Yes I Do Need Him* and *No They Fucking Well Won't Find Him* and *I Really Hate My Old Room*. They meant well. Sometimes people do. You know? But they drove me batshit. So I ate their food and stayed in my room and got more and more pregnant until I had to tell them. And, you know what? They were great! That was a shocker! My Dad did out my sister's old room with hanging kiddy mobiles and a cot and all baby stuff. And me and Mam went to Mothercare. A lot! It was lovely actually. I wasn't getting any news from Sheffield about Seb. But I knew he'd get in touch if he ever came to light. And he didn't get in touch. So I knew he hadn't. He was gone. I stopped hoping at that point. No choice. And, do you know, I didn't look at another bloke after I met Seb. I still haven't. Sounds daft I suppose, but there we are. This baby was going to be perfect. I still had this little bit of Seb see? Here.' her palm circles where her pregnancy once lived. 'And that was going to be my future. Me. Our baby. My Mam and Dad helping out. I wanted to be a great Mum to me and Seb's child.'

Rita's face flushes. Her chin pinches up. Gerda goes back across the room, sits against the sofa, and leans against Rita's leg. Cadellin yawns. Tarm gets a bottle of Jack Daniels from the drinks cabinet and starts pouring generous measures into glasses.

Rita pulls hard at her vape. 'But. Jesus fucking Christ. The best laid plans and everything! Kate was beautiful. Loads of hair. She looked like Seb. The poor little sod. I named her after Kate Bush. You know Seb loved Kate Bush? And she was a big old bugger as well when she came out. I thought I was going to go off pop!' She wipes an escaped tear away. Ptarmigan reaches into his pocket and brings out tissues. This he was not expecting.

'I breast fed her. She was starting to put on weight. And the Health Visitors were pleased with her. Mam was knitting little clothing things and she insisted they were bloody pink. And then Kate died. She died in the cot my Dad had brought down from the attic. Me and my sister's old cot. Sudden Infant Death Syndrome. No reason. Just a bit of bad luck. Here one second. Gone the fucking next. This baby had started to mend me. And now all those wounds from the year before opened up again. And it's taken all these years for them to heal. If they ever have healed. Do they heal? Do you reckon? Really?'

They sit. Over the speakers, Fiona Apple is singing about the Universe. Rita blows her nose

with a tiny honk and smiles a tiny smile. She
picks up her bourbon.

'My god Rita,' Tarm is stunned.

'I'm so sorry,' says Gerda. 'Poor you. I can't
imagine.'

'No. Well. Anyway, Mam and Dad wanted a
proper chapel service, and I said no way! God
had poured his fucking blessings down upon me
hadn't he? So I arranged a cremation. And her
little ashes are in the Garden of Remembrance.
There was a Humanist ceremony. It wasn't
much. There wasn't much to say. She was so
little. So. Anyway. That's where I was today.
Talking to Kate.'

Rita drinks Jack Daniels. She looks resigned to
her tragedy.

'I know that Kate might have died anyway.
And I know that if I'd told Seb about it there's
no way he would have gone that night. But I
didn't tell him. So he went. I also know that,
directly or not, whatever happened that night
took not only the love of my life, but it took my
child as well. That's why, if you want the truth, I
didn't take much persuading to come here on
this lunatic visit. Apart from seeing you two
again.' Rita smiles 'And that's why I want to find
out what the hell happened. And that's why, if I

can, I want to fucking well do something about it. Now, Tarm, stick some more Jack in this glass will you? We're getting drunk!'

It is late. Rita has gone to bed. She went, less unsteadily than she had any right to, saying she was glad that she'd finally got that off her chest. Gerda and Ptarmigan are still sitting on the settee.

'I think I've bitten off more than I can chew here,' says Tarm, 'God alive!'

'Well, only you know Tarm. All that stuff in that folder you've dug up from God only knows where. We're all here now. After all this time. Think about it. Sleep on it. If it feels difficult tomorrow, you can just say, I don't know, that it was all stupid. We can still have a nice time with Rita here. She's still really great isn't she!'

'She is,' Tarm gives Gerda's arm a squeeze. 'What time is it?'

'Erm… Christ it's gone two! Let's turn in.' Gerda yawns.

'I'll be in there in a bit. I just want to run through everything. I know what I want us to do tomorrow. I just need to get things straight in my head. Maybe I'll grab some cheese on toast.'

'That's why you're plump.' says Gerda.

SHEFFIELD GENERAL CEMETERY

PTARMIGAN WANDERS INTO the living room and finds Rita up and watching Sunday Brunch on the TV. Today she's wearing baggy army fatigue trousers and a Lemon Twigs tee shirt. Her hair is down and loose. It falls on her shoulders, all silvery-grey. She has made some proper coffee and, again, has Cadellin on her lap. She smiles at Tarm as he sits opposite her. Cadellin yawns and looks at Tarm, hopeful for food.

Ptarmigan says, 'Did you sleep okay?'

'Brilliant!' says Rita. 'Best kip for years I reckon.' She puffs on her vape.

'Bloody cheat!' Tarm says, pointing at the metal box hanging around her neck. 'Me and Gerd gave up before all this e-cigarette stuff. We did it. But we still hate it!'

'I packed it up when I was pregnant like I said,' Rita says. 'There wasn't much information back then but fags started tasting like shit anyway, so I gave up.'

'You smoked Bensons. They really did taste like shit.'

'Silly arse!' says Rita.

Ptarmigan gives her a friendly kick with his slippered foot, and then goes into the kitchen to pour himself a coffee.

On the big TV, Simon Rimmer is making something with a chicken. It is being spatchcocked. Flattened and walloped.

Tarm sits down and regards Rita.

'So. l want us to go up the road today.'

'Okay. That's okay. Where?'

'Well, I'd like us to end up in the front bar of The Barfield playing pool. But I want to take you somewhere. Gerd knows we're going but she doesn't know anything else about all this. She doesn't really know any more than you do right now.'

Rita strokes Cadellin. He purrs like a bee.

'Okay Tarm. I'm pretty much in your hands.'

'I know. Not a situation I'd anticipated. I've gathered all sorts of stuff. But I want us to go up the road first.'

Gerda emerges with her hair in a sleepy flutter.

'Morning!' she says. 'How did you sleep Rita?'

'Terrible!' says Rita. 'That bed's dreadful you pair of bastards!' Rita rolls around laughing on the settee with Cadellin until the cat gives up and wanders off to sit somewhere less active.

Ptarmigan prepares breakfast while Gerda and Rita drink coffee and watch the TV. An author is being interviewed. He's making Tim Lovejoy laugh.

Fried eggs, fried tomatoes with Burdell's gravy browning, fried bread, fried potatoes, buttered toast, baked beans, chipolatas, fat sausages and crispy bacon. He presents it on a huge platter and, hungover as they all are, they fall to it.

'What the hell is this in the tomatoes?' Rita asks around a mouthful.

Ptarmigan is chewing. Trancelike. Gerda elbows him. He says, 'It's something my Mum used to do. Burdell's Gravy Browning. God only knows what in it. It makes them more savoury. Although that's *umami* these days. They okay?'

Rita spreads squashy tomatoes on a thick slice of toast. 'They're tremendous. I love you Tarm. You massive knob!'

Rita fancies a shower after yesterday's journey. Afterwards she emerges with her washed silver hair still down, parted in the middle. It suits her so well that the colour looks deliberate. Ptarmigan feeds Cadellin. 'Here you go lad,' he says, wrinkling his nose at the smell. 'You're bloody welcome to it!' Then he goes down to the car park to open the doors and let the morning's heat out of his old orange VW Camper Van.

Ten minutes later they clamber in. Gerda next to Tarm, and Rita on one of the cushioned benches in the back. Ptarmigan pulls away. 'Split windscreen!' he cries as they pull onto Abbeydale Road South. Gerda turns round to look at Rita and they both raise their eyebrows. Another ten minutes and the Camper arrives at the main gate of the Sheffield General Cemetery. Ptarmigan looks at Rita in the rear-view mirror. He realises that she doesn't know where they are.

'Reet,' he says, 'We're here.'
'Where?' asks Rita

'Let's get out Rita. It's actually okay.' Gerda says.

Ptarmigan slides open Rita's door. Rita steps out and looks up at the great gate.

'Jesus! This is the cemetery.'

'It is,' Gerda says, taking Rita by the arm. 'Come and see.'

They go through the Great Gate with its curled snakes and watchful, winged world.

And Rita is overwhelmed.

There are vivid flowers as far as she can see down the hill, all bursting with colour. Purples. Pinks. Yellows. Reds. Blues. All bowing their scented heads in the gentle high-summer breeze, inundated with bees and butterflies. Among the flowers are schoolgirls. Or maybe Brownies. They are collecting leaves to press from the low tree branches. Great monuments, cleaned of years of grime and filth, stand amidst the flowers and shrubs. They gleam in the sun. Rita, Ptarmigan and Gerda walk through a lush hollow with a neatly gravelled space in the centre. Trees surround them, filled with brightly singing birds. This is a place replete with life.

Gerda and Tarm lead Rita along a beautifully maintained path into a clearing where a squat monument shines in the sun. There are two elderly couples on benches sharing sandwiches, and a young family is playing on a neatly curated grassy bank opposite them. Ptarmigan stops and sits on the grass. Rita follows suit. She looks around her. 'What?' she says, blinking. 'When the fuck did this happen?'

'It happened in 1989. Pretty much.' Ptarmigan tells her. An ice-cream van plays Greensleeves outside The Great Gate. Gerda sits on Rita's other side.

'Rita. You okay?' she asks.

'Yeah. Just… Jesus! I never came here but I know damn well from people who did that it was a proper horrorshow.'

'It was local people who decided to make this place into something beautiful,' Ptarmigan tells her. 'It took a lot of time and a lot of work. The Star was full of it while it was going on. It's pretty much what it was originally. Or better. The bigger structures are Grade II Listed. It's a Designated Conservation Area as well. It really is beautiful isn't it?'

'It is. It's wonderful!' Rita is entranced.

'Yes. Okay. Well, I've been here a few times and I've been collecting some maps online. I've still got Simon and Bunny's, which is actually back to front for some reason. Me and Gerd came here the other day. To be as sure as we can be.'

Gerda is looking past Rita at Ptarmigan with a resigned look on her face.

'Anyway. As far as we can figure out Rita, where we're sitting is pretty much where Seb disappeared thirty years ago.'

Rita's face goes blank. She looks around again at the playing children and the flowers with their iridescent butterflies and humming bees. At the old couples eating their cheese and pickle sandwiches. She looks into a tree where a blackbird sits, opening and closing his bright orange beak and singing. She can hear excited children at the ice-cream van. She hears swifts shrilling in the blinding blue sky. She sees the little girls excitedly pulling off low leaves to press.

And then she crumples. She throws her head into her hands and takes a deep and reedy breath. She sits, hunched like this for a few seconds. Then she raises her face to the sky and begins to wail. She draws her breath in jagged slices. She sings her belated lament now, in this place. She keens. She has not grieved. Not really. Not properly. Not enough. Not for her love. Not for her dead child. And now, in this bright place, she screams from the pit of her soul. And from the deeps of her gut. She howls at the world and the beating it has given her. The family and the elderly couples look studiously elsewhere. But the children have all stopped what they are doing and watch, marvelling.

Gerda puts both her arms around Rita and holds her very tightly. Rita's arms stay by her sides but her head rests on Gerda's shoulder. She roars her despair until she is empty of it and her hitching chest calms. Rita breathes. She sniffs, and Tarm places a tissue into her hand. She gently pushes Gerda away and blows her nose with another little honk. Her face is red and blotched and wet with the decades of her grief, but her eyes are more peaceful than they were. She gets to her feet and looks at the spectators apologetically. One of the elderly ladies offers her a sympathetic look. The Brownies go back to their leaves.

'Let's go now. Can we?' She has to get out of here. This place has done its job now. They walk slowly back to the van. Ptarmigan opens the doors again to allow the fierce heat to escape.

There are headstones set into the high walls on either side of the Great Gate. Rita and Gerda spend a few moments there, hand in hand.

'Look!' Gerda says. She points at a tombstone set in the middle of the left-hand wall.

Clive Ather
1827 - 1864
Husband, Father, Grandfather
Sorely Taken From Us
'I am unsafe here
Deliver me from this'

'Anyone fancy an ice-cream?' Ptarmigan says.

Rita, getting into her seat, says, 'Why don't we go to The Barfield and play pool?'

POOL

tarmigan parks his camper van back at the flat's car park, lets himself in, and runs upstairs to get change for the bus. Rita wants to get her sunglasses, a spare vape battery and a bottle of e-liquid. Then Gerda says she may as well use the toilet while they're home. Twenty minutes later and they are waiting at the bus stop with five other people. Rita sucks on her vape. She hasn't said much since they left the cemetery. Tarm and Gerda leave her with her thoughts until the bus arrives.

'You two go up,' says Ptarmigan. 'I'll pay.'

'Jesus, these things have changed!' says Rita as she climbs the steps to the bus's upper deck.

Gerda follows her up. 'God yeah. It's all Stagecoach now. I don't think we appreciated being in the Socialist Haven of The North back then.'

They sit at the front. 'Why do I always want to sit here?' Gerda ponders. 'I get right hacked off if

I can't get the front seat. I've got a bloody Master's in Physics and I still pretend I'm driving buses!'

Gerda has not quite lost her West Country drawl, but now it's peppered with the odd clipped Yorkshire vowel. Ptarmigan hardly has any accent. Other than a bit of Sheffield he's picked up over the years. He says he's not an Accent Hoover.

He comes up the stairs and sits next to Rita. 'Alright?' he asks.

'Better than I was. Or better than I've been. I think. I'm not sure. Jesus, I need a bloody drink though. I know that much.'

Tarm grins, 'Snakebite?' he says.

'Fuck off!' says Rita. And she tries out another small smile.

She looks out of the window as the bus slowly rumbles along. 'Everything's changed! Millhouses Park looks the same though.' She turns to Tarm and Gerda. 'Did it always look so... grubby?'

'Probably.' Ptarmigan taps on the windscreen glass. 'So much has changed. The Hole in the Road's been filled in. The eggbox Town Hall's been replaced. Then again, we've been here all the time. So, I don't suppose we've noticed the other stuff. A bit like when you haven't seen someone for ages and they're suddenly decrepit.' He gives Rita a smirk.

'Bollocks!' she laughs.

Gerda prods Ptarmigan. 'Here we are,' she says. 'Ding the bell.'

Ptarmigan dings. The bus wheezes to a stop with a huff of air brakes, and they get off with two of the other passengers. The Barfield stands slightly back from the road. It has brown square tiles under the windows, and the pub sign with its jolly farmer and feather-footed carthorse hasn't changed since the 1940's.

Rita looks like she might cry again. Ptarmigan puts his arm around her. 'I never thought I'd see this place again. Not after.' she says quietly. Then she gathers herself. 'But I'm glad I do! Let's drink beer!' She stomps through the open door, blinks against the sudden gloom, removes her sunglasses and goes straight to the bar. The room is empty apart from them.

'Front bar!' Rita laughs. 'What are you two having?'

'Castle Eden!' Gerda and Tarm say, almost in unison. Ptarmigan does a little dance and they go and sit at one of their old tables, near the window and opposite the pool table.

The friendly barmaid pours their pints and Rita brings them over on a tray. The tray features a photograph of a 1970's man with a perm on it. He's holding a pint mug in one hand and is doing a thumbs up with the other, wearing a chunky gold jumper and grinning at the long-ago brewery photographer.

'Some things haven't changed!' says Gerda, eyeing the tray.

Rita looks at it and her mouth drops open slightly. 'Jesus!' she says. 'Too weird. Cheers!'

They all gulp the first pint down in one. Rita and Tarm look at Gerda, who obliges with a huge belch that brings the barmaid back to the bar.

Rita laughs, 'That hasn't changed either!'

'You've seen nothing! Wait until we grab a Gandhi later!' Tarm gets a clout on the arm from Gerda, who goes to order the next round.

Three people enter the bar. One woman and two men. One of the men is losing his curly ginger hair. He has a full ginger hipster beard and looks like a miniature Hagrid. The other man goes to the bar. His head is shaved close. The woman looks around the room. She has a short and angular dark bob. Her circumnavigation finished, her eyes click back to Ptarmigan. Then Rita. And her gaze lingers on Gerda at the bar. Gerda has seen them and dithers, watching them from the corner of her eye.

'Do you think it's just our generation who drink like this?' Rita asks Ptarmigan, leaning back on her seat.

'Probably.' he says. 'Pre-AIDS, pretty much. Pre-the Government telling us what to do. We had a proper boozing culture back then. Parties all the time. No real supermarkets to speak of. Not selling alcohol anyway. I suppose that behaviour sticks. We had to go to the offy or the pub for a pint. Or the club...'

'Oh my god! The club! Is it still going?' Rita watches a man picking up after his dalmatian on the verge over the road.

'No. The whole row's been demolished. Ages back. They haven't done anything with it either, apart from flattening the place. Sad really. But if that dust could talk!'

They drink. Rita puffs on her vape.

'Do you ever see Jack Marx?' she asks

'Jack? Jack died. Suicide. A few years back. Overdose. It was out of the blue according to his wife. They'd just had a little girl."

'Jesus. That's pretty awful.' says Rita, taking a swig. 'Poor Sim.'

The trio who were at the bar have bought their drinks and sit just across from them in the otherwise deserted bar. Ptarmigan feels a spark of recognition. He glances over at them to make sure. Her face has hardened with the years, and her mouth has become a stern line, but it's definitely her.

'Have you seen?' he hisses quietly to Rita.

'No. What?' Tarm gestures over his shoulder. Rita squeezes her eyes.

'What?'

'Reet! It's Emma Smith and McBride and Nick Cave's Dad!'

'Really?' Rita looks across at them. 'Jesus Christ!' She raises her brows and whispers. 'They walk among us still, Tarm!'

Emma Smith's mouth has been pursed since she sat down. Now she gets up. She walks across to their table. She looms over it with the authority of those seldom contradicted. Then she jabs a finger full of rings into Ptarmigan's shoulder.

'You've got a nerve coming out in daylight you fucking bastard.' Ptarmigan takes a breath and finds he can't breathe it out properly. He stares at her.

'You need to crawl back under your rock!' she seethes. Emma Smith's accent has become pure Sheffield.

She looks at Rita, who is open mouthed.

'And you. You fucking hypocrite slag. We all loved Seb. And off you swanned. Like nothing had happened. Something to hide? *Little Girl*?'

Rita is so surprised by this outburst that she has frozen.

'Yeah. Think on.' Emma Smith looks from Tarm to Rita. 'I know people. I know bike gangs. One word from me and you're dead. Like your fucking boyfriend. The fucking lot of you.'

Emma Smith marches out of the pub. Her consorts pretend to do something else for a moment and then sidle after her. Rita and Ptarmigan are rooted to their chairs.

Gerda comes back with the tray, having heard the tirade. They reach for their drinks.

'What the bloody hell was that?' Ptarmigan's breathing is returning to normal, slowly.

'That woman is a textbook narcissist.' Gerda squeezes Ptarmigan's arm. His eyes are shocked wide.

'Jesus! Well *she* never grew up did she?' Rita vapes greedily, running her slightly trembling fingers around the top of her glass. 'What the fuck was all that about? Gerda? Do you know anything about her nowadays? Is she just fucking insane now?'

Gerda looks at Ptarmigan. He can't read her expression. Somewhere between pity and disgust he thinks. 'Well, her and a few of her little cabal run some sort of vintage clothes shop. I can't think what it's called. Apparently it's the sort of place where you're unlikely to get served if they don't know you. There's other stuff too. Not now though. Later. Don't worry about her.'

Although his mind is not put at total ease by this, the very strangeness of the confrontation allows him to put it to the back of his mind for the time being. He takes a draw of his pint.

'Reet,' says Ptarmigan, 'It's July 1st on Tuesday. I think we need to be ready for then. I don't know why it happens then, but we really do need to prepare ourselves. It's July. Every thirty years. And I know it sounds like Stephen King or something, but I have a whole folder full of stuff at home. And I want to go through it with you both. But not tonight. Tomorrow. Tonight, I think, we need to relax. We need to have fun. We need to drink in this pub, with our beers on this stupid tray. We need to grab a Gandhi and we need to eat it and love it. You know, me and Gerd haven't been in the place since. Or this place.'

'Really?' Rita is surprised.

'Really.' Gerda says. 'And we haven't seen Emma Smith in the flesh since either. That was a stroke of luck. Oh lordy! We've missed her so much!'

Ptarmigan smiles at them both. 'So. Tomorrow the work starts. Whatever it is. We're all fifty or getting there. We're not kids. That's in our favour. I think.'

'Shame nobody told Emma Smith.' Rita is still filled with adrenaline.

She takes a breath and rests her hand on Ptarmigan's knee. 'Right then. Tomorrow. So, right here and now, which one of you two idiots wants to get thrashed at pool?'

They play five games in the empty pub. Rita wins all but one game against Gerda. Then it is nine o'clock. They take a bus to the Gandhi. Ptarmigan orders lamb masala and chips. He likes Sheffield masalas because they always have sliced boiled eggs on the top. Gerda gets the same. Rita has a prawn bhuna with onion bhajis.

They take their feast back to Gerda and Tarm's flat and eat it from the aluminium trays on dinner plates because the lads at the Gandhi are very generous with turmeric. And turmeric is the devil to get off ceramic. The meal is wonderful. They drink cold lager with it. Cadellin smarms around them on the scrounge. And, afterwards, Gerda mixes up some Pimm's with ice and lemonade, and pops in a handful of frozen berries. They sit, with Alien showing on Netflix, in a snug silence. As Sigourney Weaver puts herself and her cat into stasis, Ptarmigan pours them all a Jack Daniels. They are tired and happily drunk. Rita empties her glass, excuses herself, and turns in.

Gerda puts her head on Ptarmigan's shoulder. The late news is now on. Sheffield United have won. 'I have no idea what's happening Tarm. And the physicist in me says it's all bollocks. But the rest of me doesn't. Everything's coming round again. Like those snakes on the cemetery gates. Alien on the telly? That stupid tray in The Barfield? My neck hairs are on end all the time. And when should we tell Rita about the dreams?'

They can hear Rita brushing her teeth in the bathroom. Tarm kisses the top of Gerda's head.

It smells of soap. 'Tomorrow,' he says gently. 'This is why I've kept quiet about the things I've found out. Those dreams are part of this thing. I think I know why too. But tomorrow, okay? When we're all sober and awake and we've all slept on today's... events. Okay?'

'Yeah, okay' murmurs Gerda, 'Let's turn in, Mystery Man.'

DREAMS & OLD PAPER

THE DINING ROOM TABLE has been cleared of everything but its tablecloth, a pot of leaf tea, a jug of milk, a sugar bowl and three mugs. It is the middle of the afternoon.

They all had Ptarmigan's Mum's breakfast again this morning. And they have all showered. Gerda has shared a purple rinse with Rita, but her hair is darker so at least they don't look like twins. For two women who only knew each other for a relatively short time in the eighties, they get on amazingly well. Ptarmigan thought this would be the case. Hoped so, anyway.

He has his folder in front of him and now he opens it up and pulls out a wad of paper.

'I know everything's online now,' he says to Rita and Gerda, 'But if we need to refer to this stuff later, I'd rather be carting paper about than a laptop or an iPad.

'Makes sense.' Rita says.

'Right. Here's what we do know.' He unclips a wad of paper from a paperclip.

'Bunny Reeder and Simon Glass went to the Sheffield General Cemetery in July 1954. It was still an active burial ground, but it was in a state of disrepair. They had both, we think, taken psilocybin mushrooms. It looks like they were trying to recreate a similar experience to Aldous Huxley's in *The Doors of Perception*. They vanished.' Ptarmigan lays out the newspaper prints of their disappearance. 'And they were eventually pronounced missing...'

'... presumed dead.' says Rita

'Yep. After seven years. Families and loved ones have that right. I think it stems from a time when people wanted to marry again, and couldn't if their missing spouse was possibly still alive. That would be bigamy.'

Gerda and Rita examine the press clippings.

'Now. We also know that Seb disappeared in July 1984. Sorry Rita.'

'It's fine,' she says, 'It's fine. Go on lovely.'

Ptarmigan loosens some more sheets. 'I'm guessing you've seen these? There was a police investigation. And Seb was eventually pronounced Missing, Presumed Dead in 1991. Again, seven years. It was his Mum and Dad who approached the High Court in Sheffield. Did you see anything about this Rita?'

'There were a few bits in the local paper, with Seb being a local lad. I didn't read them though. His Mam and Dad are both dead now as well. Pass those sheets over please.'

Tarm slides the prints across the table. Rita reads them one-by-one. She is very calm. Sleep, thinks Ptarmigan. It heals.

When Rita passes the pages back, Ptarmigan looks across at Gerda. She hasn't said anything.

'You okay love?' he asks her.

'Just trying to make sense of this. I actually have no idea where you're going with this Tarm.'

Ptarmigan slides a sheet of paper to Gerda.

'I sent this to Rita. On email. When I first got in touch. I haven't showed it to you. But here it is.'

He passes the sheet of paper to Gerda. She reads.

Sheffield Evening Telegraph. August 9th 1894.

'UNUSUAL EVENTS IN SHARROW'

The people of Sharrow, Sheffield, are afraid to go abroad in the vicinity of Frog Walk at night following divers reports of a ghastly creature who gives chase and can leap great distances with seemingly little or no effort. The last sighting of the beast was on Tuesday last, when a group of friends were frightened by the apparition which was travelling at great speed along the far bank of the Porter Brook stream at Frog Walk.

John Furnise, a cutler's apprentice, told the Telegraph, 'It was 7 foot tall or more with a long face and white eyes and an open mouth and it can run and jump without making a sound. There is as well a stink about it like flyblown meat. It seemed more than anything on earth to be gliding fast along the pathway. It is real and I wasn't the only one to see him. He chased us up the lane on the other side and all we saw was the tall thin figure whose flesh shook like jelly as it moved. Then it jumped across the stream with ease near to where we was then we ran like mad. This is all true!'

Local historian Thomas Broad, who is a Professor of Science at the new Firth College, holds that the witnesses to this grim phenomenon are victims to visions brought on by drink. He stated, though, that a dire creature known as 'The Hallowe Man' was written about and described in similar terms within certain pamphlets at the time of the English Civil War. Professor Broad's hypothesis is that persons unknown may have knowledge of this arcane legend and are making merry with the people of Sharrow by means of a cunning disguise, probably abetted by friends.

Hardly three-hundred yards from Frog Walk, on the steep hill to the south, lies the Sheffield General Cemetery, from whence many fear the specter creeps. Constructed on the sloping bank of a former quarry by the architect Samuel Worth 50 years hence. The cemetery buildings therein are Egyptian and Classical in design. Ouroboros and a winged globe decorate the main gates and the whole vast burial ground is terraced in the Italianate style, much resembling a vineyard of that country. The main gateway resembles a charnel arch, meaning that entering the cemetery is symbolic of the crossing of the river Styx, the River of The Dead from antiquity. This graveyard, intended initially for the deceased religious nonconformists of the city, was opened for burials in 1836. Mary Ann Fish, a victim of consumption, was the first to be interred here. Between 1836 and 1846 ten bodies were laid to rest in a primitive catacomb dug into the hillside. The resulting miasmic stench of rot was sufficient to persuade the city fathers to end the practice, although the bodies were limed rather than re-buried.

Some, with perhaps a more pragmatic outlook, have suggested that the residual miasma from these poor corpses is affecting illusions and fantasies to those in the lower Frog Walk where foul mists will pool, and that they perhaps see nothing once they have made their escape because the inhaled impressions of such horrors have been vanquished from them.

Regardless of this, on Saturday nights, gangs of young men are now patrolling the environs carrying sticks, cudgels and hatchets with which to attack this Hallowe Man but have thus far met with no success in that they have not been confronted by it. The fear of those living locally is such that the locksmiths are reducing their prices in order to strengthen doors and windows in order to help guard against intrusion by the abomination.

Gerda slowly passes the sheet of paper back across the table. She looks at Rita. 'You've read this?'

Rita sucks on her vape and exhales a fragrant cloud. 'Yeah.'

'Gerda knows I've been digging about online, but before I go on… Rita. Have you been having dreams? Nightmares? I don't mean generally. Recently. Vivid stuff?'

'Vivid's right!' Gerda says.

'No I haven't. I hardly ever remember dreams.' Rita says.

'Okay. I'll come to that.'

Gerda fires a look at Ptarmigan then looks down at the table.

'Right. Exhibit Two. From what I've picked up on the Internet, it's clear that many local kid's rhymes contain nuggets of local history. Children's rhymes and nursery rhymes weren't written down until the 1700's, so they were all passed down by mouth. Generation to generation.'

Rita and Gerda nod.

'There's actually a village in your neck-of-the-woods, Gerda. Kilmersdon? Do you know it?'
'Never heard of the place.' Gerda says.
'Thought probably not,' Tarm pulls out another sheet of paper. 'It's tiny. Apparently it's where the 'Jack and Jill' rhyme originated. You know. Jack and Jill went up the hill? Anyway, in the 15th Century there was a young unmarried couple living in Kilmersdon. They used to meet on top of a hill near the village. These trysts were most unseemly back then. Jill became pregnant, and, just before the child's birth, Jack was mysteriously killed by a rock that fell from the hill. A few days later, Jill died giving birth to their love child. There are actually stone markers set along the hill path telling the story.'

'Wow!' says Rita. 'Sounds like me and Seb when we were kids. We had to keep our trysts secret to begin with as well.'

Ptarmigan slips the paper across the table. He sips his tea.

From 'Sung But Not Forgot. A Compendium and Study of British Children's Rhymes' by Frederick Piper-Morris. Published 1897 by Bentley & Sons, London.

> There was an old Lollard lived under the hill,
> If he's not gone he lives there still.
> Of babbys and chillen he ate in pies,
> And he's the old Lollard who never dies.

Southern Yorkshire Skipping Rhyme c1650 - Present.

Although the provenance of this short rhyme which is still sung, predominantly by girls of the lower classes around the City of Sheffield today, is unclear, it is not believed to refer to the primitive 14th to 16th Century Catholic-reform movement. By the 17th Century the term 'Lollard' had become a derogatory term for any person of foul or unclean habits or appearance. However, as with Mildenhall, Suffolk's 'Lady Rainbow' chanting rhyme discussed earlier, the real meaning behind the words is now lost to us.

'Lollard.' Gerda shivers. 'I always thought that was a vile word. Makes me think of dead people with their tongues all hanging out.'

Rita also gives a noticeable shudder. 'Jesus Tarm. This is just… weird.'

'But it makes sense doesn't it,' says Ptarmigan. 'I started collating all this stuff last year. I didn't know if I'd find anything. But, you know. Search terms. Keywords. Think about it. We're the first people in history who know about this who've had access to this amount of data. If where I think this is all going is right, that puts us in a unique position.'

'Good!' Rita says, pouring tea into her mug.

'So, here's the next bit of information. It's incredible what's hanging about out there on the internet. If you know what you're doing and you don't mind pinching stuff. Which, you know, I don't.' Ptarmigan beams at them.

Another single A4 sheet. He passes it across the table.

*C*urious *Report regarding Refidents of SHARROW panic-stricken by Apparition of great Gray giant in the ENVIRONS of Sharrow ; workers defcribe TERROR as monfter runs abroad.*

The ftreets of the Village of Sharrow near the CITY of Sheffield are living in fear of a ghoul refiding somewhere within the vicinity ; though it is known not whence by any soul therein. Thrice this month has the specter attempted to ABDUCT or harm, though it is a mystery of great import as to motive or likely effect, as the aforementioned affront or injury was by chance avoided by all three intended victims.

In all cases known the innocent villain was about their Night toils at the new Sharrow ftone Quarry near Porter Brook when a HUGE beaft made its presense plain by means of "growling and WINNOWING" as of a "High and sturdy tree warping in great winds."

Samuel Worth, a quarryman at these Works was about his bufiness on the night of July 15th 1744 when he was startled and amazed by the WRAITH ; who bore down apon him with great haste indeed, being more swift in his motions than any Chriftian man may muster on this earth.

The witneff stated here that "This creature was vast and GREY with a charnel smell of rot like only to a month old corse and made such rending sounds as I have never heard. I shout'd to my friend nearby who came quick with his lamp and pick and the fierceness left it and it vanished. My friend then fell into a faint and was needed to be revived with strong ale and cold water. My sons shall not venture forth here at night and I shall neither."

Two further attemptf were made by this DAEMON to no avail owing to the engagement of the quarry workmen, who speak of this as "The Hallow Man". It shall be here said that a CHILDE of one Quarry-man of but three years has been vanished since July 17th AD and her wheabouts remain unknown to all and such child did vanish at night and quietly so.

A service shall be held at St Paul's Church in the CITY of Sheffield on Sunday Auguft 1st to pray for surcease.

Ptarmigan looks closely at Gerda. 'You okay?'

'I'm going to be sick!' she says. Gerda pushes back her chair and scurries to the bathroom down the hall. There is the muted sound of liquid vomit hitting toilet-water.

'Fuck me Tarm!' Rita has gone pale.

'I know Reet. It's bad. But we know more in this room than anyone else has. Ever. Just hold that thought. Please? Okay? Bear with me.'

'Yeah. Just. Fucking Jesus! A quarry?' she says.

A few minutes later Gerda comes back into the room and sits down. She is pale. 'You okay?' asks Tarm.

'Been better.' she says, smoothing the tablecloth.

They sit in silence. Rita reads the piece again.

'Remember that quarryman's name.' says Ptarmigan.

'Why?' Rita skims the old text. 'Samuel Worth? Who's he?'

'Well I'm not totally certain. But he might be important. I'm hoping so.'

Rita looks from Tarm to Gerda. 'And Hallow Man?'

'Yeah. Again. Not certain. I've got some ideas. Anyway. The General Cemetery was built on the site of the quarry.'

Rita's eyes widen. 'Fuck off! Really?'

Gerda takes a swig of tea, grimaces, adds sugar.

'It was. It was described as a remote and undisturbed location. They got that right. By the time they designed the cemetery at any rate. For hundreds of years before then, industry was powered all over the place around Sharrow, including at the quarry, by the water flowing along Porter Brook. There was a cutlers workshop right near where the Cemetery is now in the early 1600's. The Porter Brook waterwheels powered that too. All of that industry had died out by the 1830's, obviously. I guess The Industrial Revolution and steam-power did for all of those little works. Now, if you look back to the 1888 Telegraph article, this thing was seen on Frog Walk. Which runs alongside the Brook. And something else I found out.' He hands a map across the table. He has circled a couple of grids in red marker.

Gerda and Rita look together. 'So,' Rita says. 'The path along Porter Brook opposite Frog Walk is...'

'Stalkers Walk.' Gerda finishes. 'Stalkers Walk? That's horrible.'

'That's the Sheffield A-Z for this year. Sometimes things just stick.' Tarm looks down. 'There are some more. But do you want to take a break?'

'No.' Rita takes a draw on her vape and smooths the plait of her new mauve hair. 'Let's get this information so we can process it. Gerda?'

'Yeah. Come on. I'm okay'

Ptarmigan pours himself another mug of tea and presents another printed sheet.

In regard to That Real & Trublesfome Hallowe Man of Sharrow Field. I hath devised this miffive to bring the notice of good Christian Men of honour in this vicinity to ye vilest Monstre of our land. As fuch the Great Hollowe Man doth roam at Darke about Godf Earth in defilement of His law and unto God And Jesus Chrift we pray to be delivered from such dread death or injury as he may inflict. Thif year of 1594AD ye Hollow Man hath devoured of two young girls of this Parrish of Sheffield and they Mothers are right sore with grief and weep along the day and the night. We pray to Our Lord that He watch over us lest his Hellish Appetites do smite us too and we place our faith and truft in God that he deliver us from such horrors as have been seen abroad here. Hallow Mann, so this he be, hath both hight and strength and fastness of his ways not seen in Mortal Men and yet his cowardice liveth in his choosing poor ripe children for his feast for he feareth The Lord within men. For they which needs must be warned Hallow Man is of great stature with a Great hoarish aspect of grate length and terror and hath the power of dreams over Christian Men of great and Worrisome Vividity. His stink of foulness doth preceede wherever he does show himself, and that only after sunset, for this again shews his fear of the goodness of God and His good light. Mine fairest & Gretest desire is to see him gone from this place and all places under God for he is an abomination under God. I pray this offers aid and succour to all within his hunting fields of Sharrow and that with the Grace of God Almighty and His Only Son, Jesus Christ, we here may be safe from the predation of Ye Hallowe Man. In the name of Jesus Christ.

George Talbot, 6th Earl of Shrewsbury. Sheffield. July 30ᵗʰ 1594

'1594?' Rita has read this twice now and still cannot quite take it in, even after all the rest. 'That's over four hundred fucking years ago!'

'Yes it is.' Tarm says and pushes his chair back. 'Gerd. Where's Cadellin?'

'He's out I think.' Gerda says. She is reading the document again.

'Right. I'm getting him in. Things are wrong. It probably sounds stupid. But I want everything and everyone I'm bothered about to be in here and safe.'

Ptarmigan goes downstairs and opens the door. Gentle padding paw-steps up the stairs. Then Cadellin bounces into the room and heads straight for Rita. Ptarmigan stands looking at the car park through the window.

Gerda asks, 'Who was George Talbot?'

Tarm is still standing. 'He's quite famous. He was charged with being the keeper of Mary Queen of Scots while she was being shunted about the country. She was held prisoner down the way at Sheffield Castle for fourteen years. I guess that's when he wrote this. Elizabeth the First wouldn't let him retire from the position either. He was a witness at Mary's execution.

Quite a violent man by all accounts. Then again, who wasn't back then?'

The cat has been curling around Rita's feet. 'Hiya little orange fella. Coming up for a cwtch?' Cadellin leaps onto her lap.

'A what?' Gerda says.

'A cuddle. It's a Welsh thing.' Rita smiles and strokes the big ginger cat. She pushes back her chair to allow him access. Cadellin leaps up and stretches out across her legs, waving his tail in her face. He starts to dig his claws into her knees. Left paw, right paw, left paw.

'Bloody cats. I'd forgotten they do this! Makes my eyes water!'

'Chuck him off if you like.' Gerda says.

'Nah. He's alive and he's warm and happy. So I'm happy.' Rita strokes the cat and he purrs back at her.

Rita reads again around the rumbling Cadellin. 'Hallow Man? Hollowe Man? Hallowey?'

'From what I can find out it comes from *Hallowed* or *Hollow*. Maybe *Harrow*?' I'm not certain. But, looking at all of this, any of those will do.' Ptarmigan wipes his forehead and licks his lips. '*Hallowed* hasn't always meant what it means now, religiously. It actually used to mean "uninjured", or sometimes "impervious".

Ptarmigan sits back down, looking at Cadellin and at Rita, his cat's new best friend.

'Okay. Exhibit whatever it is now. This was the second weirdest thing I found. Beauchief Abbey. It reminded me of when I'd just moved here. I asked Mrs Bron where *Bowcheef* was. She nearly wet herself. It's *Beechiff*. You know that though. Anyway. I got chatting to, of all people, a drummer with a band who were in about a month ago. Turns out he understands this stuff. He didn't write anything down. I didn't ask him to either. But he told me what it means, pretty much.' Ptarmigan passes a further A4 sheet to Rita and Gerda.

Fratres hominis ABBEY DE Beauchief IMPRIMIS abbatis cum hospitibus et Augustus Salomon dedi transitum ad plebem Sharrowus qui metu iniecto secundum gratiam Dei quae est per horroris erant consecratæ HOMO IN NOMINE DOMINI NOSTRI JESU CHRISTI et secum adsumere JESU CHRISTI et honoraverunt apud populum pauperem et bubulcus de plebe Sharrowus retrahentem INFERIUS CAERIMONIUM abductions ILLINC IN ubi vero custodire IN ventrem usque ad obitum pertulerunt fugaces belua est cognomen, SANCTUS EST eo quod videntur FORMIDILOSE ILLI pago ab TEMPUS quo non extat memoria petimusque AUSONIUS ad matutinum, sexta, nona pro archangelis, ut in ipso percutiat SANCTUS ET facere finem cum regnum terroris AD PRIMUM BOOK anni haec multos annos in nomine Patris filii et Spiritus Sancti Per omnia saecula saeculorum Amen

Facsimile of Manuscript *circa* 1324. Beauchief Abbey, Sheffield. © The British Library. 1979.

'Latin. What did your friend tell you it means?' asks Gerda.

'In effect, ' says Ptarmigan, 'The monks of Beauchief Abbey down the road went to help the peasants. They were being terrorised by the Hollow Man, or Hallow Man, who was trying to abduct or eat children. There's also something in there about "death in the belly." And "three decades". Something was terrorising Sharrow Field, which is now Sharrow, where our old house on Vanguard Road was. And where the cemetery is. And the old quarry. And Frog Walk. And Porters Book. And Stalkers Walk. It could make people fall "unto death",' Tarm looks at Gerda. 'And it contaminated peoples' dreams. Now. Gerda. Over to you.'

Gerda looks at Rita. 'Ptarmigan asked you about dreams.'

'Yeah. I know we all have them. I don't remember many though. Never have. Bit boring really, although, Jesus! Listening to other people droning on about their dreams in detail is even duller! "Then the coffee table ran away and I realised I was at work and I was naked and then I was taking my driving test."

Gerda snorts. 'Me neither. Not until last week anyway. We both had the most appalling dreams on the same night. It was the day after we went to work out where Seb was taken from. Down at the cemetery,' she pauses. 'There weren't any coffee tables.'

'Go on then. What was it?' Rita is fascinated.

'Okay.' says Gerda.

She closes her eyes.

GERDA'S DREAM

'I wasn't myself. I don't know who I was. I was in a dream about long, long ago, I know that much. And it was real. It was more than real. When I woke up I was shrieking my head off, but Tarm had just his dream too so we were no help to each other at all. We just laid in bed until it started to get light outside.

I was on my knees, barefoot, gathering up loam and needles and leaves from the floor of a forest near my village, wherever that was. The forest I was in was mostly dead. The trees were chalky-white, and a lot of branches had fallen onto the soil and were crumbling to dirt. Woodlice and spiders kept creeping onto my feet. There was water nearby. I could smell it.

But it was stagnant and poisonous and smelled lethal. A square tomb monument was thrusting up out of the soil nearby, and I threw my leaves and muck down against it, so that I could rest there if I needed to. The people of my village stood around me, dotted among the trees, motionless. They were like scarecrows. Or those Gormley statues on Crosby Beach. Only their chests moved as they breathed, and their faces looked like they were all having terrible, motionless seizures. I knew that something dreadful was about to happen. Some people came into the village. They were tall. They had beads in their hair. My people just stood watching. I could smell smoke. And the Moon was up. I think it was screaming. Someone was.'

Ptarmigan puts his hand on her arm. 'Okay?' Gerda, eyes closed, nods.

'The moon and the dark and the soil and the rot were everywhere. And there was smoke. As I watched, my people began quickly dying all around me. They were suddenly just dead where they stood. They were milk-eyed and reeking in seconds. I breathed them in and out with the smoke. Then, just as quickly, the rankness went from them, and they just blew away with the leaves in the wind. Like shucks.

Then I woke up.

I was alone, it was nearly dark. I was looking up at the day fading out, then I turned over. I kept myself low to the ground because I knew something was watching me. I could feel the cold soil between my fingers and toes and a there was foul smell.

And then something huge crawled over to me through the leaves and the insects and dirt. I could see its open mouth. It was all out of shape. But the rest was in shadow. It came closer. And then, rather than looking at it, I used my thumbs to put out both of my eyes. I felt them pop. And then it took my hand.

And then I woke up properly.'

They sit at the table. Gerda pours more tea. Downs it in one. 'That's grim. Tepid.' She smiles thinly and reaches out to stroke Cadellin's head. 'I don't know if it means anything as such. It's more a feeling. Just hopelessness. Ruin and sudden death. But I'm sure there's something else. A shiftiness about it. And the fact that it's still completely clear in my mind. That's really odd. Dreams happen during deep REM sleep. And once we've woken up, the hippocampus can't store them for very long. Only seconds usually. That's why we forget them so quickly. This thing is as clear as a TV show I've just watched. Yours is as well, isn't it Tarm?'

'Clear as a bell. Unlike my bloody head right now. I'll do this and then there's one more thing.'

Ptarmigan looks up at the ceiling.

He closes his eyes.

PTARMIGAN'S DREAM

'I was an officer in a huge police station. Me and the others were in the canteen when there was the sound of shooting coming from just outside the station. We immediately put our weapons on with those shoulder-sling things, and made our way to the main entrance. I don't know why we had guns. There was a lot of gunfire and blood had started to pool under the entrance doorway. We couldn't understand what was happening. A man came through the station door wearing a tree costume. The costume was enormously tall. I couldn't understand how he'd managed to get through. There was a knot at the top of the tree, like a hole. It was getting bigger. We were shooting at him. But the tree-man just kept on coming through into the station. The bullets didn't hurt him at all. He stood in the foyer, or whatever it's called, pulled out this huge fucking automatic machine gun and started blowing people to shreds.

I ran and hid with some other officers in the cell area downstairs. We stayed quiet and still.

Then, calliope music started coming from the main building.

We agreed to carefully go back up, our weapons drawn.

The steam-driven music got louder and louder as we climbed, like a fairground was going on.

I elbowed open the door to the main station and was immediately tumbled off my feet. The floor was rolling like a ship. On the Upper Deck, which looked like something from a pirate movie, stood the guy dressed as a tree. He was decapitating people with a huge blade, making sure the bodies fell into the sea while the heads rolled about on the floor.

We worked our way around the door, only to realise that everything about the station had changed. There was a smell of old rope and tar. The floor was heaving in the swell. A bell was ringing somewhere, and I could hear the distant mourning of a whale. We edged our way along the deck. Waves broke to starboard.

The calliope music was so loud that I could feel it moving my guts around.

One of the other guys was shot. His back exploded. Bits of spine hit me. Then another. The tree-man had turned towards me. His mouth was a massive hole. Then all of my team died. All of them. Right there. They suddenly shrivelled. They were like dry leaves pressed into a book and they just blew away into the sea.

I ran towards what I thought was an exit. A small door in the side of the corridor. The door slammed behind me, trapping me in a little dark room. And in the little room, a dead, white-faced baby wagged its head from side to side like its neck was broken.

The calliope music got louder and louder and I covered my ears. And then it stopped. Suddenly. Silence. And a great grey face came out of the dark.

Its mouth looked like it was being pulled apart. Its body was solid in the dark, but almost transparent when the light hit it. I think it was the tree-man, but it was different.

There was something moving inside its belly, but I couldn't see what it was.

Then the dead baby came again only it was enormous. It reared up in front of the thing with the broken mouth.

The baby wagged its head and screamed, 'I am but death-soap! But I was once as you. And you shall be as I. And all I shall suffer!'

Then Seb came into the tiny room looking old, and said, 'Death soap?'

The giant baby vanished, and the mouth thing was back. Now it was bigger than the dead baby. It covered its belly with its great hands for a moment. Then it wrapped me in its giant arms. And then it was gone.

And then I woke up in bed with Gerda asleep next to me.

I turned onto my back and a foot-long mouth was silently screaming into my face, and its huge, greasy body was straddling me like a crab.

And then I woke up properly.'

'At this point I'm sick of being sober,' says Rita. She looks at her watch while sucking hard on her vape. 'It's four o'clock. Sod it. I can go and buy something.'

Gerda waves a hand. 'Don't be a berk.' She goes into the kitchen and returns a moment later with three small ceramic beakers and a litre bottle of Tullamore Dew on the Greenall Whitely tray.

'What the hell?' Rita is looking at the feather-cut man on the tray.

Ptarmigan says, 'I popped back to The Barfield and asked that barmaid if you could have it. I told her the bloke in the jumper was your Dad.'

Rita is on the settee again with Cadellin and the tray and a glass of Jamesons. She is laughing. 'Tarm. You're… Well, you're something.'

Gerda says, 'You have no idea.'

Ten minutes later. They are drinking measures of Irish whiskey around the table. There's a bowl of melting ice as well, but nobody can be bothered with it and the condensation is slowly soaking into the tablecloth.

'Okay.' Ptarmigan says. He looks at them both. 'This is the thing.' He takes a drink. Then he grabs his folder again. And he pulls two printed photographs out. There are two more sheets as well. He folds these up and slides them into his trouser pocket.

'I found this photo on an intranet I had no business being on. It was, as far as I can discover… well I think it was taken in 1924. This was just after the time when you had to stand bolt-upright for five minutes while the photographer took his picture. But not by much. The cemetery was still in use then and there were two parts. Anglican and Nonconformist. There was also a small area for Dissenters and some sort of demarcation wall. If I'm honest I don't understand that. It's probably irrelevant. I couldn't find out which part this is of. Anyway. Here it is.'

Ptarmigan slides the print across the table.

Gerda has been looking over at Ptarmigan.
Making sure he's okay. Now she looks at the
photograph with Rita.

'Creepy!' Rita says. 'But it was a cemetery. It
was going to be creepy. It doesn't look in very
good nick for a working cemetery does it?'

Gerda studies the picture. 'It looks like a
negative doesn't it?'

'The whole site was becoming a bit overgrown
by then. A little bit neglected.' Ptarmigan lowers
his eyes and quietly says, 'I examined,
recoloured and enhanced that photograph. It
took some doing. Especially because I wasn't
sure what I was looking at. Gerda, I'm sorry
love. This may bring something back. It did for
me.' He pulls the final item from his folder. And
slides it across to them.

'It's this.' says Ptarmigan.

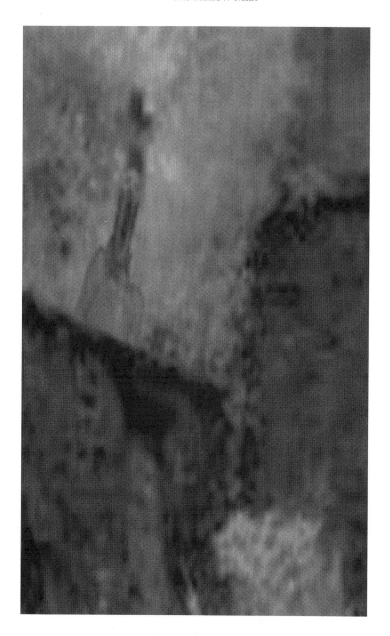

THE PARK IN THE SUNSHINE

THEY HAVE TAKEN a brief, silent bus journey to Millhouses Park. They walked in the bright sun past the picnicking families and football-playing, hollering teenagers. The boating lake is busy with dads and little kids. An ice-cream van plays the Popeye music. A green woodpecker makes its swooping flight between trees. It lands on a trunk and fires up its pneumatic drill. Four grandmothers are fielders in a large extended family's cricket match in the flat middle of the park. Ptarmigan has held Gerda's hand since they got off the bus, and Rita had her arm through his on the other side as they walked. Now they sit near the park brook in the shade of a towering horse chestnut tree. A woman upstream throws a stick into the water, and her dog, a young collie, leaps after it. A small splash. A loud splash.

Gerda didn't say anything when she saw the photograph. The blood fell from her face. She made a hitching, clicking noise in her throat. Then she said she needed to get out of the flat. Rita has been silently grinding her teeth since they left. They have brought the big bottle of Tullamore Dew with them in a canvas shoulder bag, and are passing it between them occasionally. The change of scenery, the normality, has begun to sweep away their heavy, sickly mood.

'Did it bring back any memories?' Tarm asks Gerda.

'It's the thing from my dream.' Gerda is still pale.

'Is that what took Seb?' Rita asks them, fully knowing the answer.

They watch the normal world go obliviously about its business. The sunny, unremarkable world. It is late afternoon now.

'I want a fag.' Gerda says suddenly, watching the collie shake itself. 'Really. I know it's stupid. But I've never wanted a fag so much in my life.'

Rita looks at her lanyard. 'Fuck it. Me too. You can always move to a vape afterwards. It's a site cheaper!'

Tarm hops to his feet and jogs towards the park exit.

'Where's he off to?' Rita points after him.

'Oy Tarm!' yells Gerda. Ptarmigan turns round. 'Keep it up. Mister Plumpy!'

Tarm flicks her the v's and carries on towards the gate. Rita is on her back with her eyes closed. She giggles.

'Jesus you two are brilliant!' Gerda passes her the booze, and she props herself onto her elbow. 'Boy!' Rita says after taking a slug. 'This is great stuff!'

'Yeah! I'd like to pop to The Barfield later I think. So I'm taking it a bit easy.'

'Me too!' Rita takes a huge swig and cackles.

'So, what do you make of all this?'

Rita puffs at her vape. 'It's real. All of it. I've always felt that there was something wrong about absolutely everything that happened over in that house. Like someone was making decisions for us or something. I don't know. And as for the part of me that's going "But Things Like That Don't Happen!" I have three answers.'

'What answers?'

'Coelacanths, Tardigrades and 9/11.' Rita looks up. 'Mind out. Here comes Mo Farrah.'

Ptarmigan is breathing more heavily than he'd like, especially considering the nature of his errand. He sits down and tosses a pack of Twenty Benson & Hedges at Rita. Gerda gets Marlboro. He has Camels in his pocket.

He nods at Rita. 'They'll still taste like shite you know.'

'Cheers Tarm!' says Rita.

Gerda has opened hers and has one in her mouth. She points at the end. 'Light?'

'Ah fuck!' says Tarm and gets up again.

'And They're Off!' yells Gerda. The extended family look over. She gestures towards the dwindling form of Ptarmigan. 'He's in training!' Gerda tells them, cupping her hands like a loudhailer. 'For Cheltenham!'

The family laugh. Rita tells Gerda to shut up or she'll pee herself.

Later still. They sit smoking. The collie and its owner have gone. The family are still playing their game of cricket, shouting at each other now and again. Couples on blankets are spread out around the park greens. The loudhailer man at the boating lake tells number 56 that its time is up. A man has started fishing with a short, thin rod a few yards downstream. Gerda notices a squirrel, beady-eyed and curly-tailed, in their horse-chestnut tree.

'Look!' Ptarmigan points at a dark undulating shape in the clear stream. 'There's a trout.'

Rita turns to Tarm. 'We were talking about… what we were talking about earlier. The photos and the rest.' She sends her cigarette-end flying into the brook. The trout darts away. 'You said to remember that bloke's name. The quarry worker?'

'Samuel Worth.' Gerda's cigarette follows Rita's into the water. The angler shoots her a look.

'Yeah. Him. Well. Like I said it could be a coincidence, and I can't find any more information about the quarryman. But Samuel Worth designed the cemetery buildings and the main gate.'

'What? That Samuel Worth?' says Rita. 'Can't be.'

'Not that one. But look. The Samuel in the pamphlet worked in a quarry in the 18th Century. We know he had sons. We know he was from Sheffield… Sharrow specifically. And we know, if it's accurate, that he packed his job in. The night shift anyway. People used to keep names within families. My great, great-great and great grandfathers on my Dad's side were all called Rupert.'

Gerda grins.

'Laugh away. It doesn't make my ancestry investigation all that easy. Anyway. This man, the 1744 Samuel, told his sons about his experience. It's not much of a stretch to think that the next two generations told their kids as well. Now, 1744 Samuel had witnessed this thing being seen off by a bloke with a shovel or whatever. And I think he knew more than he told whoever wrote that piece. He wouldn't have said he was telling his kids not to go out at night. He certainly wouldn't have given the quarry owner any kind of ultimatum after just that one incident. And you had to be careful what you said back then as well. You know. The Witch Hunts were long gone. But having any kind of esoteric knowledge would have been suspicious. These people were incredibly religious. Fanatically so. Added to which, the quarry owner would have held incredible power over his workers. This was pre-unions of any kind.'

He takes a nip from the bottle and rolls the fragrant, fiery liquid around his mouth. He glances over at Gerda and Rita.

'Bear with me okay.' He takes a breath. The trout has returned. Ptarmigan watches it. He hopes the man downstream doesn't catch it.

'Only two generations later and we have 1830's Samuel Worth. He knows this family secret. Or set of secrets. And then he is tasked with designing these cemetery buildings.'

'Did he design the whole thing?' Rita asks.

'No. A man called Marnock did the landscaping. He designed the Sheffield Botanical Gardens as well. The General was opened as a "Garden Cemetery". Before then, people were quite untrusting of nature and the landscape. In the early Victorian era it started to become fashionable to appreciate the natural world. The Lake Poets like Coleridge and Wordsworth changed the national psyche and helped kickstart tourism. Weird eh? No. Samuel designed all of the buildings. And the gate.'

Gerda gets up and stands, looking into the water. The sun is falling lower in the sky and her shadow stretches out behind her. A family of ducks paddles towards them.

'Anyway. I did more excavation online. Nineteenth Century Sam wrote a book. Well, more of another pamphlet.'

'What?' Rita sits up straight. The ducks have rounded a corner, swimming with the gentle current.

'In 1829. It was a kind of allegorical story from what I can make out. It was called Cronus Return. There are only fragments dotted about and I had to go from reference to reference in other old scholastic texts to find anything at all. Took bloody hours.' Ptarmigan straightens his legs and pulls out the two pieces of paper from his shorts pocket. 'Listen to this. In the pamphlet, a father is educating his son. I don't know what's happened before this lesson because there's no record whatsoever. Apparently he only had about fifty pamphlets printed. Makes you wonder why doesn't it? Anyway. These are the father's words.'

Ptarmigan flattens out the creases on one of the sheets and reads aloud.

'And so, in looking to vanquish the beast we must first understand the nature of the beast, for fierce he may appear, he, though may be fierce in visage alone. The Devil himself is a coward and holds good people in thrall by his renown alone. Though he has the power of fantasie, his is the power of impotence. Though he looks

mighty, he shall quickly fall. Were the brave to
smite him, Satan would turn and flee. Our
brothers in the Old Times of Egypt had this
knowledge and by their wisdom did banish
divers monsters. In this way the rope of eternity
is severed and the Sun shall have dominion. Like
a dark mirror on the miracle of birth, Satan
keeps those within and extinguishes them like a
candle as further nourishment approaches.
Denial is the door. Courage is the key.'

Ptarmigan looks up. Gerda and Rita are
motionless. 'The son's name was Samuel.' he
tells them.

'Remember the George Talbot thing? 1594?
That talked about cowardice as well. I think
Samuel is saying the same thing. Basically, it's
all very well doing a Freddie Krueger and
messing with people while they're asleep. And
it's all very well taking three-year-olds and
people who are off their faces on hallucinogens.
But perhaps you're not so good against someone
your own size.'

'This is brilliant!' Rita says. She gets up and
brushes grass from her legs.

Seb folds up the paper. 'And look, we all read the piece from The Star about Jack Marx being the last person to see Seb? Apart from us? It says that the police had released information about that pile of waxy stuff they found? Animal in origin, apparently. It made me think about Samuel Worth saying that Satan keeps those within and extinguishes them like a candle. Wax? You know. When something better comes along? Or something… fresher? I don't quite understand. Not yet. I think I'm getting there though.'

The day is becoming dimmer, the shadows more diffuse. Pinkly glowing streetlamps have begun to turn on along the main road. Although it is still warm, Gerda shivers. The stream is a dark gurgling path now, only occasionally reflecting the last of the day. 'Can we go home?'

They gather their things, including the half-empty whiskey bottle, and make their way to the gate. Seeing the gate jogs Ptarmigan's memory back to where it was going.

'And also. Remember what's on the big cemetery gate we went through the other day?'

'Ouroboros and a globe with wings.' Gerda says.

'Yeah. Well, it's actually a sun with wings.'

'Oh is it?' They reach the bus stop.

'It is. Right in the middle. Right where you have to walk through. I'll show you the last thing on the bus. The last thing for now anyway.'

Full dark now. It is only three stops to Ptarmigan and Gerda's, but the traffic is heavy. They are at the front of the top deck again. Rita is yawning. Long afternoon. It is almost ten o'clock.

Smoothing out the last piece of A4 paper, Tarm reads again.

'The oldest-known ouroboros was discovered within the tomb of Tutankhamen. It dates from BC 1,300.' He looks up. 'That's over three thousand years ago.' he looks back to the text.

'The symbol, also one of the most commonly used in alchemy, refers to the mystery of cyclical time, which flows back into itself. In effect the symbol can mean both infinity and the disruption of infinity. The ancient Egyptians understood time as a series of repetitive cycles, instead of something linear and constantly evolving. Ring any bells?'

'Yes. Okay,' says Rita. 'So what about the globe? Sun thing?'

Ptarmigan reads on. 'The Winged Sun is a symbol that existed even before the Egyptian civilization with which it is most associated. Archaeologists have found winged suns carved onto very ancient stones, making this symbol one of the earliest recorded in human history. The Winged Sun represents divinity, courage, power and the light and goodness of the world. Old Sam is telling us something.'

Rita and Gerda look at each other and smile. Gerda says, 'He is isn't he.'

Later. In the flat. 'That's the problem with this sort of heat.' Gerda scrapes liquifying cat-food into the recycling caddy, 'Everything's minging in five minutes.'

Cadellin rubs around her legs while she gets a fresh dish and spoons his new food into it. 'Although, in your case, cat, it didn't have far to go.'

They are all tired and about to turn in. Ptarmigan turns to Rita. 'It's July at midnight.'

'I know,' she says, yawning again. 'I know. I'll see you tomorrow. I'm turning in.' Rita pads down the hallway. 'Night Gerda!' she says. 'That cat stuff really stinks!'

'Tell me about it. Night Rita.'

Gerda comes through from the kitchen, leaving Cadellin slurping his dinner up, and sits next to Tarm on the settee. He is looking at a map of the cemetery on his iPad.

'An hour until July,' he says, closing the cover. 'I'm going back to the cemetery tomorrow. So I'm off to kip. You coming?'

'In a bit. I'm going to watch something cheery. It's been a bit of a day.'

Ptarmigan kisses her hand. 'I know. I'm off. I'm beat. Love you.'

'Love you too, Chubbychops.'

NIGHTMARE

OUTSIDE, FAR BELOW the flat, the road is quiet. A lone vixen skitters along the sodium-lit gutter, sniffing for food. She has five cubs back in her den. They're growing quickly and are constantly mewling for their milk. She finds a rejected chicken burger and quickly eats it. High in the bushes across the road a family of sparrows suddenly spark into twittering life and just as suddenly subside. In Millhouses Park, the trout moves his tail in time with the current. He is asleep, but his sensitive lateral-line is always awake, feeling for predators or prey. Two badgers tumble down the gentle bank of the makeshift cricket field. The extended cricketing family are all asleep in their separate houses. The four grandmothers are gently snoring. Ptarmigan and Gerda sleep deeply. Their curtains sway softly in the now-July breeze. In the Sheffield General Cemetery, apart from a barn owl silently hunting its scurrying quarry, all is still.

A ragged shriek, loud as a bullet. Ptarmigan and Gerda are immediately awake. Tarm turns on the bedside lamp. Another high scream, ending in what sounds like a sob.

'Rita!' Gerda is out of bed and wrestling with her dressing gown. A further ululating shriek. Piercing. Terrified.

Gerda knocks perfunctorily on Rita's door then goes in. In the hallway light she sees Rita sitting up in bed. Her face has gone. Then Gerda sees that her violet hair is wrapped around her head like a veil. She rushes to Rita's side. Rita is breathing so rapidly that she is in danger of hyperventilating.

'Reet!' Gerda puts her arm around her stricken friend. 'Rita. It's me.'

Rita tries to focus. She reaches shakily to the bedside table for her glass of water. Gerda gets it for her. The bedside clock says 3.03am. Ptarmigan appears in the doorway, his hair sticking up on one side. His shadow falls on the bed. Rita gasps.

'It's okay. Rita.' Ptarmigan turns on the bedroom light.

She obviously sleeps naked, and she is beaded with sweat on everywhere that is exposed to the light. She sips water. Her hair, now that Gerda has gently moved it away from her face, is lank with moisture. For a moment Rita looks confused and then she puts a hand under the duvet. She starts to weep. 'Jesus Gerda. I'm so sorry. I've wet the bed.'

Ptarmigan comes and sits on her other side. 'Hey that doesn't matter. We've all done it. We protect all of our mattresses anyway. Because of the cat.'

On cue, Cadellin slides through the door and jumps onto the bed. Rita grabs him and hugs him. Cadellin purrs.

'You're honoured. Last time Tarm tried that he nearly lost an eye.'

Rita manages a weak laugh.

'What happened?' Ptarmigan is rubbing sleep from his eyes. Gerda reaches up and flattens his hair for him.

'Dream,' Rita says, she sips more water. 'Nightmare. Fucking… fucking awful. Shit! Oh Jesus I'm sorry about the bed.'

'Shut up.' Gerda pulls at her arm. 'Come on. Get up and get in the shower. I'll sort this lot out.' She shoots a look at Ptarmigan. 'And you can bugger off out of here.'

'Oh. Yeah. Sure. Sorry. Shall I put the kettle on?'

'Yeah. That'd be good,' says Gerda. 'After you've buggered off.'

It is nearly four o'clock in the morning. Rita wanted the TV on, so the BBC rolling news is whispering in the background. Rolf Harris has been convicted of indecent assault. While Rita was in the shower, Gerda changed her bedding. 'Wasn't much!' she mouthed to Tarm on the way to the washing machine with the damp bundle. It was, she thinks, mainly sweat.

Now Rita sits, freshly showered and hair washed, nursing a mug of decaffeinated tea, eyes on the television.

'That was fucking horrific,' she suddenly says. 'And I remember every moment. Like you two. I want to tell you. But where's the cat?'

'I'll get him.' Ptarmigan disappears into Rita's room and comes back dangling Cadellin. As soon as he puts him on the floor, the cat leaps onto Rita. He plods for a few seconds and then comes to rest with his head hanging between her knees.

'Silly sod.' Gerda laughs. Rita strokes his head. She closes her eyes.

RITA'S DREAM

I was pregnant, at my Mam and Dad's. I couldn't figure out why because I knew they were both dead and that Kate was dead. I was huge. My Dad came down from the loft with me and my sister's old cot and set it up in Kate's old room. He had a washing-up bowl and a cloth. He was washing it down and he kept saying, 'I can't get the stink out of this thing.' It looked okay to me, but he kept scrubbing with the cloth. The water was getting more and more filthy. He went and filled the bowl with fresh water and washed it again. And the same thing happened. He was washing and washing the cot and he couldn't get it clean. He looked furious. Sweat was pouring down his face. He cleaned and cleaned until he'd cleaned all of the little Bambi's and rabbits and flowers off it. And he still carried on washing it.

My Mam came into Kate's room with a tray of sandwiches. The tray was that one from the pub, with the Greenall Whitely man on it. I tried to ask her where she'd got it from, but I couldn't open my mouth.

'Your favourites!' my Mam said. There were tuna sandwiches and cheese and pickle and egg. My Mam said, 'Help yourself Reet!' She put the tray on the floor but she trod into the food when she left the room. There was marge and egg and tuna all trodden into Kate's bedroom carpet. My Dad was still scouring away, saying, 'Fucking stench. Fucking filth.' My Dad never swore! And then he stopped. He smiled at me and said, 'Now then. I've done it. That's better. Look Reet! Look my lovely!'

The cot was bones surrounding a beshitted mattress. Long bones with veins and fat still sticking to them. Like something an animal had gnawed and got bored with. My Dad kept smiling at me and his teeth were all black. There was a sort of wet noise from the kitchen. I got up and went in. My Mam was sitting at our old kitchen table, with its tiled top, rocking back and forth. She was breast feeding Kate. I couldn't scream at her or ask what she was doing because my mouth had gone. Kate was taking great sucks and gurgling like a sick stomach.

My Dad came into the kitchen. 'I've cleaned the cot!' he yelled. His teeth were falling out onto the tiled floor. They made a tinkling sound like tiny Christmas bells.

Kate pulled away from my Mam's thick, yellow breast. She shuffled off my Mam's lap and stood. Kate was a tiny baby! She was nowhere near crawling, let alone standing. But there she was. Her lovely hair was all matted with dirt and sour milk. There was smell of smoke.

Then my Mam and Dad died. They just died and desiccated. Like a timelapse film of two old seed-pods drying out. They were gone in a second. Just two vague piles of dusty hair and skin on the kitchen floor. I reached up and tore at my mouth. The tough rind that was covering it broke, and I screamed. That might have been when you heard me first.

Kate walked towards me with her arms out. She said, 'I am unsafe here Mam. Deliver me from this. Please Mam!' Then she shrivelled too. She died. Right there. While I watched, with my ripped-open mouth and my great belly. And from my belly, a noise like old trees bending. I fell to the floor and opened my legs. First a great sinewy arm burst out of me. Then another. I was being torn in half. Then the head. This great head, leeching and guzzling as it came out of me. It turned and looked me in the face. Its mouth was impossible, and its eyes were stupid. And then the rest of the huge body fell out of me in a burst of filth and blood. It turned over and there was something inside it. Like a larva. And I woke up here, in bed.

Then the great head with the huge mouth on the pillow next to me turned over, and it looked at me with something like love.

And then I woke up properly.

PTARMIGAN AT THE CHAPEL

IT IS TEN IN the morning. Ptarmigan has left Gerda and Rita back at the flat. Shortly after Rita had described her terrible dream to them, he had excused himself and gone back to bed. In situations like this, he thinks, women need other women. A man clumsily dancing around on the perimeter is less than helpful. When Tarm got up at eight o'clock this morning, they were both curled up fast asleep on Rita's newly made bed with Cadellin sprawled between them, dreamily flicking his paws. Tarm had crept around the house trying to be quiet so as not to disturb any of them. This is always a pointless exercise in his opinion. He always thinks it's like someone telling you not to laugh. Impossible. He's not sure why didn't just go banging about the place like usual. He'd have made less racket.

He has driven to the cemetery. He wants to have a proper look around with a current map, and to study one place in particular. The Sheffield General Cemetery Trust, the organisation who run the place now, have produced the very thing. And he has it in his pocket.

The Great Gate looms before him. He notes the winged sun and ouroboros and he tips a silent wink to old Samuel Worth. He opens the map. The path through the gate first takes him past Ernest Shuttleworth's memorial. It is one of those low-slung marble slabs. Highly polished and still loved, it commemorates both Ernest, who perished during The Great War, and his father, who died several years later in 1922. Samuel Holberry's memorial is next, on Tarm's left. Just a plaque near a tombstone really. But this man was a key figure in the Chartist Movement in both Newport, close to Rita's home, and here in Sheffield. He died of tuberculosis in York Prison in 1842, and 50,000 people attended his funeral here at the cemetery. There is a fountain named after him in the Sheffield Peace Gardens in town. Ptarmigan tries to imagine 50,000 people.

Birds are in full song above him, and the shrubs and flowers are abuzz. He sits on a bench for a moment. He breathes in the scents of sweet, verdant life. Marrying this beauty with the barely remembered and filthy terror that he, Gerda, and especially Seb experienced in 1984 is impossible. They are different places in different times. He starts walking again, map in hand.

He knows where he is heading. The stone memorials to Mark Firth and James Nicholson, the local steel magnates, loom ahead. Nicholson's, with its mourning angel and her open book, is all in green. Firth's is a towering and draped urn, all in grey.

How long did these peoples' immortality last? Ptarmigan wonders. He himself has visited his own parents' graves twice. And would it have been different if they were beneath a great edifice like this rather than a shiny marble gravestone? Or just down the road? He doesn't think so. Who lays flowers on their grandparent's graves? Let alone their great grandparents'?

Ptarmigan turns left along the path. Past John Cole's obelisk and George Bennett's chunky marker. George Bassett's dour monolith is visible from where he now stands. This was the man who gave the world Liquorice Allsorts. Tarm thinks a great big Bertie Bassett, in full colour, would have been more acceptable to this jolly sweet maker.

And now he stands. Looking up at Samuel Worth's Chapel. It looks like The Pantheon, or an Egyptian or Roman temple. A cross-fertilisation of Greco-Roman and Egyptian architecture, he thinks. Samuel Worth was obsessed by this stuff. And Tarm, Gerda and Rita are the only people on earth who know why. This thought gives him pause.

Although. The only people? Maybe that isn't the case. It's something they need to find out. But, for now, this great monument was made by the man Ptarmigan is laying his hopes on. Are there any further lessons? He walks up the stone steps. He walks around the great building twice, searching for information. Four great columns span the porched entrance. They remind him of the club. There are eight oblong windows, four on each side. But there are no carvings or inscriptions.

He goes inside. Where there once must have been bare brick, possibly plastered, there are now clean white walls, tastefully lit by what look like LED lamps. It is more like a conference centre or registrar's office than a chapel. Anything Samuel Worth had commissioned to be etched onto the walls will be totally covered now.

He examines the whole edifice closely once again. It takes him ten minutes. There is nothing.

But he knows that, even though this was a fruitless journey in one respect, the Hallow Man is no longer here. He can't be. So where is he? It is now July after all. The killing month.

Ptarmigan leaves the chapel. He sits on a step. Texts Gerda to tell her that he is on his way back.

TARM: I've done what I need 2 do.
GERDMISSUS: Find anything out?
TARM: Yes & no. More no. But also yes.
GERDMISSUS: Christ! U tosspot. Hungry?
TARM: Yes I am.
GERDMISSUS: Before I 4get I remembered what Emma Smith's shops called.
TARM: Lovely. Go on then.

There is a pause.

GERDMISSUS: It's called Xlusive.
TARM: Cool n hip. How many autocorrects did that come up with?

GERDMISSUS: Plenty. Ffs. CU inabit. x

Gerda and Rita have made a huge late breakfast. The usual, and Rita has attempted Ptarmigan's Mum's tomatoes and they're pretty good.

'Burdell's!' Ptarmigan says.

'Burdell's to you too matey!' Rita says. She has recovered from her dream, but says it is still so intense that she can taste it. Cadellin wheedles around the table legs. He is either looking for scraps or waiting until Rita has finished.

'Rita?' Ptarmigan says when they have all eaten and are back in the living room.

'Ptarmigan?' says Rita, with Cadellin's nose in her face.

'How are you? You lot were all flaked out on your bed when I left. But it was pretty full-on last night. So. You okay?'

'You know when we were in the cemetery?' Rita says with her brows raised.

'Well, of course.'

'And I howled and shrieked like a biblical widow?'

'Yes.'

'Well, after that, everything's got clearer. Plainer. That fucking dream last night.

Something isn't what we think. I don't know why. But I'm excited. We're right and we're wrong.'

'Okay.'

'So, what did you find out today? At the cemetery?'

'Rita. It isn't there. The Hallow Man? Whatever he is. There are no new messages either. We need to look elsewhere. We don't have long now. It's July. I think we should go and look at the old house. See what memories it jogs. A lot of this seems to be about memory.'

'Vanguard?'

'I think so. Can't hurt.'

'No. It can't.'

VANGUARD ROAD

IT IS ONLY a short drive, but it's a tumbling
backwards of all of their time. They all
remember, to some extent. The Willow Pattern
crockery. The ticking cooker. The cellar with its
damp secrets and its failing meters. The useless
torch. The lozenge clock. The yellow curtains
and the geometric living room carpet. The nights
out and the nights in. They remember watching
the huge erratic television. Sometimes it showed
Alien and sometimes *Top of The Pops* or
Blockbusters or *The Professionals* and sometimes
The Thing. They remember the Gandhi curries.
Ptarmigan remembers his quiet nights alone
here before Seb and Rita even came. Those
gentle, solitary nights when he was here on his
own. Before Emma Smith. Before everything.
Gerda remembers her first nights with Tarm.
The warmth and exploratory headiness of new
love. Rita remembers Seb. His laugh and his
buffoonery, all hiding a bright, probing
intelligence. She remembers the bedroom study

desks, one facing one wall and one facing the other. They try to remember Simon and Bunny. And they remember the sound of Sex Gang Children pounding in the club while the girls with dreadlocks marched about on the stage yelling *Jezebel!* Ptarmigan looks across the road to where the Sweet Centre used to be. He remembers *Grandstand* and curry-on-the-bone and kicking a football around with Mo. It's someone's house now. The curtains part and a face peers through the window. Tarm wants to tear those curtains down and demand food. Goat curry on the bone please. The first line of an old book comes into his mind. *The past is a foreign country; they do things differently there.* They remember being here. In this place. All those years ago.

None of them have been back to Vanguard Road since 1984. In addition to simply not wanting to come, Ptarmigan and Gerda have had no reason to return. They have both sailed past the road's entrance on countless buses. They have always known where the road is. How could they forget? But they have bypassed it without a single thought for thirty years. Maybe they felt a nudge of distaste and sadness about the place. But in reality, apart from their subliminal feelings, Vanguard is a narrow road and leads neither to-or-from anywhere. Rita, in South Wales, has had even less reason, or opportunity, to revisit their old house.

And yet here they all are, getting out of Rita's little Corsa, outside their old house on Vanguard Road, on a late early-July afternoon.

'Jesus!' Rita looks at the dark green front door. That door never opened because, when the room was his, it was part of Ptarmigan's bedroom. 'It's the same fucking colour.'

'I think they stopped selling that shade of green in about 1920.' says Tarm. 'Penicillin Green. Cashing in on Fleming.'

They stand outside, looking up at the windows. 'That was me and Seb's room.' Rita points to the left. She shades her eyes. 'It's a bigger room than it looks from here. We were really happy.' Gerda gives her a little hug.

Rita presses her key fob and beeps her car shut. The phone box is still on the corner, but it has become some sort of book-lending library. They head around to the yard at the back, through the narrow alley.

'Look!' Rita says quietly, 'That's old Mrs Brons's angel!' The three-foot figure stands in a well-maintained little garden. It has a heavy brow. Its stern face seems to look both towards and away from the observer with the suggestion of wings covering its body. Silica and quartz glitter all over it.

Rita, Ptarmigan and Gerda look at each other and then they look upwards. Three magpies are hopping along the roof apex. They clatter backwards and forwards until something spooks them and they take to the wing, shrieking.

Ptarmigan walks across their old yard and leans on the ledge, looking through the downstairs living room window. The glass is smeared. The room is bare. No curtains. No furniture. No carpet.

'That's weird isn't it?' he says, wiping his hands on his shorts. 'Prime student rental. Empty. I wonder how long for?'

'We could ask a local estate agent?' Gerda offers. 'It's a bit peculiar.'

Rita wipes the windowpane with her sleeve and presses her face against it. 'Maybe it's been condemned?' She can just see into the stairwell. Just see Tarm's old bedroom door. The place looks forlorn.

'I'm trying Mrs B's old place,' Ptarmigan opens her gate. The click sounds familiar.

Tarm knocks on the door. There is no response. He peers through the window. The curtains are drawn. He thinks they are the same curtains that were here thirty years ago.

'Okay. Nothing here.' Ptarmigan says. He is disappointed. He stands in the little alleyway between Mrs Bron's fence and the adjoining terrace of houses looking up. Expecting magpies. Gerda and Rita go back to the car. They get in.

There is a noise from Mrs Bron's house. Startled, Ptarmigan ducks down behind the fence. A moment later the door opens. Ptarmigan stands up. Mrs Bron. She looks at him with dead button eyes. She looks around. She hasn't changed. Not one bit.

'Can I help you?' she says. 'You're on private property you know.'

'No. Thanks. Sorry to have bothered you. I was looking for a friend. Wrong address.'

Ptarmigan walks calmly away. Mrs Bron's gaze follows him. He climbs back into Rita's car. He begins to shiver, panicked. 'Bloody hell. That was Mrs B. Drive Rita!' he says quietly. ' Just fucking drive! Now!' Rita pulls away.

'That was her? How come Tarm? She must be, what? A hundred by now!' Gerda sits behind him. Rita drives.

Ptarmigan looks round. Mrs Bron is nowhere to be seen. 'Yeah. Well she isn't. She's the bloody same as the last time I saw her in 1984.'

Gerda looks at Rita in the rear view mirror, who shrugs back at her with eyes wide. 'Tarm. Tarm!' she shakes his arm, 'It's impossible.'

'No Gerda. No. No it isn't.'

REVELATIONS

THEY FALL BACK into the flat. Ptarmigan makes for his laptop. Gerda heads for the booze. Rita stands in the doorway.

'It was her. It was Mrs Bron. I don't think she recognised me. I've changed. She hasn't. She really hasn't. I don't get it.' Tarm is fidgeting, unsure what to think. 'Right. If she was a Mrs in 1954, she would have had to be sixteen that year at the very least. If she was a blushing sixteen-year-old bride when those lads disappeared that would make her, what? 76 now? And she told me that Mr Bron had long gone to wherever by 1954. She must be 80. Gerda, she looks our age!'

Rita is still hovering in the doorway. 'Are you sure it wasn't a daughter or something?'

'She didn't have any kids,' Ptarmigan sits down. 'There weren't any next door anyway. Not when we were there. You know that. It was just Mrs Bron.'

He is badly shaken. There must be some explanation. He takes deep breaths, and he tries to calm. All of this is taking them to places he didn't expect. Then, as if his mind wants to change the subject, he remembers the conversation in the park about yesterday's encounter with Emma Smith.

'Gerda,' he calls into the kitchen. 'What was she on about yesterday?'

Rita goes to the kitchen, gets a pint mug from a cupboard, comes back in and sits down too. 'Yes. And "hypocrite"? What did Emma fucking Smith mean by that?'

Gerda comes into the room with the Greenall Whitely tray. It has a jug of Pimm's on it. 'Pimm's o'clock!' she says, a little unsurely. 'I'll tell you in a bit. You as well Reet.'

Rita pours a pint of Pimm's into her mug. Gerda goes to refill the jug and then puts it back on the coffee table. It is now eight o'clock. The sun strikes the houses opposite the flat, making the bricks fiery.

Ptarmigan has closed his computer. He looks at his pack of Marlboro. Takes one out. Lights it. Walks around the living room.

'We'll have to fumigate the place after this!' Gerda isn't serious, but Tarm is losing himself in shock and confusion.

'You fucking decided that smoking was back on the agenda!' he says loudly, dropping ash onto the carpet. He sits back down.

'Hey!! Gerda says. She kneels by him. 'Hey! Hang on. Take a breath. Just take a breath.'

Ptarmigan does. He sits. Breathes. In. Out. In…in… in. Out. He subsides. Gerda pours. They drink the sweet and welcome alcohol.

Later. Gerda sits in front of Rita and Ptarmigan. They are now calm. They are ready for a revelation.

'Back at Uni,' Gerda says, 'Emma Smith made a career out of hanging about with all of the great and the good in Sheffield. Maz Carter. Simon Gouldman. Martin Frew. Abby. The lot. She got here as a first year in 1983 and she was suddenly all over the place. According to some people at work, nothing changed after she left. And she was still shagging half of the Sheffield Glitterati last I heard.' Gerda's mouth forms a moue of distaste. 'She was at the Poly doing Art with all of her ludicrous mates, and then they all dropped out. I suppose dropping out was the height of fashion for half an hour at some point. That was about a month after you had your little thing with her, Tarm.'

Ptarmigan whistles for Cadellin. 'I'm not surprised. She'd have got a first in hierarchies and pack-animal behaviour, but other than that...'

Gerda clutches his arm. Caresses it. 'After you'd split up. Well, look. She left it a while. A year or so.'

'Left what a while?'

'Ptarmigan. She virtually pinned me against a wall in the ladies. In The Barfield. Just before, you know. Before Seb disappeared. She told me that you raped her.'

Ptarmigan has left the house on foot. He has taken the half-full bottle of Tullamore Dew with him in its canvas bag. How does he feel? Is he angry? Yes he is. He's angry. He is ablaze with fury. Does he feel like the world has dug a hole for him and then disguised it with a low-comedy banana skin? That too. Now he understands the struggle to perform in Sheffield with his band. And the effort it took to get Ptarmigan Sounds out of the blocks. Who wants to support a fucking rapist? He wonders what he could have done differently. And what argument would he have had anyway? It didn't happen M'lud? His word against hers and that of her friends. Why would I M'lud? Well, that's male power and

arrogance right there. He feels filthy. Soiled. He
walks, occasionally coming to a halt under a
streetlamp to swig whiskey. He reaches the park
gates, sure they would be closed. But they aren't.
He steps onto damp grass. *Why? Why you fucking
awful bastard? For a laugh? Because you could?* He
walks across the dewy-wet grass, turns around,
sees his footprints like dark stalking ghosts in
the half-light. The fact that three decades have
flown past means nothing. It feels the same to
Ptarmigan as if she'd accused him of abusing her
last night. Walking across the greens, he can
hear the brook chattering to itself. He reaches the
water and suddenly feels too warm. Sitting on
an exposed root of their horse chestnut tree from
earlier, he dunks his booted feet into the stream.
He gasps. The water is numbingly cold. Once it
has worked its way around the intricacies of his
feet, they feel too heavy to lift. So he leaves them
there, swaying in the current.

He pulls the cork from the bottle. He upends it
into his mouth. A huge gulp. The liquor is like
hot gravy, and the fumes go up his nose and
invade his gut. Heaving, he retches and then
vomits tepid alcohol to his right, away from the
bottle and his legs. His feet are freezing. He
raises lefty up. Iced water runs up his bare leg
and into his shorts. He gasps again. Lefty comes

down on the muddy grass. Ptarmigan struggles to undo the wet laces. Eventually they come squeakily apart.

Another swig. And another. Righty next. He pulls his right boot out of the water and thumps it down in front of him. He forces the sodden laces open and works the boot off his foot. It squishes slightly in his grasp. Another swill of Tullamore Dew. He pours water from his boots. He takes off his socks and wrings them out. They smell of home. He sits barefoot. The stream reflects the city-glowing sky. He wonders if the trout is still floating a few feet away, swaying in the gentle flow. *Just why? Why the hell would anyone say that?*

Ptarmigan needed this. This space and solitude. He thinks back over his brief and inconsequential relationship with Emma Smith. They met at the club before Seb and Rita had turned up and changed everything. Ptarmigan had been talking to some people he'd got to know near the bar, and suddenly a girl with black and blue hair was at his side. She was pretty in an unconventional, angular way. Her lips were glossy and her eyes were wide and not quite aligned, which gave her a quirkiness that Ptarmigan found attractive. After the club, she had gone back to the empty house on Vanguard

Road with him. The fresh sex was exhilarating
for them both. Emma Smith and Ptarmigan
began going to gigs and the club together. The
sex continued to be good, but the rest of their
interactions were soon wearing thin for them
both. Emma Smith had a group of friends with
whom she shared a house on the other side of
Sheffield. The first time Tarm had met them he
was amazed that four adults (five if you
included Emma Smith) could be so wrapped up
in other peoples' business. It seemed to
Ptarmigan that gossiping and bitching about
your friends was dull at best and toxic at worst.
Emma Smith seemed unable to say George
Cave's first name without breaking it up into a
laugh, *Geo-or-or-orge*, even though he had never
heard Cave say anything even remotely
amusing. Their mission in life, it seemed to
Ptarmigan, was to get to know as many of the
Sheffield elite as possible, and to treat everyone
else with condescension. Emma Smith had
managed this to an extent. She would frequently
drop the names of people Tarm had never or
only vaguely heard of into their conversations.
She would then look at him, awaiting a swoon or
at least some sort of reaction. Ptarmigan found
this, and the fact these people used social-
climbing and the demeaning of others as

oxygen, impossible to live with. It became clear after a month that things weren't going to work. Emma Smith saved Tarm the job of ending the infant relationship by coming to Vanguard Road on her way to a party and telling him it was over. Ptarmigan said that he knew there was no future in it and wished her all the best. She stood up, called him a bastard, and stormed out of the house. Tarm had remained in his chair for a while, expecting her to come back and explain what the hell all that was about. But she didn't. At the time he thought that maybe she'd been drinking. Armed with this new information though, he can see, as Gerda had said, textbook narcissism all over this baleful exchange.

But why allege rape? Short of murder isn't that the worst accusation possible? Did his nonchalance at her termination of their affair stick in her important and mighty craw? He thinks that maybe it did. He slides his wrung-out socks onto his freezing feet. His boots go on, although they stick to his socks on the way through.

A noise behind him. Someone is coming towards him across the park with a torch. Ptarmigan stands up. Stumbles. Realises just how drunk he has become. The torch beam blinds him.

'Oh fucking hell Tarm!' Rita cries. She runs at him and almost knocks him into the brook. She wraps her arms around him. Gerda is behind her with the torch. 'I thought you might be here. You okay?' she says.

Ptarmigan has Rita's hair in his mouth. He pulls it out. 'Well, I'm better than I was. Watch where you stand. I threw up over there. I'm drunk. But I've got it clear in my head. More or less. Probably less.'

Rita is shuddering against him and pulling in huge wet breaths. He holds her close and looks quizzically at Gerda in the dim light. Gerda shakes her head and mouths when she's ready.

Later. They sit together on the bank of the stream and drink the last of the Tullamore Dew. Gerda checks her watch. It is past two in the morning. A moorhen hoots somewhere in the dark.

'Gandhi?' Ptarmigan suggests to Gerda.

'Think again, Mister Squelchy. They wouldn't let you through the door.'

'Probably not. Let's go home.'

They walk through the park gates. Under the sodium light, Tarm can see that he is filthy. His legs are coated in mud. Rita looks like she might buckle, but he thinks she just needs some good, dreamless sleep. His boots are indeed squishing as they make for the flat.

Rita walks ahead. She hasn't spoken since she embraced Tarm.

'I told her after you'd gone.' Gerda says quietly.

'Told her what?'

'That Emma Smith told everyone who'd listen that Rita killed Seb.'

SOMEWHERE, NOT TOO DISTANT

SOMEWHERE, not too distant, the woman sits in the dark. She knew who the man in her yard was today. She would recognise a person once seen from their skull alone now. She has seen so many faces. So many lives that have come and gone. Like flowers, these fleeting bursts of existence bud, bloom and are no more in an instant, their only real legacy rot and desiccation. For now. These souls blow away in the lightest breeze, like ash. For now. Soon, she hopes and hopes and hopes again, that they may all go around again. If she is able. She may sleep soon. Sleep is no longer necessary for her. She enjoys her dreams though. Sometimes her dreams are of a quiet village by a forest, alongside a clear brook alive with fish, her people going about their gentle lives. Sometimes, men and women toil, laughing, to build great stony memorials to their lost loves that will last forever. Sometimes her children come to her in her dreams, and she gathers them into her arms and spins them around, basking in their laughter. Sometimes her man is there, touching her in the burning dark. She looks up to her low ceiling now and feels the years weighing heavy upon her. Maybe now. This time. Maybe.

PTARMIGAN MAKES A LIST

CADELLIN MARCHES into the living room. He spies Gerda in an armchair and throws himself at her. Gerda lets him snug his wet nose against her cheek. He circles her lap twice and collapses, apparently comfortable.

It is eleven o'clock on the bright morning of Wednesday July 2nd. Ptarmigan awakes. He is hungover. His legs, although he showered last night, still feel gritty. That's just dirt though. Just river mud. He feels filthier inside himself. Dirty. Like shit. Outraged at the idea that people might think he is a rapist. He cannot begin to imagine what Rita feels like.

Emma Smith. Human toxin.

Gerda is already up. Ptarmigan needs to see her face, so he throws on his old purple dressing gown and his slippers. He pads into the living room. Gerda sits in an armchair. Cadellin is upside-down on her lap. His pink tongue is poking out of his mouth.

Gerda smiles at him. 'Quite the week we're having isn't it, Mister Lovely.'

Tarm feels a strange relief, as if the fake-guilt has been slightly erased.

'Hullo,' he says. 'It's full on for sure. Rita?'

'Still asleep. I think she needs it. She really lost it last night when I told her.'

'I'm not bloody surprised!' Ptarmigan can feel his anger rise again and decides it won't help.

He asks, 'Proper coffee?'

'Ooh yes please. And come here.' Ptarmigan sits at Gerda's feet. She grabs his ears and puts her face close to his. 'I've known about that woman's crap for years. She told me about it in the ladies at The Barfield in 1984, just before Seb. I heard her. I looked at her. I heard you. I looked at you. And it took less than five minutes to figure it all out. She was poisonous. Still is, by the looks. And as for poor bloody Rita. She was nowhere near Seb when he went. We were. But why let facts stand in the way of a good bitch? Or a good laugh? Or whatever these people survive on? Emma Smith has sailed through her life destroying as many people as she can.'

Tarm kisses her mouth. He is relieved all over again. 'I love you.' he says. And he goes into the kitchen to make proper coffee.

The smell has roused Rita from her bed. She plods into the kitchen and falls into a chair.

'Rita,' Ptarmigan says, 'I am so sorry.'

'Why?' Rita looks at her vape and decides on a Benson & Hedges instead. She lights up.

'For dragging you into this,' Tarm pours coffee into mugs. 'It's not what I thought it would be. I thought, you know, an investigation into Seb. A finding-out. Now we've got Emma bloody Smith back and Mrs Bron… so weird. I wouldn't blame you if you just sodded off back to Wales.'

Rita accepts her coffee and sugars it. 'You know Tarm. You're a cracking bloke. But you aren't half bloody thick.' She goes into the living room, leaving Ptarmigan bewildered and sipping his proper coffee.

Later. They are back at the kitchen table and back to business.

'I wanted to make things manageable,' Ptarmigan says, putting a new writing pad on the table. 'So we know what we're doing. And so we have an itinerary.'

Rita laughs. 'An itinerary eh? Get you!'

Tarm smiles. 'Right. What do we know? And I want to keep Emma Smith and her fraternity or whatever it is out of it.'

'She's dangerous.' Gerda says.

'I agree. So. Let's start from the very beginning.' He writes, occasionally referring to his folder of papers and some notes he has made. Gerda and Rita go into the kitchen for twenty minutes. He looks up at them occasionally, milling around. And then he finishes.

'Okay' he says. He tears off three sheets and passes them over.

1. 1324. Monks of Beauchief Abbey dispatched to spiritually help the people of Sharrow Field. The Hollow/Hallow Man had been seen and had abducted a child/children from the area. Scribe stated that this thing could influence peoples' dreams. The words "death in the belly" appear. And the manuscript says that this Hollow Man could make people fall "unto death".

2. 1594 (270 years, or 9 x 30 years later). Pamphlet written by George Talbot. Easier to

get info as is relatively modern English. Here he is *Hallowe/Hallow Man. Corruption of "Hollow"? See death in the belly above?* He is described. Great height and strength. He was nocturnal. Was this part of his nature? Or was he, as the document implies, fundamentally timid? The Talbot paper does NOT report an abduction. It does say that he *hath the power of dreams over Christian Men of great and Worrisome Vividity.* Describes the HM's smell in detail.

3. 1744 (150 years, or 5 x 30 years later). Quarryman Samuel Worth paper. The HM had attempted to abduct three children. Failed. Hardly omnipotent then? Samuel was approached by the HM, and his friend saw him off with a pick and an oil lamp. A certain weakness. Note that the friend "fell into a faint". Was this due to the aforementioned ability to make people fall unto death, or did this man faint having seen the HM? Rank smell is mentioned again. And a child went missing, "quietly" shortly after Samuel's experience. Samuel says that his sons shall not venture forth here at night and I shall neither.

4. 1894 (150 years, or 5 x 30 years later). Article from the Sheffield Evening Telegraph. HM was seen moving at speed along Stalkers Walk or Frog Walk and actually jumping across Porter Brook. This only mentioned in the Telegraph document. He is 7ft tall or more. No mention of any smell. No abductions/disappearances either. References some Civil War literature that mentions HM. I have been unable to find this source.

5. 1897 (date N/A). Frederick Piper-Morris children's rhymes book. I looked at this again last night. Everywhere else in Britain, this rhyme goes:

"There was an old woman
Liv'd under a hill,
And if she ben't gone,
She lives there still."

It is only here that the Lollard version was sung by children.

6. The photograph. Unless someone was very skilled in 1924, it's genuine. It's proof. It doesn't answer any questions though.

7. Simon and Bunny want to recreate the Huxley book. They vanish.

8. Seb.

When they have read, Ptarmigan says, 'Fiddly isn't it? But these are the points that appear in more than one of the items.' He has been writing.

A. He was big.

B. He took children, but we don't know what he did with them.

C. He was possibly easily spooked.

D. He could make people pass out or faint.

E. He could get into or people's dreams.

F. He only came out at night.

G. There was something about his belly.

H. There is a smell about him.

ADDENDUM: If we're honest, we don't know what "he" or "it" is. If we're still being honest, I don't think it actually matters.

'That last bit's right,' Gerda passes the paper back.

'I know. So that's pretty much it, from the literature and our own experiences,' Ptarmigan says. 'Until we get to Samuel Worth's own work. He called his allegory *Cronus Return*. Any ideas?'

Gerda and Rita are rivetted, but they both shrug.

'Cronus is the Greek Saturn, in effect. He was the father of Zeus and, I'm glad you're sitting down, because he ate his own children.'

'Jesus!' Rita whispers. Gerda stares at Tarm.

'So let's have a look at what Samuel Worth says in some more detail," Ptarmigan has the document before him.

'*And so, in looking to vanquish the beast we must first understand the nature of the beast, for fierce he may appear, he, though may be fierce in visage alone.* So. Timidity. Cowardice? *The Devil himself is a coward and holds good people in thrall by his renown alone.* And again! *Though he has the power of fantasie, his is the power of impotence.* That's the dreams, I think. In fact, I'm convinced. *Though he look mighty, he shall quickly fall. Were the brave to smite him, Satan would turn and flee.* Easy to defeat if you know what you're doing. *Our brothers in the Old Times of Egypt had this knowledge and by their wisdom did banish divers monsters.* So there's a reference to Egypt. Think of the cemetery buildings? *In this way the rope of eternity is severed...* There's the ouroboros on the gates! ... *and the Sun shall have dominion.* There's the winged sun! *Like a dark mirror on the miracle of birth, Satan keeps those within and extinguishes them like a candle as further nourishment approaches.* The belly. The mirror reflecting birth. The candle! We've talked about that. And at the end, *Denial is the door. Courage is the key.* And I don't think this means "denial" as in saying that something isn't true. I think it means not allowing The Hallow Man to achieve something. I think that, if we can deny this thing what it wants, and it wants it every thirty years, then we'll find out what happened to Seb, Bunny, Simon and all the others.'

Ptarmigan looks at Gerda and Rita. Nobody speaks.

'Now, Gerda. You know what I think about horoscopes and astrology don't you.'
'Same as me. It's bollocks.'

'Quite. But bear with me. Saturn Return, or Cronus Return in the case of old Sam Worth's little book, is a planetary transit that occurs when the planet Saturn returns to the same ecliptic longitude that it was in when people are born.' Ptarmigan smiles wanly. 'I don't know if it's relevant. And I don't profess to understand it.'

'I do!' Gerda's face is suddenly flushed. 'I really do! It's every thirty bloody years!'

XLUSIVE

THURSDAY. EARLY. Ptarmigan has both the *Star Online* and the new *Sheffield Tribune* streaming live on his iPad and laptop. He is watching for any news about disappearances. Or anything else that might be relevant. The devices give a little bong sound whenever a new story appears.

He was the first awake this morning and looked up Emma Smith's Xlusive shop on the internet as soon as he had a cup of tea in front of him. Tea is the only way to start the day. The website is highly polished and performs equally well on his phone as his laptop. Gerda said that the shop was on the other side of Sheffield, so he was expecting a little store somewhere. Like a vanity project. But Xlusive is now on Fargate, the main shopping area in the city. The website says they upscaled back in 2006. There was a grand opening that November (invited guests only) and it was covered in The Star. Tarm only buys the paper on Fridays, for the music news, so he must have missed it. Gerda doesn't read it at all. The photograph on the home page shows the shop, a handsome, historic, double-fronted boutique, nestled between a Thorntons and The Body Shop.

The website home page reads: *For ten years, Xlusive has been the most highly regarded haunt for the trendy and style-savvy in Sheffield. We burst onto the scene with a small boutique in an out-of-town location in 2005, specialising in retro clothing for the hip, hipper and hippest. Demand was so fierce that we upscaled to our current prime city-centre location on Fargate in November 2006, and we have never looked back. Xlusive's unique vintage product range appeals to a loyal band of regular customers, celebrities and newcomers alike.*

Ptarmigan is intrigued. He goes onto the Companies House website.

The filing history for Xlusive Vintage Boutiques Ltd is all up to date. In Overview, under Previous Company Names, is a shop in Burngreave called Nobby Styles. Tarm grins. It's a far better name than Xlusive. He looks at the

People page. There are five Officers, Companies-House-Speke for Directors:

SMITH. Emma Carol
HANDY. Fiona Tracey
SWIFT. Caroline
McBride. Simon Noel
CAVE. George Tarquin

'Tarquin!' Ptarmigan can't wait to tell Gerda and Rita about that. Other than Cave's middle-name, it was what he had expected.

Something makes him click back to the Overview page.

NOBBY STYLES

Period: 05 Dec 2005 - 03 Oct 2006

Ptarmigan is no whizz at mathematics, but he does run a business. And moving from a dingy Burngreave shop underneath a bedsit to a premier trading location on Fargate after trading in second-hand clothes for only 10 months is an extraordinary achievement.

He trots downstairs to turn off the studio intruder alarm and call Cadellin in. The cat is spending most of his time, awake and asleep, with Rita. Tarm whistles a few times. No cat. He goes back upstairs and puts the oven on. It is now nine o'clock and he's hungry. Ptarmigan can't understand how people get bored with the same food over and over. Finances and time constraints mean that he and Gerda don't have these elaborate breakfasts all the time. But over this break from work, and with a guest, they are both very enthusiastic about them. And Rita seems almost ecstatic. He slices tomatoes, lays them out on a baking tray, and taps gravy browning onto them. Letting them absorb the umami improves the flavour no end. That's what his Mum told him. Only she had said savoury.

The kettle goes on for Proper Coffee. That should bring the others out like those cartoon dogs floating along with their noses in charge.

The oven pings ready. He puts sausages and thick bacon on the tray alongside the tomatoes and slides the tray into the oven. A low heat and a slow cook. His mum told him that as well. He sets the timer. The kettle boils and clicks itself off. Ptarmigan spoons coffee into their large cafetiere and counts to sixty to make sure he doesn't scald it with boiling water. As soon as he pours, the rich, almost burned fragrance begins to fill the room. And then it fills the flat.

He sits back at his laptop. The rape and murder allegations are haunting him. And something is now gnawing at him about Xlusive.

As he predicted, Rita and Gerda materialise at the same time. Both bleary-eyed and dressing-gowned and beslippered.

'Good morning ladies!' Tarm says as they fall into two armchairs.

'How long have you been up, Mister Wakey?' Gerda yawns. 'Where's the coffee?'

'Yeah! Tarm! Coffee! Where?' Rita has caught Gerda's yawn, and hers ends with a whinny.

'Ages actually. Done some digging. Money stuff. Emma Smith stuff. You wouldn't be interested.'

Rita looks alert all of a sudden. 'Fuck off Tarm! What?'

Ptarmigan laughs. 'Let's eat first.'

"Actually yeah. Jesus I'm starving. Where's the grub, Bub?'

Ptarmigan thinks it's a bit Harry Potter. All this sitting about shovelling down food whilst engaging in mysteries and deceit. But he likes it.

After they have eaten breakfast, he loads the dishwasher and turns it on. Then he sits between Rita and Gerda on the settee, opens his laptop, and loads up the Xlusive and Companies House pages. While trying to read, they jostle him so much that he gets up and leaves them to it. He pushes open Rita's door and is unsurprised to find Cadellin luxuriating on the Rita-scented duvet.

From the living room, loudly, 'Nobby Styles!'

Sitting on the bed he smooths the big ginger's soft coat. Cadellin fires up his outboard motor. Ptarmigan nuzzles him a little until the claws start to unsheathe. 'You're an idiot, cat,' he prods Cadellin gently on the belly. The cat rolls around. He's not going to leave this room, Tarm thinks. Not until we change the bloody bedding again anyway.

From the living room, 'Tarquin!'. Raucous cackling.

Gerda and Rita have separated onto different chairs when Tarm wanders back in and they are both smoking.

'We'll have to get this place fumigated after this," Ptarmigan offers Gerda a beaming smile.

'Balls! Anyway. What do you think?' she is thoughtful.

'Well. Didn't you say that she was still shagging half of Sheffield? I think you used the word "Glitterati."'

'Did I?' Gerda laughs. "I can think of a handy rhyming slang. But yes. That's what I heard at work. Some of my colleagues… how should I put this… "knew" her. Back in the day. And subsequently.'

'Lucky old them!' Tarm sees that Cadellin has wandered in. 'Jack Marx?'

'Most definitely! And not that long ago either in the scheme of things.' Gerda smooths back her hair. She stops, mid motion. 'Hold up Tarm. Hold up! Let me look at that again. Pass me that laptop.'

Rita has been silent since she looked at the two websites. 'I want to destroy that cunt.' she says. And she goes back to her room.

They watch her go.

'She okay?' Ptarmigan says quietly, watching the bedroom door close.

'I'm not sure. I think so. That piece of shit accused you of rape. I know there's a slim demarcation line my lovely. But murder? That's the zenith of false accusations. Rita loved Seb and he loved her back. Emma Smith. She's been like an oil-slick. For three decades.'

Gerda taps on the keyboard for a few minutes. She finds some Sheffield Star articles. She turns the screen to Ptarmigan.

'Let's have a proper look.'

The Sheffield Star. Wednesday September 6th 2006

"FAMOUS SHEFFIELD MUSIC PRODUCER DIES"

The death has been reported of legendary Sheffield record producer Jack Marx. Mr Marx, who was instrumental in furthering the careers of The Mass, AFK, Abby and others, was found dead at his home in Nether Edge, Sheffield, on Friday.

The Sheffield Star. Tuesday October 10th 2006

"JACK MARX DEATH SUICIDE"

Following an inquest, the death of internationally renowned music producer and engineer Jack Marx, who was found dead at his home on Friday 1st September, has been recorded as suicide by Sheffield coroner James Swinning. Mr Marx leaves behind his wife Simone and their four-month-old daughter Esme.

A service is to be held at the Walkley Woods Crematorium on Wednesday November 1st. The family have asked for privacy at this time.

The Sheffield Star. Wednesday November 1st 2006

"A SHEFFIELD LEGEND'S MEMORIAL"

Family, friends and colleagues gathered at Walkley Woods Crematorium today to bid farewell to Jack Marx. Marx was instrumental in furthering the careers of many Sheffield acts in the 1980's and 1990's. He achieved international fame in 2003 with New York band Morine Pole's "Flowers &

Shadows" album, which reached Number Two in both the UK and US Charts.

He leaves behind his wife, Simone, and their five-month-old daughter Esme.

'And Emma Smith was shagging him?'

Gerda takes back the laptop. 'That's what I heard.'

'Any idea when?'

'Not off hand. I think I can find out though.'

RITA IN THE FLAT WITH CADELLIN

PTARMIGAN AND GERDA have gone food shopping, leaving Rita and Cadellin alone in the flat. Rita had offered to give them some food money, but they told her not to be daft. She has checked in with her office and everything is sailing along without her, which she is strangely disappointed about. Now, pulling Tarm's notes out of their folder, she lays them in order on the table, next to her cup of tea and the ashtray.

'Bloody smoking again Reet,' she murmurs. 'Mam'd go nuts!'

Cadellin comes in and mewls. Rita looks at the clock. Eleven in the morning.

'Let's see if I can find your grub mateyboy.' She goes to the cupboard and locates a tin of cat food. She lifts it down and finds a bowl. The tin has one of those ring-pull tops and some of the jelly gets on her wrist as she peels it away.

'Jesus!' She runs the arm under the tap and rubs the muck off. Then she gives the cat his dinner, and he stops bustling around her legs.

Rita goes back to the laptop. To take her mind off Emma Smith's hideous claims, she has been looking at the Sheffield General Cemetery Trust website. It is obvious to them all that the Hallow Man, whatever he is, no longer resides in the Sheffield General Cemetery. The whole place is lit-up like a Christmas Tree at night now. And, as well as tourists and local families trudging all over it, there are gigs, art shows, weddings and all kinds of events happening every other evening. Many of these take place in Samuel Worth's Chapel. She thinks he'd be delighted.

Cadellin has finished and strides in, smelling slightly fishy. Rita goes back into the kitchen and washes his bowl. Too many flies at this time of year.

Back at the table, Rita wonders where an eight-foot-tall monstrosity could possibly hide in modern Sheffield. The fact that she is posing herself this question at all takes her by surprise. But, as she had said to Gerda, the impossible is only impossible until it's possible. Tardigrades? If you told someone from George Talbot's time about creatures that live in ocean-depths, rainforests, ice and volcanoes and can survive extreme temperatures, extreme pressures, suffocation, dehydration, radiation and starvation; they'd laugh in your face and probably call you a witch into the bargain. She knows that Sheffield has changed almost beyond recognition even since the eighties. And she doubts that someone who was last around here in 1954 would know where the hell they were at all.

Gerda's disclosure of Emma Smith's venom seems to have taken their minds away from the earlier events of that day. The pamphlets and newspaper clippings were uncannily familiar, suggesting terrible things have been happening in Sharrow for centuries. But the photographs had chilled Rita to her core. There are two possibilities here, she thinks. Either Gerda and Tarm are playing an incredibly cruel and elaborate trick on her. Or this whole thing is real. She knows it's real.

Her mind keeps returning to their house on Vanguard Road. This is the one link that Tarm hasn't really considered, even after Mrs B's sudden, strange, youthful appearance. Things sometimes hide in plain sight, she thinks. And being accused of rape, surely a very private crime, may cut far deeper than the ludicrous charge of murder. It is certainly harder to deny. It is weighted. Rita isn't surprised that Ptarmigan's mind is elsewhere. Simon and Bunny lived there, in the same house. They put the house on their funny old map. She lived there. Tarm lived there. Seb lived there. Gerda spent a lot of time there. She finds the 1954 clippings. She feels strangely untethered.

Their neighbour, a Mrs Bron, said today that she may have heard the students leaving their house on Vanguard Road in Sharrow late on the night of the 24th, but could not be sure.

She pictures the back yard. Their student house led straight out onto it. Mrs B next door had a fenced garden that protruded around ten feet, leaving a narrow alley between the adjacent houses and her fence. There was no other way in or out of the yard. It was the only way to get into their house. Nobody had used the front door for years. The low brick front wall even went across where the garden path used to be. And the place was an acoustic soundboard. This is why they were always careful not to be stereotypically noisy students and kept the noise down.

She thinks back. Her time there with Seb. Her absolute conviction that they would be a couple forever. Utterly together. Ptarmigan being there, like a skinny pony and happy for their company, when they arrived back for their second year of study. Jesus, how badly that could have gone! If they hadn't sparked an immediate friendship. No, an immediate love. That easy acceptance of each other. Something was magical. Coming back to that house, laden with books and ambitions and work. Coming back to the house laden with snakebite and Gandhi curries. And Mrs B polishing that angel she had in her garden. What was that thing? She finds she can't quite remember. The quietness of the place. Sometimes the only sound was their old and cranky TV. That stillness.

And the night Seb went. It was the last house he ever left. His last ever home. That's why they are all here. All here and together again.

Their neighbour, a Mrs Bron, said that she may have heard the students leaving the house late on that Saturday night but could not be certain.

Mrs B's bedroom was at the back of her house. Rita is certain of it. She wonders if she can check the weather from July 24th 1954. She imagines trying to do this in the Dark Ages of the Eighties. Impossible! She hunts online for a few moments. Bingo! Here is a handy *What was the Weather Like on my Birthday?* app. Rita types in the date. The website says that it was 24°C. 75°F in old money. Rita considers. That's open-windows weather in those houses. And with the bedroom window open, unless she was asleep, which she said she wasn't, there is no way on earth she wouldn't hear two big lads, especially two big lads tripping on mushrooms, leave the house. Or mistake them for something else. Cadellin jumps onto Rita's lap and purrs in her face. He smells like a mackerel.

Later, Gerda and Ptarmigan return home with bags of shopping. As they unpack, Rita runs through her thoughts with both of them.

'Makes sense to me,' Gerda puts pasta in a jar. Cadellin is back in the kitchen milling around and almost trips Tarm up.

'Bloody cat! Hang about sunbeam.' Ptarmigan puts the bowl down and spoons a measure of cat food into it. Cadellin humps down and eats.

'I fed him about an hour ago. Sorry.' Rita says when she realises.

'Bloody cat!' Ptarmigan can't help but admire his cheek.

Sitting in the living room, the very full cat on Rita's lap again, Ptarmigan says, 'You're right. The allegation, or libel or slander or whatever it is. It's taken the floor from under me. I can hardly think about anything else. And you're also right in that it could have happened. We know you were at Cat's when Seb went, Reet. I don't even know when I'm supposed to have raped Emma Smith. I'm guessing it was the night she came round to end it and I didn't collapse at her feet like fucking Chatterton or something. Just a guess. It'd probably fit the narrative.'

'She never said,' Gerda tells them. 'But probably. No witnesses one way or the other. Look. I know you, Tarm. Your friends know you. A few of them also know Emma Smith. Or they know *of* her anyway. And I have a phone call to make at...' she looks at her watch, '... 9 o'clock tonight. That might offer up some ideas.'

'Oh, really?' Ptarmigan reaches over and strokes the cat.

Gerda looks at Rita and Ptarmigan.

'So. What are we going to do? We can hardly knock on Mrs Bron's back door and ask her if she knows anything about a centuries-old murder legend based next door.'

'Well, no,' says Tarm. 'But we can knock on her back door and ask her how she is. We were neighbours thirty years back. Rita's up in Sheffield. We're being friendly. We're revisiting old haunts.'

Gerda says, 'But Tarm. She saw you the other day. She'll think you're dangerous or something. Or she'll think you're a bloody idiot. And what about her not being any older?'

Ptarmigan rubs his beard. 'She might not go out in the sun much? I don't know. I may have overreacted. Anyway, if she's as old as we reckon she is, I doubt she'll remember what she had for breakfast, let alone seeing me.'

And in bed that night, Gerda tells Ptarmigan who she spoke to on the phone. And she tells him what they said.

EMAILS (2)

Email
From: tarm@ptarmigan.com.uk
To: simonemarx2323@smarto.net.uk
Saturday July 5th 2014

Dear Simone

I hope you don't mind my emailing you out of the blue. I found your email address on your Facebook account, assuming it's still current. I'm hoping this doesn't just go into your Junk folder.

Anyway, we've never met. But I knew Jack. I run a recording studio and our paths crossed a few times through work. I was very sorry to hear about his passing. He was a great engineer and producer and is sorely missed in Sheffield and beyond. My late friend Seb and he were quite good friends in the 80's. And his ex-partner, who I am still in touch with, always speaks very highly of him.

There are a few things I would like to talk to you about. I know this must sound really strange, but I believe they may have a bearing on why Jack did what he did. I have a question too, which will probably also seem odd. Do you still live in the same house as you did when Jack passed away?

If you are uncomfortable with all this getting dragged up after all this time, and I wouldn't be even remotely surprised if you were, then please ignore this email and please also accept my deepest apologies and condolences.

Many Kind Regards

Shaun Houghton

Email
From: simonemarx2323@smarto.net.uk
To: tarm@ptarmigan.com.uk
 Saturday July 5th 2014

Dear Shaun

Thank you for your email. I knew Seb too and was very saddened to hear of his death, as was Jack. I do not know what information I can give you regarding Jack. Although in answer to your question, yes. We still live in the same house.

Best,

Simone Marx

Email
From: tarm@ptarmigan.com.uk
To: simonemarx2323@smarto.net.uk
Saturday July 5th 2014

Dear Simone

Thanks for getting back to me so quickly. In fact, thanks for getting back to me at all. And thanks also for answering my question.

Okay. As I said, my friends and I believe we can shed light on everything that happened to your family back in 2006. My partner, Gerda, spoke to one of her colleagues yesterday. He had some information. The colleague didn't think it meant anything. But we do.

This is going to sound really odd. But can I come over at some point? I think I know where something is in your house. By all means have bouncers and guard dogs in the room. But I really think I can answer the questions you must surely

have been asking yourself for the last eight-or-so
years. Please let me know.

Kindest Regards

Shaun

Email
From: simonemarx2323@smarto.net.uk
To: tarm@ptarmigan.com.uk
 Saturday July 5th 2014

Dear Shaun

Now I am intrigued. I have no need for bodyguards
as both Esme and myself study Taekwondo and
Judo. Unless you come armed, we are in no
danger. And I think it unlikely that you will come
armed. Let me know when you would like to visit.

Best,
Simone Marx

A HIDING PLACE

PTARMIGAN FEELS AN inner shiver as he retraces Seb's journey from all those years ago. His pockets are full of old mobile phone chargers. He hopes he will need one of them, even though it's a long shot. Hopes that this isn't some wild chase after shadows. The speed at which this venture has taken shape is astonishing in itself. The fact that Simone Marx has so readily agreed to a total stranger coming to root around in her house even more so. It is Sunday. Tarm only emailed Simone yesterday. He wanted to do this as quickly as possible, but he didn't expect to be here so soon. Gerda and Rita were still asleep when he left, Cadellin spread out on Rita's bed like a stole.

Another bright blue day. The morning sun is mimicking evening with its long shadows. A cool breeze occasionally plays around his head as he walks. The road is lined with fine old trees, the bark of their trunks green in the early light. Ptarmigan wonders why people use brown when they paint tree trunks. They are grey or green more than anything. Sparrows and magpies are gossiping in the leaf-full branches.

The occasional jackdaw interrupts with his squeaky-pig cry.

The gate opens with a squeal. Tarm sidesteps a large azalea whose fronds cover much of the path and approaches the shiny black door. He stands and takes a breath. Then he draws back the old-fashioned bell-pull. It dings twice somewhere in the house. A moment later he hears small slippered feet on a tiled floor. The door opens a little and a young girl peers out at him.

'Are you Shaun?' she asks.

'I am. Are you Esme?'

The girls smiles. 'I am. Come in.'

Esme closes the big front door behind Ptarmigan. Her mother comes out of a room halfway down the hallway to the right. Simone Marx. She wears round glasses, has blonde hair tied back in a ponytail and is wearing loose joggers and a tee shirt with "Paris!" written on it in big sloppy letters. Simone Marx is tall and studious-looking She extends a hand. Tarm takes it.

'Shaun.'

'Well, most people actually call me Ptarmigan.'

Simone raises an eyebrow.

'Or Tarm. It's a long story. From Canada. When I was a kid. I stroked a wild bird. Like a sort of white partridge thing.'

Both eyebrows raised and a brief smile. 'I didn't think we'd need security.' Her voice is warm and Northern.

Simone leads him into the high-ceilinged living room with its burnished floorboards. Esme follows.

'Have a seat.'

'Thanks.'

Simone sits in an armchair across from Ptarmigan. 'So. Tarm. What do you think you're going to find in our house?'

Ptarmigan looks around.

'I don't actually know Simone. But I think I know where to look. It might sound strange, but I'm really pleased you didn't carpet this room.'

Esme, sitting across from Ptarmigan, says, 'I said I wanted a nice carpet. Mum says the floorboards look classy.'

'You only wanted a carpet so you could jump about on the furniture and not break your neck if you fell off!'

'Says you.' Esme is a precocious eight-year-old.

'Says me. Now go and do something. Roger's coming later and it's the pictures.' Esme wanders off and Tarm hears her feet on the stairs. Simone looks at Ptarmigan. 'Roger, Fiancé. Movie, *Paddington*.'

'Nice!'

'So, what do we do now?'

'Simone, I'm going to do something peculiar. It's nothing dangerous. But I think I can answer some questions for you. And for me. And Rita. Well, we do. Me and Rita. And my partner Gerda's work colleague,' he realises he is waffling. 'Anyway. Here goes.'

Ptarmigan takes off his boots and socks.

Simone watches him as he walks around her living room in his bare feet, leaving foot-shaped smudges and nudging the floorboards with his heel and instep. He looks apologetically at her. She appears to be both amused and slightly disturbed, but he carries on. He trudges from one side of the room to the other, moves some chairs, and starts again.

'Here!' he says suddenly. At the front of one of the easy chairs, a small piece of board has moved fractionally. He treads with slightly more heft. 'Here!' he says again.

Tarm is on his knees. He tries to get his fingernails under the edge of the wood, but the gap is too small. Simone gets to her feet and walks out of the living room. There is the sound of drawer-rummaging. She returns a moment later with a flathead screwdriver. She passes it to him.

He gently slides the thin metal head into the narrow gap. It gains purchase. My god I hope I'm right about this, he thinks. The board comes loose. The screwdriver raises it. He grabs it before it can fall and places it carefully down to his left. In the exposed void sits a black plastic container about the size of a shoebox. It is only slightly dusty. The hole in the floor smells old. *Chapelly*, Seb would have said.

Simone kneels next to him.

'My god!' she whispers.

Ptarmigan lifts the box out and sits it at his side. He peers into the void. Nothing else. Then he replaces the board. It settles back with a little thud.

'Under the floorboards?' Simone is astonished. 'Very Poe.'

The lid's hinges don't even squeak. Everything within the box has been hidden away for at least eight years.

Ptarmigan begins to unpack it. He is glad Esme has gone upstairs.

A large baggie containing shrivelled weed.
A large baggie containing wraps of whiteish powder.
A very large baggie containing dried psylocibin mushrooms.
And an Apple iPhone 6.

VANGUARD ROAD AGAIN

tarmigan parks the campervan halfway down Vanguard Road. It is Monday morning. Rita and Gerda were overjoyed by the treasure discovered at Simone Marx's house yesterday. Simone had made him tea and he had charged the mobile phone while they drank it. She had been understandably upset by what they unearthed. But they have an understanding. An agreement. Ptarmigan even got to meet Roger. And he has promised Esme that he will look at her Frozen collection when he goes back

He glances at Gerda next to him and at Rita in the rear-view mirror. They both look uncomfortable and a little unmoored. Tarm supposes he does too. Gerda and Rita are smoking. Tarm has avoided having one so far today, but he thinks it won't be long. They sit. A family strolls past, Mum in a hijab and the little kids jumping up and down. The Mum smiles at Tarm and he smiles back. He can see the old Sweet Centre from where they have parked. It looks forlorn as a house. Ptarmigan feels the tug of loss again.

'Right' Rita shakes herself about in the back and looks at Tarm and Gerda in the front. 'Come on.'

Tarm presses his key fob and locks the van with a squink sound. They walk slowly towards the house. Gerda takes Ptarmigan's hand. Why do they all feel so strange?

'I feel sort of seasick.' Rita says.

'Yeah. Since I got up.' Gerda looks up at Tarm. He just feels sure that something is going to happen here.

They turn a corner and are all back in the Vanguard Road yard. Mrs Bron's garden fence still creates that narrow alley. They spread apart as they enter the yard itself. They look around.

'It's the same!' Gerda whispers.

Ptarmigan looks at her and heads to their old living room window. They all look through. It is empty.

'Jesus! Weird.' Rita breathes onto the glass and rubs it with her hand. 'The place is deserted. Why?'

Gerda is amazed. 'What's happened here? We were here, what? Thirty years ago? How is everything so changed? Thirty years? That's nothing. Is it?'

'Hang about,' Ptarmigan says. 'We've already done this. We were only here the other day. We looked through this window. It was bare then.'

'Did we?' Gerda frowns. 'No we didn't!'

'Yes! We were here. I saw Mrs Bron. She was still young.'

'When?' Gerda is looking scared. She feels like she did when they woke up in the cemetery thirty years ago. Disoriented. Somehow fooled.

Rita looks though the window again and gasps. 'Jesus! The telly's back. Look! It's Bob Holness. But he's dead isn't he?'

Gerda and Ptarmigan crowd against the old window. There are people inside, beyond the yellow curtains. They are drinking tea.

Gerda clasps Ptarmigan's arm.

'It's us.' She says this as if it was fully expected.

Rita's spiky hair is just visible inside the room, framed by the now open window. A Gold Run about to start. Blockbusters. There are two girls with crimped hair and heavy make-up on the big, square TV, and a smug-looking boy wearing a public-school tie. Rita's head is moving. She is rolling a Benson & Hedges around in the weird twirly ashtray. She might be talking about the Rebecca Riots. There is a smell of tobacco smoke, but all sound has gone. The yard and the house are silent but for their breathing.

Across the room, on the sofa, a young Gerda sits playing with her hair. Her face is slightly flushed as if she has had a hot bath. She is wearing a beige waistcoat covered in badges. Her hair is feathery and white. There is a mug in her hand, and she is smoking a cigarette. Tarm sits next to her, looking at her. Beardless and smiling. His black hair is carelessly backcombed.

The Gerda in the room suddenly looks straight at them. She says something. Rita's head spins round, but she sees nothing. Ptarmigan, the Ptarmigan watching Blockbusters, also looks blindly in their direction. Next to them sits Seb. He is grey and drawn and old. He looks through the window and into their eyes. He mouths: 'Death Soap?'

Birds again. Traffic. An aeroplane whispering high above them. Ptarmigan tears himself away from the impossible scene inside his old living room. He looks up to the roof. There are three magpies there, on Mrs Bron's side. They hop along the roof ridge yelling their cracked music. Then they fly away.

Gerda is shivering. Rita glances into their old and once more deserted living room again. The window is closed.

'Why can't I remember?' she whispers.

'No reason.' says a voice behind them. Mrs Bron stands outside her gate.

'For your old place being empty I mean. No reason I can understand anyway. Could be house-prices or bloody Julian Torode looking to make money without lifting a finger. The little shite.'

They are all shocked into silence.

Ptarmigan is right. She hasn't changed. Mrs Bron studies them. 'Rita. Ptarmigan. Ptarmigan's lady.'

They stand in the yard, in the glorious July sun, and simply stare at her.

'I think you'd better come in now.' she says. She holds open the garden gate. 'It's getting on.'

Mrs Bron opens her back door and goes through it. Ptarmigan, Gerda and Rita walk through her garden past the stone angel.

They step into her house…

HANDS UP WHO WANTS TO DIE!

… AND THEY ARE back in the club. It is dark. The Birthday Party's manic, tribal drums are pounding.

Have you heard how Sonny's burning? Like some bright erotic star?

They look at each other and they all the same as they were when they left the car. But here they stand. Back in the club.

The bar is busy. The dancefloor is full of bodies. On the stage, the girls with the dreadlocks are walking up and down. They're ready to scream *Jezebel*! when the Sex Gang Children come on. *Uncertain Smile* by The The begins playing and the dreadlock girls go back to wherever they sit.

Ptarmigan, Gerda and Rita make their way to their usual table. They sit on the familiar bench seats. Three plastic glasses of snakebite are already there waiting for them. So is Jack Marx.

'Jack?' Ptarmigan says, 'I was in your house yesterday.'

'Of course you were.'

They sit, trying to make sense of all this. Rita keeps glancing at Jack Marx, who doesn't appear to notice. After a while, a small man with a neat beard strides over to their table. He wears an Elizabethan ruff, and his clothes are all purples. Velvet and silk. He brings with him a scent of cloves.

'My friends.' this man sits with them. 'How do I find you?'

Gerda is looking at this Elizabethan, and at Jack Marx, with horror. Rita is somehow more sanguine.

'Hallo.' she says.

A cheer goes up as Killing Joke's *Love Like Blood* comes on. The club is more raucous than they remember it. The dancing more aggressive.

Ptarmigan somehow replies, 'We are very well, thank you. Do you know what's going on here?'

George Talbot takes Gerda's hand and kisses it. Gerda looks at Tarm. She is dismayed.

'I am so sorry my dear friend. I have nothing to tell you. My missive was all I had to say upon this matter. But, Rita. Your moss-bear intrigues me.'

George Talbot smiles. Then he sits. He watches the dancers.

Two men in grey monk habits make their way over from the bar. They have pints of snakebite in plastic glasses. They sit at the table next to theirs and begin to talk animatedly in a dead language. Gerda looks at Ptarmigan again with absolute terror on her face.

'What the fuck is this Tarm? Did someone slip us something?'

'I have no fucking idea!'

'No. Nobody has slipped you anything.' Jack Marx assures them. He watches the dancers with his black-rimmed eyes.

Nag Nag Nag begins to play. The Monks of Beauchief Abbey grin as they get up to dance. The dancers flock around them, fascinated by their whirling habits and their tonsures. The monks begin to loosen their robes. They both flick their tongues suggestively. In unison. Like reptiles. The crowd cheers. The Beauchief Abbey brother monks start to wrap themselves around the Doric pillars. They arch their backs and stamp and grind their flabby hips in time to the music.

George Talbot glances behind himself, smooths his moustaches and beard and says, 'My friends. A poet is amongst us!'

A tall, slender, almost starved-looking man makes his way through the growing crowd of dancers and sits between Jack Marx and George Talbot, opposite Ptarmigan, Gerda and Rita. He wears a grey suit with a high, starched collar. With a sigh he takes all of their hands in his and immediately bursts into a paroxysm of weeping. 'You have no concept of my sorrow.' he cries. 'I am so sorry!' Tears cascade down his long cheeks.

George Talbot reaches up and squeezes the man's shoulder. 'My good friends, this sorry spectacle is Frederick Piper-Morris. He once wrote a book about playground rhymes and chants. *Sung but Not Forgot.*' George Talbot gives a little wince. 'Didn't you, sir? He missed the fucking point here though. Didn't you?'

Talbot is on his feet now, bent over, shouting into the cringing face of Frederick Piper-Morris. Piper-Morris whines. Nobody in the club has noticed. They are all still dancing and watching the monks undress. They shake their fat behinds and begin to touch each other. On the raised stage, the dreadlock girls are strolling around.

'Didn't you? Didn't you? Fucking Fred-Er-Fucking-Ick?'

'Fucksakes George!' says Jack Marx

'None of your business at this time Jack.' George Talbot smiles at Jack Marx. Jack Marx shrugs.

'Please. Please. Don't!' Piper-Morris holds up his hands as if at prayer. He wails.

George Talbot grabs a handful of Piper-Morris's hair. He pulls his head backwards and punches him hard in the face, again and again. Tarm, Gerda and Rita watch in horror. The beating seems endless

Piper-Morris is still crying. His blood gouts onto the bench on which he sits. A clot hits the table. His ruined face crumples as if it were just tears holding it together. George Talbot releases him from his grasp. Frederick Piper-Morris collapses to the floor. He is gone. His suit is empty. He leaves behind a smell of old paper.

George Talbot gives them all a little wink and gets up to dance to Theatre of Hate's *Nero*.

The club is hot now. Sweat and dark, thick blood is drooling down the walls and onto the slick carpet. Emma Smith is sitting at a table across the room. She is on her own for once. She looks uncertain and lost and pathetic.

A small, round man in a high-collared suit has taken Talbot's place He looks at them through tiny spectacles. His moustache glistens with some kind of oil or preparation. His voice is almost a whisper, but they can hear every word.

'Rita. My chapel. Yes. I approve of the festivities. A place of the dead ought to be the happiest and most peaceful. Their cares are gone. The living have their woes. If the dead can lighten the burden of existence momentarily, then what harm is there?'

Rita looks at him. He offers her a small, tight smile.

'Samuel?'

'My clues, yes? I hope your futures will benefit from them. My great grandfather. A character by all accounts. I never met him. But he wrote well. For a quarryman. Nobody knew where he learned.'

'Samuel Worth?' Ptarmigan feels like he is on board a ship. The club is swaying. He looks towards the entrance, half expecting to see the tree-man. Jack Marx places a steadying hand on his arm.

'I am sorry about George,' Samuel says. 'He is something of a hot-head. My poor contemporary Frederick knew nothing. Why would he? Still. He will be fine in the end. We are all fine in the end.' Samuel laughs briefly. 'Or we are not.'

'The snakes and the sun with wings,' Gerda takes Samuel's sleeve. He looks down at her hand. 'You knew?'

'No. I suspected. I'm a Georgian, Gerda. And later a Victorian. We had none of the clever devices which you three enjoy daily. But my father showed me the old Samuel's jottings. *Cronus Return*. I did not, though, know about *her*. How could I? Rita. Ptarmigan. Gerda.' Samuel Worth pulls out a pocket watch and flicks it open. 'It is imperative that you do as she asks.'

He replaces his watch, reaches into his jacket pocket, and produces a small dagger. He examines it over his spectacles and hands it to Rita.

'The handle and bolster are ivory. The spine and blade are meteorite. Not that I suppose it matters.' Samuel glances over his shoulder. Two young men are making their way across the dancefloor towards their table.

'I must leave you,' he says. He stands, gives them a small, quick bow, and walks rapidly away.

Jack Marx picks up his drink and, patting Ptarmigan on the shoulder, finishes it and begins to head for the exit. He pauses. Comes back. 'See you soon, Tarm.' he says with a sad smile. And then he is gone. His empty snakebite glass sits on the table. A small nugget of froth slides down its side.

The two boys sit. They both have snakebites. The one with the glasses turns around to survey the club. He pushes hair from behind his lenses. A group of tall and ornately-dressed men and women with red clay beads dangling from their hair have appeared and are trying to start a fire on the stage near the girls with the dreadlocks. The boy with glasses has a red, circular shape embroidered onto the back of his blue drape jacket. He turns back.

'Ptarmigan, Rita and Gerda.' He says, nodding to each of them in turn.

'Yes?' Gerda is now somehow getting used to this upending of her reality.

'Samuel gave you a knife?' This is the other boy. He has a West Country manner of speaking that Gerda recognises.

'Yes.' says Rita.

'He's right. It doesn't matter.' Bunny is very handsome. He looks young and lost. 'But it will suffice. I think.'

'Have you read the Huxley?' Simon asks Ptarmigan.

This is so unexpected that it takes Tarm a moment to formulate a reply.

'No. I saw Brave New World though. The film.'

'There isn't a film. Not a proper one anyway. You're thinking of 1984. What do you reckon Bun?'

'Yeah. 1984. Peter Cushing. Donald Pleasance.'

Simon shrugs. 'I don't think that matters either. That's a different story. We asked Aldous to come. He declined. It's a shame because we like him. But it's unlikely he could have thrown any light onto the topic at hand.'

Bunny sips his drink. 'Not now anyway. Maybe at some point. Like most other things here. It doesn't matter.'

Gerda and Ptarmigan reach for each other's hands. This is a nightmare thirty years in the making. They hold tightly.

The music has changed. Now it is the harsh droning of some kind of horn. The dancers are moving slowly, faces contorted with pain. They all look as if they are having seizures. The tall, strangely dressed people on the stage have started their blaze. One of the dreadlock girls is alight and screaming. George Talbot is by the stage, capering and applauding.

'What is he? The Hallow Man?' Rita asks the two boys.

Simon laughs. '*He*? He's nothing. He's just a graveyard. It's her. She was a fury. She was hate and vengeance. Something happened. We don't know what. But now she's tired. She's been tired for years. For centuries.' He looks at Rita.

'Are you tired?'

Rita's head sinks towards her chest. She whispers, 'Yes.'

Bunny slams his palm against the table. 'Well wake up!'

They all jump.

'Look at all of these.' Bunny gestures to the packed dancefloor. They look closely for the first time and realise that many of the dancers are children. Some are babies too young to even stand, but even so, they dance to the terrible, wailing, shrieking music.

'We can't go,' says Simon. 'We're just stuck. Aren't we Bun?'

'All of us. The snake needs to eat. She wanted it for us. But he took two. That was a first. It was impossible for her.'

'We haven't got long now, ' says Simon. 'But do what she tells you. It's nobody's fault. Not really. Things live and things die. Her heart broke into billions of pieces. Imagine your whole world ending in fire and death and gleeful laughter. Within a week. But it's like Bunny says. She's tired. And I think this will be an end to it. I hope so.'

Simon takes off his glasses and pushes back his hair. 'I wish we could have seen more.'

Bunny nods. 'There was so much we wanted to do. But we didn't manage. Not this time around anyway. Maybe next. Or the one after. If me and Simon can meet up later. It's possible. Please just do as she asks.'

They begin to fade into the dark of the club. They smile at Ptarmigan, Gerda and Rita and then they blow away. Like dry chaff in the breeze.

Now Mrs Bron is sitting at their table. The music has stopped. The club is deserted. Silent. She looks at each of them in turn. 'You'd better come upstairs,' she says. 'There isn't much time. He's waking up.' Mrs Bron leads them from her front room, where they have been sitting, to the stairs door. She goes ahead of them. They climb the ordinary 1970's swirly-carpeted stairs with their heads spinning, clutching the banister. Mrs Bron opens the first door at the top of her stairs. And here it is. The smell. Faint but powerful. Like dead chickens ripening in the sun.

'He's in here' she says.

THE HALLOW MAN

PTARMIGAN IS FIRST into the room. The curtains are drawn. There is no bed and no furniture. A huge, naked carcass takes up most of the carpet, from the window to the door. In the blue curtained light, it looks as if several elderly corpses have been knitted together. The legs are splayed across the floor at impossible angles. Bald, simian feet, with finger-like toes, all of which look broken and unmended, are slowly fidgeting. Two great thin arms stretch at right angles, culminating in plate-sized palms and long, nobbled fingers. The nails are grimed with old dirt. Its chest is thin. A strange ribcage, all criss-crossed with fish-like bones, holds it all together. It rises and falls with a wheezing sound like torn bellows. Its midriff is covered with a wide green tarpaulin, which is shifting around where the massive, swollen stomach must be. The head is hairless and slung back. It sits upon a neck all bunched on one side, like stacked fatty tumours. Its eyes are closed. And, worst of all, there is the huge, foot long oval of a mouth drawn into a permanent, furious roar.

Gerda and Rita are in the room now. They look at the Hallow Man's gut. It is distended under its covering. There is something moving around in there. *It's like our dreams*, thinks Gerda.

Mrs Bron sits on the floor next to the horror. She touches its arm. The skin is cool and wet. 'Oh lad!' she sighs. 'My rage has wearied with me these many centuries. Would that you had let me die with my people. So that I might go around again.'

Gerda is agape. 'Mrs Bron. Who are you?' she asks her.

The woman bows her head and says, 'Do you know, my people didn't even give ourselves a name. Because there was only us. For so long.'

'But. Who are you?' Gerda. Amazed at her own tenacity.

The woman sighs again. 'Have you heard of West Kennet Long Barrow? Wayland Smithy?'

'No.' Gerda shakes her head.

'Ah. Not even that then. We were the great stonesmiths. Gerda. When your people say, as is your wont, that mystery surrounds the builders of these monuments? They were us. The barrows. The great standing stones. Not Stonehenge. That boasting folly. No. The first, real monuments. And those places weren't called by those names then. And Bron isn't my name either,' she eyes Gerda. 'I doubt you could pronounce my name. And Howe Hill? It isn't far. Not really. We walked there. Most of us. I watched that place built. I worked on it. It was magnificent. All I have left of us is that little figure in my garden. Nothing more.'

'Those people you saw on the stage down there. The ones with the fire and the heads riven with beads. That was them. They roasted my children alive. And our men's heads and parts. My man was gentle and good and a father. And the incomers made us watch them all cook while they stood and laughed, men and women both. My children. My man. My mother. My father. My family. My people entire. Within ten days I was the only one. And soon I will join them.' A single tear slips down her smooth cheek.

'And. What is he?' Rita points at the Hallow Man as he lolls on the floor. 'And what was that downstairs? We were here, but we were in the club?' Rita feels oddly serene.

'I don't know what he is. I never have. And it's like Samuel and Bunny and Simon said. It doesn't matter. Not really. He's the bogeyman. The Lollard. He's what parents tell their children. That they might behave. He used to be quick. But he's slowing now.' The woman rests her hand upon his huge, still shoulder.

'All things have their time. There is a pine-tree over in America somewhere that's five-thousand-years old.' The woman sighs once more. 'It will die.'

Her accent is thickening. Becoming more exotic.

'I sometimes wonder if people somehow made him. My people. Or the people before us. If there were people before us. We were the first, that we knew of anyway. So yes, perhaps people made him. Out of their fear of what might lurk in the darks of the night. In the shadows. In the soil of the grave. In the rotting wood. Sometimes I think he might be death.'

The thing under the tarpaulin makes a low and empty sound, like a faraway ship's horn. The woman looks at him with something approaching love. Her hands go to her lap and fold.

'But death came in boats. Death brought with it pottery and spears and fire and cruelty. And death had its way with us. We all perished. But for me. We were the first genocide.'

'And that down there? Your club? I did that, yes. He gave me that. All the dreams and the knocking flat of senses. That was me. His gift. As long as he had his battery, I could do all of that. And I wouldn't die. Down there? Your club? You needed to see. I have been talking to you. To all of you. For years. Now I am tired, Ptarmigan, Rita and Gerda. I have been tired for centuries. I wanted this with Simon and Bunny. But he took two and voided one. It was too much.'

'Battery? Voided?' Ptarmigan can't tear his eyes away from the thing on the floor. It is like a long-rotted ocean creature, all washed up and eaten and beached. He cannot smell its stink now. He has become accustomed.

'He took. Every three span of ten years. Saturn Return. Cronus Return. Samuel Worth was right about many things. I began to regret my new life so long ago. Before the brother monks came to pray for deliverance from him. From me. In the beginning, when my rage was new, we terrorised the incomers. I gifted whole villages such dreams, asleep and awake, that all took their own lives or slaughtered each other terribly. With every gush of blood and rend of guts I saw my family melting in their great bonfires and I smiled. And then more invaders came. Equally vicious. Equally greedy for our land and our trees and waters and our great stones. They slaughtered and raped those who came before. Tide after tide of human subjugation. Conquest after conquest. I saw the same hatred on different faces again and again and again. So. He took one every thirty years. Why thirty? I don't know. Why does the Century Plant only bloom every twenty? Because it does. That is its way. He took only one. And that one, somehow, sustained both he and I until he voided them and took another.'

'I saw the report from the cemetery. The waxy leavings? Something animal? That was Bunny and Simon. The poor boys. Voided. They cannot move now. He has part of them in him. And part of him remains in what is left of them. I wanted this for them. But he took both in his need. And then there was you. Who do you think wrapped those young lads' records in old newspapers? Who do you think put the suitcase in your cellar all those years ago? But you were three. In the cemetery. Too much again. You saw. And so I had to make you unsee. I had to stun you, Ptarmigan and Gerda. Then I sowed the germ of this into you, Tarm. The wait has been long for you, and you didn't even know you were waiting. It has been the tick of a clock for me. And now here we are.'

The woman is wistful now. 'We weathered the great winters with no discomfort. I kept him hidden in Sharrow Field then, or whatever it was named. No need for shelter. He only spoke to me once. I don't even know if he used his mouth. But he spoke once. As soon as I was back and filled with my need and my vengeance. We rested for decades long within the forests. Until the forests were cut and flattened. Then we chose old mines and caves. He liked the dark and the warmth. And I didn't care. I had my hate to comfort me. The stone quarry, once it was such, was our place too. Children were easy and best. Younger, you see? Their lives were his battery. His fire. His essence. And mine. More energy in growth than ageing. You understand? I think that's why he has slowed.'

'Your people looked upon your children as both burdens and workers for so many ages. And then, when you realised how precious they are, as I did with my dead passed babies, they became harder for him to take. You began to protect them. That's when he was seen running. He wasn't hunting. He cannot hunt. He can only steal. He was panicked. That cemetery, once it had overgrown, was a good lair. I was with him there when your photograph was taken. I was with him there until this road was built. I was fatigued even then. And by then I required shelter. I left him there, but he knew where I was. And as his power diluted, so did mine, I am sure. Then he came to me here. He has been here ever since the cemetery was lightened. In this room. Where he lies. So here we are, Gerda, Rita and Ptarmigan. I am very old. My fury was spent ages since. And I believe that, once this is done, I may be with my family and my people. The visions I have given you today are my last.'

The woman folds the tarpaulin down. She reveals a stomach distended beyond anything natural. It balloons across the Hallow Man and onto the carpet on either side. It bulges four feet upwards. The grey skin is stretched and taut, run through with great seams and furrows. The belly is almost transparent. And within this womb, curled up like a foetus, is a man. The man moves.

'Seb!' Rita's face whitens. Gerda and Ptarmigan fall to their knees. Mrs Bron is calm.

'The snake,' she says. 'It needs to eat itself. We must be quick now. You must help me. Now.'

The woman takes a long grey arm and gestures for Tarm to grab the other. The Hallow Man's great head lolls backwards with a sound like ship's rigging. Together they manoeuvre the heavy body until it lays flat.

'Rita. Samuel's knife. It's as good as any. I need to close the snake. Before he wakes and voids again.'

Rita has the dagger in her hands. She moves across the room in slow-motion.

'What do you want me to do?' she whispers. Gerda and Ptarmigan are still kneeling. Incapacitated.

The woman undresses, leaving her garments in a heap. Out of her clothes her body is lithe, but reticulated with tiny lines, like skin under a microscope. She takes hold of the Hallow Man's great yawning jaw with both hands and pulls down hard. The mouth and neck stretch to the size of a high, narrow window. It unhinges like a snake, with a harsh grinding sound. He produces a bass-gurgle.

The woman whispers, 'When I'm through,' she gestures to Seb, curled within the thing's huge, glassy belly, *'Cut him out!'*

She takes a last look around the room. A final glimpse of her long, long reality.

'I'm sorry,' she says. She takes a deep breath. 'My children. My man. All of those babies. The children. Their poor mothers and fathers. Bunny and Simon. All the hundreds more. I am so sorry. And, beautiful Rita. My sorrow for you is boundless. I was there when your man was taken. I wept for you. But now you have him again. You can live as I did once. And then, who knows? We will all meet and this will be as nothing. We can all go round again now. I think. And there are worse monsters than him. Or me. As I believe you know.'

Smiling at them for the first time she says, 'Thank you.'

And she throws herself headlong into the Hallow Man's impossibly gaping mouth. And she is gone.

They can see the short, crooked neck bulge as she is swallowed down. Her slim mass circumvents the narrow chest and is gulped straight into the tremendous mound of belly. It expands as this poisonous meal reaches it. The Hallow Man's eyes open. He moves his huge head from side to side. He has tasted something dangerous. The straining tendons of his neck sound like groaning ships in a harbour. Impossibly loud.

Rita cups the ragged flesh nearest to Seb. She saws at it with the meteorite dagger. Its blade is as sharp as a cutthroat razor and the blubbery flesh gives way easily. The smell of decay increases. The Hallow Man's arms begin to thrash and bang against the walls and floor. Each movement sounds like the sudden warping of ancient planks. His legs kick sluggishly. *He's slowing now*. The enormous head rises from the floor. His mouth has shrunk back to its usual, horrific size. Rita punctures the sac in which Seb has lived, keeping the Hallow Man and his tragic companion alive for the last thirty years. The great body turns on its side, limbs scrabbling to try and stand upright. As he does so, there is a sound of skin and cartilage tearing, and a flood of putrid jelly-like fluid. The Hallow Man lifts his head in a soundless, final howl. He looks down at himself with his dying eyes, and sees Seb, still in a foetal curl, tumble out onto the carpet within a freshet of brown, stinking liquid. And he sees Mrs Bron, or whoever she once was, nestle close within him. She looks like she may be dancing. Tearing her companion apart from within. The Hallow Man looks at Gerda. Then Ptarmigan. And finally Rita. The great mouth moves, almost as if in prayer. Then the huge, mythical being lays back down. And is still.

The house begins to buzz and vibrate. Ptarmigan walks across to Seb on his knees. He uses the bottom of his tee shirt to clear the muck from Seb's eyes and mouth. An almost operatic rushing sound fills the room, growing louder and louder. Rita shoves Tarm aside and holds Seb close to her, unmindful of the reek of decomposition. Then they all cover their ears.

Seb is left, coiled snakelike, on the floor. The noise increases to a thundering howl, like a jet engine reaching its highest register. Is this the poor souls escaping from their shackles and going around again? What else can it be? Century upon century of them. All of the loss and sadness trapped within, now released. Ptarmigan can almost hear calliope music within the roar. They look to each other in terror, thinking that their heads are about to shatter like porcelain. The pressure rises. Rises. The room is becoming hotter. They all begin to scream, like Rita in the cemetery. Gerda and Ptarmigan reach for each other. And now the suggestion of vast, stony, pounding wings.

Then utter, sudden silence.

And Seb takes a massive, ragged breath.

THREE MONTHS LATER

'Xlusive.'

The male voice on the other end of the telephone sounds bored.

'Hi. I've just moved to Sheffield and need to offload some clothes.'

Silence.

'A friend at the gallery suggested I call you.'

'Oh. Which gallery?'

A sniff of interest.

'The Haunch. Mayfair. I've come up from London. Smaller place, hence peddling the clothing.'

'The Haunch of Venison?'

'That's it.'

'Did you work there?'

A nibble.

'Good heavens no. It was at my last London exhibition.'

'Oh really? Okay yes. What sort of items? We more or less pride ourselves on upscale vintage.'

'That's what my friend told me. Well, some of it was my mother's. Sixties stuff. All in vacuum packs.'

'Let me grab a pen, okay?'

'Okay.'

A pause. Paper moving.

'Can I take your name please?'

'Anna Siddle.'

'And what brands have you got Anna?'

'Well, I can't remember everything, or which garments are by whom. But I can give you an overview.'

'Great!'

'Well, there are some *Biba* pieces. *George Halley. Comme de Garcons. Dior. YSL Cardin.* A few other bits.'

'Can you hold for a moment please?'

Nearly.

'Of course.'

Hand covering the mouthpiece. Muffled, urgent whispers. A female voice.

'Hi Anna! I'm Emma. I run Xlusive. Simon tells me that you have some lovely clothes for me!'

Keen.

'Hi Emma. That's right. If you'd like to view, how do we go about it? I don't relish the idea of lugging a ton of vacuum-packed apparel into the centre of town!'

'Oh no. I'll come to you! I'll need an address obviously. When would you like me?'

Hooked.

Rita puts the phone back on the receiver.

'Good accent huh?' she says.

'Bloody perfect!' Gerda and Ptarmigan hug her.

They had left Mrs Bron's house, Rita and Ptarmigan carrying Seb, still hunched, between them. He didn't weigh much, which, for this exercise, was a bonus. Because the repulsive smell of the Hallow Man's insides was strong and suspicious, they had run a bath at Mrs Bron's house. They had scrubbed him down and washed his long hair. Ptarmigan crept from the house and drove home for fresh clothing and some ID. What they were doing was risky enough. If their charge was naked, it would have been doubly so. On the drive to the hospital, with Rita still holding Seb in the back of the Camper Van, there had been frantic discussion about what to tell the NHS staff. Gerda said that extreme psychological trauma can sometimes make people adopt the foetal position. Short of any better ideas, they decided to say that Seb had been feeling poorly while he and Rita were staying over. And that he had been in this state when they woke up this morning. Perhaps he'd had a bad dream.

As it turned out, the staff at A&E were quite unconcerned about the history of the case. Their concern was for the patient. Apart from his wasted condition, which Rita explained, with her heart in her mouth, was due to intermittent bulimia, all of his vital signs were normal. His muscles had atrophied inside the Hallow Man, but far less than would be expected had he been in a coma for a year. Gerda said it was because he had some space to move around in. That idea made Tarm feel nauseous.

Seb was in hospital for a month, under the name of Shaun Houghton. Having a dead man rock up at A&E might raise some eyebrows, Ptarmigan said. After they left Seb at the hospital, Rita had three sleepless nights in a row. These horrifying, shocking and ultimately joyous events had affected them all. But Rita was particularly traumatised. On the third night, Ptarmigan had opened a litre bottle of Tullamore Dew. And they had all got roaringly drunk and laughed and cried and watched The Thing on Netflix. Afterwards, Rita had slept for 26 hours.

After bathing Seb, they had all looked back into the Hallow Man's room. There was nothing there. No sign that anything had happened at all. There was nothing on the carpet apart from the tarpaulin. The blue curtains still hung. It was as empty and dead as their old house next door. Mrs Bron's family had all died centuries before, so there were no next of kin. Maybe someone would see the post building up eventually and maybe they wouldn't. Her long, strange life would now live only in their memories. And in the memories of the hundreds that the Hallow Man had killed in order keep them both alive. Ptarmigan kept a weather eye on the local news, but there was nothing. The still and silent house on Vanguard Road would raise eyebrows in the end. Someday, someone would gain entry. They would note the empty rooms and the layers of dust and time. And, one day, maybe some young students might move in. After all, the Gandhi was only over the road.

Rita, who Tarm and Gerda had expected to be full of hate, said that the Hallow Man was only doing what he did. No different to a big cat or a shark. And, because of the brutal slaughter of her people, Mrs Bron had railed at the world of the incomers for aeons. For long, long after the incomers themselves were dust. Rita had gone back to Wales to work her months' notice once it became clear that Seb would recover. She had decided to move back to Sheffield to be near her friends. Her years of experience running a busy fundraising organisation meant that finding work was easy. She has a start date in November, managing the Sheffield office of a large charity supplying clean water systems to developing countries.

It is 7pm on a cold October evening. Rita is in the drum room of Ptarmigan Sounds, sitting on an old easy chair opposite Gerda. She puffs at her vape. They have all stopped smoking. They lost interest after Vanguard Road. She can see the reflection of three heads in the soundproof glass of the window.

The doorbell rings both in the studio and the flat above. Ptarmigan knew she would be punctual. He trots down the stairs and opens the door to Emma Smith. She is wearing a trench-coat and her hair is more severely cut than ever. Her face, which had been wearing an obsequious smile, falls as soon as she sees him.

'You?' she says. 'What the hell are you doing here? Where's Anna?'

Ptarmigan smiles at her. 'She's in here. Come in.'

Emma Smith is as confused as she ever is. Momentarily she considers walking away. But the lure of Biba clothes, and schmoozing with a London artist, wins out. What, though, is Anna Siddle doing here with this fucking nobody?

Emma Smith sighs loudly and follows Tarm into the recording studio seated area. There is a kettle on a shelf. A snack dispenser glows against a wall. The waste-bin is overflowing with beer and cider cans. And there is a pervasive underlying aroma of sweat. Emma Smith looks disgusted.

'What's going on?' she says, her eyes following the lines of cabling running along the wall.

'I wanted a word,' says Ptarmigan, 'About a few different things.'

'What? Where's Anna Siddle?'

'All good things to those who wait!' Tarm smiles at her. 'Now. Emma. Let's talk about power and death.'

Emma Smith can think of no response. She isn't used to being spoken to like this.

Ptarmigan offers her a seat. She sits.

'There. That's better. Now, power. What do you know about power Emma?'

'I don't know what the hell you're talking about.' Emma Smith feels she might be warming to this though. She likes a drama.

'Okay,' she says, 'I'll tell you what I know about power, you raping piece of shit. That's what it was all about wasn't it, *Little Boy*! I dumped you. You couldn't handle it. So you demonstrated your pathetic masculine power. That's what you do. You lying fucking coward.'

This outburst hasn't had the effect she expected though. Ptarmigan sits smiling at her. There is a pause. Emma Smith is thinking about leaving when Ptarmigan says, 'We both know that it didn't happen don't we? But anyway. That's ancient history isn't it Emma? Well, ancient lies. So, let's move on. Let's talk about death. What's your take on death? You were a Goth for, what, ten minutes? While it was *en vogue*? You must have had a nodding acquaintance with the concept.'

'Do you have any idea who you're talking to? I know people…'

'Yeah I know. You know bike gangs. I know. But back to death, Emma. Or more specifically, murder. We really are covering all the serious crime bases aren't we?'

'Murder? The only thing I know about murder is your stupid fucking Taff mate finishing off her stupid Taff boyfriend.'

'Ah. I'm glad you brought that up.' Tarm stands up and walks to the drum room door. He pulls it open.

'Here's Anna Siddle. Say hello to Emma Smith, Anna.'

Through the open door walks Gerda, followed by Rita, who is pushing someone Emma Smith recognises in a wheelchair. Her jaw drops and her eyes widen.

'*Dior. YSL Cardin.* A few other bits.' Rita says in Anna Siddle's upper-middle-class London accent.

'Hello Emma,' says Seb, grinning. 'Long time, eh?'

Seb came out of the hospital three weeks ago. He can remember nothing after making mushroom tea at Vanguard Road in 1984. His life skips straight from that moment to an older, violet-haired Rita holding his hand in the hospital. He looks young, having been away from direct light for thirty years. But he is still weak. And he sleeps a lot. The consultant at the hospital says this is to be expected after such a trauma. Even though the consultant can't imagine what that trauma might be. He has lost some of his hearing. But he is fond of telling people that this probably would have happened anyway, considering the volume at which he listens to music. Seb can manage the stairs now. Up is easier than down. Rita has cut his hair, which was down to his waist, back into a facsimile of the style it used to be in. It is grey in a few places, but he quite likes it. So does Rita. She says he can use her and Gerda's various dyes as he gets more grizzled. Ptarmigan and Gerda are amazed at how easily he has got used to his new reality. His new life. Rita isn't. She says it's Seb all over.

Since she met him, as a fourteen-year-old punk rocker, Rita has seen Seb analyse and process every negative situation. She has seen him twist it into something either hilarious or at least viable. One night in 1979 the drunken Butts, the hard lads in their valley, thought they would have some violent fun with them. It was their appearance the music they liked these lads objected to, but anything would have done. Seb had talked them down in ten minutes. And they had all finished the evening drinking beer and singing Sex Pistols songs on the valley side, while he played the guitar parts on his old acoustic.

And, when it looked like Rita's Mum and Dad were about to ban her from seeing him altogether, he had knocked on their door. Once invited in, he had discussed the Rugby and Bob Dylan with her Dad. And her Mam had ended up making them egg, tuna mayonnaise and cheese and pickle sandwiches and asking Rita why she hadn't invited him round before. Seb's calmness and humour impressed them both. She hasn't told him about Kate though. Not yet.

Rita pushes Seb into a space between the chairs, applies his brakes, and sits next to him. Gerda sits next to Rita.

Seb grins at Emma Smith. 'Alright Emma! Rita here tells me she killed me. That right?'

'How the fucking hell are you here?' Emma Smith has a premonition that this is just the start. She is beginning to panic. 'You were dead in, what…'

'1991. It was 1991,' Rita looks at Emma Smith like she is vermin. 'And you told everyone that it was down to me. You are, and I'm being honest here, the worst person I have ever met.'

'Yep!' Seb smiles. 'You were a right bastard. Still are, apparently.'

'And so are your toxic little coterie,' Gerda says.

Emma Smith starts to gather herself to leave. Ptarmigan sees this and he locks the studio door.

'You can't make me stay.' she says under her breath. She still has some fight in her.

'Oh? You'll be surprised what we can do. Now. About Jack Marx.' Tarm says.

Emma Smith blanches.

Ptarmigan strolls into the mixing suite. He turns on the internal microphone. 'Testing. Testing. 1-2-3. Am I coming through?' Seb and Gerda give him a thumbs-up through the glass.

'Good. Now, Emma. What do you know about text to voice technology?'

His voice through the speakers is bass-heavy and clear.

Emma Smith sits. Her nails are fascinating her.

Seb is still smiling. 'It's bloody brilliant! Ever so clever. Isn't it Reet?'

Rita sits, glowering at Emma Smith.

Ptarmigan's voice again. 'I've made one of the voices male. And I've made the other one female. Made sense, considering. I've also recorded a little preamble. Are you sitting comfortably everybody? Good. Then we'll begin.' There is a slight click over the speakers. Then Ptarmigan's recorded voice comes into the room.

'The following are text messages copied from an Apple iPhone 6, which was located at the house of Simone and Esme Marx on Sunday July 6th 2014. Thanks for the now-forgotten floorboard info, Seb!'

Seb raises his hand and grins. Emma Smith looks like she might faint. There is dab of sweat on her forehead and patches of moisture have appeared on the underarms of her trench coat.

'I became curious about the relocation of a small second-hand clothes shop in Burngreave called Nobby Styles, to a plush venue on Fargate in Sheffield City Centre. I looked at the Companies House page for Xlusive Vintage Boutiques Ltd. Nobby Styles ceased trading on 03 Oct 2006. Then Xlusive opened with some fanfare in November that year. Emma, knowing what an astronomically vile human being you are, and with Gerda's help...'

Gerda takes a small bow in her chair.

' … regarding your extracurricular activities, I paid a visit to Jack Marx's widow. In the place Seb had alluded to in 1984, and which I happened to mention in my statement to the police, I found an iPhone. And on the iPhone I found these texts. The text messages span the period between Thursday 24th August and Wednesday August 30th 2006. The moment I have played these to you I am emailing the whole soundfile and relevant supporting documentation to South Yorkshire Police. As I say. One male. One female. Happy listening!'

There is a short pause, another click.

Male Voice: *Emma please. I told you this as soon as I found out Sim was expecting, It's over. We've been trying for years. You know that. I'm sorry. I can't do it any more. We had this discussion in Mr Kites. Can't do it. I'm sorry Emma. Really I am.*

Female Voice: **Really Jack. I thought you knew me better than that. You stupid fucking man. I've got your number. I know your address. Nobody throws me out with the rubbish you raping piece of shit.**

Male Voice: *What? Emma. Look, come on. We had fun. What do you mean by raping?*

Female Voice: **It's quite simple, Little Boy. You're a fucking rapist. I can get Caroline to say you assaulted her as well. It doesn't matter if it's true or not. I've done it before. You know that. Fucker. Wonder what lovely Sim and her precious fucking Baby Bump will have to say about that? Daddy's in prison! Hahaha.**

Emma Smith is crying.

Male Voice: *You're not serious. Emma, this is nuts. Please don't do this.*

Female Voice: **Well I tell you what, big old famous old Jack. Money. How much is your pathetic little nuclear family worth to you?**

Male Voice: *Emma. Please. Don't. This will kill me.*

Female Voice: **Not before time either. We've done some calculations. Bank transfer. £120,000. Today.**

Male Voice: *Emma, I am begging you. Don't do this. Please. Please. Please.*

Female Voice: **Tick. Tick. Tick. My fingers are dangerously close to the phone. Tick. Tick.**

Male Voice: *Okay. Christ. I'll do it. Email me your bank details.*

Female Voice: **Good call, Loverboy.**

Female Voice: **Thanks for the cash. Now. How does it feel being £120,000 poorer and not knowing who's going to be talking to the fragrant Sim next time the phone rings. Sleep easy, fucker.**

There is silence in the room, apart from Emma Smith's quiet sobbing. Ptarmigan comes back in the room. He looks at Emma Smith.

'That last one from you was sent on Thursday August 31st. About three hours before Jack killed himself. Leaving his wife widowed and his daughter without a father. Simone let me copy all of this. She has the iPhone. The email has gone off to the police. I'm pretty sure you were all in on it. Cave and McBride and the rest of your little herd of children. Blackmail Emma. Serious stuff.'

Rita is still staring at Emma Smith. 'You. You're a walking insult to every woman who actually is raped or abused. Every single one, you poisonous bastard. And every murder victim too. How fucking dare you? You sleazy, self-obsessed piece of shit. I can't think of any words for my contempt for you. Fuck off out of my sight.'

Gerda stands. She taps Emma Smith's trenchcoat shoulder. 'You can go now.'

Gerda opens the studio door and the back door.

Emma Smith looks like she is in hell. She walks out.

'Sleep easy, fucker.' Gerda says as she closes the door on Emma Smith.

They all go back upstairs and open a bottle of Tullamore Dew. Cadellin lays sprawled between Seb and Rita, purring like an engine.

.2015.

THE MIRACLE

RITA AND SEB have bought a house close to Ptarmigan and Gerda's flat. It is a three-bedroom semi with big rooms and high ceilings on a nice, quiet road. Squirrels live in the trees that line it. Seb's recovery is still ongoing, but he is now comfortable in his body again. Rita says he has got plump, and Seb is proud of this. He has started calling Ptarmigan *Fatbro*.

Not long ago, Rita told Seb about Kate and her sad, baffling death. She drove him to the Garden of Remembrance in Wales one weekend They walked around the grounds. They met some more recently bereaved parents of dead children. Seb had to sit on the benches scattered around every so often because he was tired. And on one of these, he had cried. They visited his late parents' house, now occupied by strangers. Seb had opened the passenger car door and looked at the changed garden with its unfamiliar plants and children's toys. And he had cried again.

Eventually, Seb called the police and announced his reappearance after thirty years. There were some headlines in the local and national press. But it wasn't much of a story beyond that. He simply said he couldn't remember anything. There was a flurry of mail and emails from psychics and mediums and hypnotists, all offering to help. Rita and Seb ignored them all. The Fortean Times published an article entitled *The New Kaspar Hauser*? But it didn't take long for the world to move on.

Following a short trial, Emma Smith and her four minions were found guilty of blackmail and were sentenced to between nine and fourteen years in prison. Simone Marx and Ptarmigan gave evidence. The defendants' lawyers had few arguments in their lawyerly armoury when confronted with those damning text messages. The edition of The Star with the headline *Fake-Rape Blackmailer Jailed* is framed and displayed on Gerda and Tarm's living room wall. When Emma Smith received the maximum sentence, Ptarmigan, Gerda, Rita and Seb went drinking in The Barfield. And they had their first ever sit-in meal at the Gandhi to celebrate. Afterwards, Rita

insisted on going back to Tarm and Gerda's flat
to give Cadellin a massive cwtch.

Rita and Seb's miracle happened in August.
Although she is now forty-nine, Rita became
pregnant almost immediately Seb was well
enough for them to start sleeping together again.
On the day the test showed a blue plus-sign,
Gerda and Ptarmigan had come to their house
with flowers and chocolates. Rita looked flushed
and happy. She looked *motherly*. Rita insisted
that Seb and Tarm walk to The Barfield and
leave the flowers and chocolates to her and
Gerda. When they returned, with a Ghandi
takeaway, they stood in the kitchen singing
Can't Take my Eyes Off You until Rita told them
to shut up or the neighbours would start
complaining.

The growing life inside her has made Rita
remember Kate. How she would talk to her
about Seb while the baby moved around as if she
was in a hurry to come out and breathe the air.
Early on, Rita had a few weeks of tearful
mourning for their first child. Seb did all he
could to comfort her. She often visited Gerda
during this time. And in the mornings, they

would often be found by Ptarmigan, asleep together in Rita's old bed in the flat.

To begin with, Cadellin sensed the change in Rita and kept his distance from her, preferring to sleep on Tarm's bed. Gerda looked this behaviour up on the Internet and it appeared to be normal for cats. They either went one way or the other, she said. Either a purring nuisance or aloof. This upset Rita all over again until the cat had a change of heart a week or so later and reverted to his previous fondness.

The morning sickness was bad for her. And not confined to mornings. It lasted for weeks. While it was going on, Rita couldn't bear bananas in the house. She said she could smell them three rooms away. Seb was convinced she was carrying a boy, and they agreed to have a gender reveal as soon as possible. Like most expectant parents, they weren't concerned about their baby's sex. Just its health and its happiness.

They are back at the hospital today, for their twenty-week scan. They announced their news to Ptarmigan and Gerda after the first twelve-week scan showed a perfectly healthy, if grainy-looking, speck of baby with a lively heartbeat. Because of her age, a consultant obstetrician, Ms Chaudery, has overseen Rita's pregnancy at every stage. Ms Chaudery is delighted with Rita's progress, saying that she has the womb of a young farmgirl. Seb yells 'Ooo-Aaar!' at her whenever the opportunity arises. She has given up vaping. But she says it's just for the duration. Seb's tobacco habit has disappeared altogether.

Rita lies on her back, with Seb on a chair by her side. Ms Chaudery wraps a blood pressure cuff around Rita's arm and pumps the bulb. The cuff tightens then relaxes, and the consultant says, 'All fine'.

She removes the cuff then says. 'This will be a little cold, but it's just my stethoscope.'

Seb says, 'Death soap?'

Rita's head spins towards him. He looks blank. He shrugs. Ms Chaudery gives him a grin.

'Steth-o-scope Seb.' She waggles the apparatus at him and then listens to Rita's heartbeat. 'All fine as well.' She says. 'Over to Jo. I'll see you in a little while.' Mrs Chaudery gives Rita's foot a little squeeze and leaves the room.

The sonographer, Jo, squirts ultrasound gel onto Rita's now-healthily-showing tummy. The cold fluid makes her gasp. Seb smiles at her and holds her hand. They know how lucky they are. Passing the probe over Rita's belly, the sonographer turns the small TV screen around so they can both see the baby. A galloping heartbeat comes over the speaker. Rita is delighted. She turns her head back towards the screen as her child comes into focus.

The baby hangs inside her like something stale. Its long arms curl towards its chest. Rita looks to Seb in panic and back at the screen. Seb's face is grey.

In eight weeks, it has developed much further. The sonographer drops her clipboard, says something unintelligible, and leaves the room.

From this aspect they can see the ragged crenelations on one side of the neck. The legs splayed at impossible angles. The thin, concave chest above a bloated stomach in which something squirms. And, atop all of this, the elongated head. And the great yawn of a mouth, pulled downwards into a perpetual, noiseless scream.

.THE END.

AUTHOR'S NOTE

While I was casting around after the bones of narrative for this Sheffield-based novel, my wife, who I first met in Sheffield in 1985, told me about a local legend. I was fully aware of the London version of Spring Heeled Jack. My band, Siiiii, even have a track about him on two of our albums. But I was unaware that his mythos had extended as far as our former city of Sheffield.

Spring Heeled Jack, in his London guise, became an early urban legend. He was described by those unfortunate to come across him as having a "terrifying and frightful appearance, with a diabolical physiognomy, clawed hands, and eyes that resembled red balls of fire." In these tales, Jack wore a helmet and, beneath his diaphanous cloak, a black and white garment "like an oilskin". Jack was capable of leaping great distances with little effort, hence his nickname. He also blew great blue flames from his mouth.

His reign of terror in London began during the very early 19th Century, when he was initially known as "The Hammersmith Ghost". Strangely, at the same time, similar sightings were also reported in Southampton. He was christened Spring Heeled Jack in about 1837. And in 1838, the Lord Mayor of London, Sir John Cowan, reported that he had received a correspondence from "a resident of Peckham" regarding various mischiefs and molestations that had been carried out by the brute.

Possibly the most famous tale about Spring Heeled Jack is the Alsop Case. I actually used this occurrence in the Siiiii lyric. On the night of February 19th 1838 there was a knock on the door of a girl called Jane Alsop's house in London. A man, who claimed to be a policeman, told Jane to bring out a candle. He claimed that that he and his colleagues had caught Spring Heeled Jack, and that he was detained in the lane. Jane did as she was bid and fetched a candle, at which point the "policeman" discarded his cloak and "presented a most hideous and frightful appearance". He vomited blue and white flames from his mouth, and his eyes were, again, like "red balls of fire". Jane began to scream which brought assistance. The assailant then fled.

Tales of Spring Heeled Jack's antics began to be picked up by the press. Many of these articles appeared in pamphlets and *Penny Dreadful* magazines, but he was also reported on in The Times.

The London Spring Heeled Jack breathed his last in the 1870's, when the News of The World reported that Peckham was "in a state of commotion owing to what is known as the "Peckham Ghost". This strange person was "quite alarming in appearance" and the editor claimed that it was Spring Heeled Jack.

Sheffield's Spring Heeled Jack was first seen earlier, in 1808. A piece in The Sheffield Times reported that year: "Years ago a famous Ghost walked and played many pranks in this historic neighbourhood, he was nicknamed the Park Ghost or Spring Heeled Jack." He was able to leap enormous heights and he terrified the people of Sheffield with his dreadful mischief. The paper said that he was "a human ghost, as he ceased to appear when a certain number of men went with guns and sticks to test his skin."

Although similar in appearance to the London Jack, the Sheffield Jack had rather more longevity. His last sighting was during the 1970's when police were inundated with calls about a man with glowing red eyes who assaulted women and beat up men in the Attercliffe area of the city. Subsequently though it has been suggested that this particular Jack was just a local drunken brawler. Unlike in London, carvings of Spring Heeled Jack can be seen across Sheffield. One is still visible on the wall of The Old Queens Head pub on Pond Street.

I realised that I wanted to incorporate Jack into my story, but realised that he just wasn't scary enough. All those flames and glows from the Age of Steam. So I added a little bit of spice and made him a cross between Jack, Grendel and, frankly, The Bogeyman. I was happy to reference this colourful Sheffield myth in the shape of Jack Marx, erstwhile drug-dealer and adulterer.

I chose the perhaps unusual character names of Ptarmigan and Bunny after my wife and I collaborated on a new take on an old traditional number called 'The Hearse Song'. My wife played the part of 'Abigail' and her Yorkshire pronunciation of the names was so affecting that I couldn't not use them. This is the link. This is the link. Don't watch it while you're eating.

https://www.youtube.com/watch?v=gZZeBjJF
xHw

When I first moved to Sheffield in 1983, like
Ptarmigan, I lived alone in a house in Sharrow
for a few weeks until the students came back
from their Summer Holidays. One of these
student returnees was a chap from Shropshire
called Joe. One warm September evening, Joe
and I decided that we would intoxicate
ourselves almost to a standstill with mushroom
tea and then walk the ten minutes to the
Sheffield General Cemetery. The place was, back
then, exactly as described in this book. It was
derelict and neglected. Those two hours are the
most unnerving I have ever had. Dangerous
drops. Pitch dark. Getting lost. Useless dead-
battery torch. Unexpected noises. Thankfully,
though, we got out and went home. And we
probably watched *Alien*.

Please visit the Sheffield General Cemetery
Trust website at https://www.gencem.org/ to
discover how utterly beautiful it is today.

Acknowledgments and Thanks

I am indebted to The Sheffield General Cemetery Trust for maps and reminders.

My thanks to Loki for the cover art wizardry.

My thanks to everyone who purchased and said such sweet things about my first two books.

My thanks to Mohammed Fazal (proprietor of the real Gandhi, the Shabab Restaurant on Chesterfield Road, Heeley, Sheffield) for all the free grub back in the early '80's.

And finally, my thanks, as always, to Linzi, the love of my life. For everything.

Goodbye